TAKING IT
TO THE LIMIT

STEVE HERNDON

TAKING IT
TO THE LIMIT

BY
STEVE HERNDON

As in the case for snowflakes, no two human flakes are quite the same. Succeeding accounts herein exemplify these notions. Brief episodes lead the unwary from the intriguingly ribald into fables of sex, murder, and insanity. Echoes of Stephen King's macabre style manifest when least expected.

THE FOLLOWING YARNS ARE WORKS OF FICTION. Names, places, and incidents are the products of the author's imagination. Any resemblance to any actual persons living or dead, events or locales are purely coincidental.

Gotham Books

30 N Gould St.
Ste. 20820, Sheridan, WY 82801
https://gothambooksinc.com/

Phone: 1 (307) 464-7800

© 2023 Steve Herndon. All rights reserved.

No part of this book may be reproduced, stored in a retrieval system, or transmitted by any means without the written permission of the author.

Published by Gotham Books (June 7, 2023)

ISBN: 979-8-88775-248-8 (sc)
ISBN: 979-8-88775-249-5 (e)

Because of the dynamic nature of the Internet, any web addresses or links contained in this book may have changed since publication and may no longer be valid.

The views expressed in this work are solely those of the author and do not necessarily reflect the views of the publisher, and the publisher hereby disclaims any responsibility for them.

TABLE OF CONTENTS

Turkey Trot 1

Fool's Rush: Prior To Alaska 39

Dog Daze 47

The Last Song.. 74

Manhunt: For a Son-in-law 83

Happy Hour: An Excerpt From An As Yet Unnamed, Unpublished, Manuscript Written By Steve Herndon 98

Torchy Burnbaum's Moment of Truth.................... 119

Draw The Latch: Maximum Security Homicide Ward Oregon State Hospital for the Criminally Insane 133

Toy Soldier.. 156

The Pink Zebra 169

Stood Up 186

Going Out With Grace 199

TURKEY TROT

I see myself from near, yet afar. As I wander in and out of that ether world between sleep and semi-consciousness, I'm aware that I'm either dreaming or hallucinating. The woman I adore is there, on a beach towel beside me. We're somehow transported to a tropical paradise — just the two of us. Palm trees sway on a gentle breeze. Appaloosa clouds graze contentedly in azure blue. Sadly, she vanishes. And when I'm so down I think I'll just check out, she reappears.

She's in a white bikini — propped on an elbow facing me: Rhonda enraptured, sexy, tan, and fit. I reach behind her back, deftly undo a string. Her bikini top slides, slowly, subtly, as if that mini-hanky is in on the seduction plot. She smiles: her beautiful eyes, glazed with lust. The mystique of her sensuality has never failed to light my fire.

The top slides another quarter inch. I'm fully aroused. In my periphery, a slit moon of dark brown is revealed.

Bingo Bango! My heart does the tango. My fingers, of their own volition, inch down, down. The climax of the game waits in the form of a brush patch beneath that little white triangle. As our tongues tangle, I cough, snort, and wake with a start. I come to completely befuddled. I'm alone in a travel trailer on an island in Southeast Alaska. (Key word here is *Alaska*). I squinch my eyes. I concentrate with all that's in me, but the harder I try — well, you know. You've been there, that *particular hell* — the need to return to that uninhibited dreamscape. It's the worst strain my brain will ever experience, but my desire will not be fulfilled, no way. I pry open my mattered lids to the gloom of another pisser of a day.

There's a strange white luminescence outside. Snow! Its white weight dispassionately endeavors to crush our *RV* trailer under its relentless, unforgiving weight. I regress into deeper sorrow. *Thanksgiving Day*. I've never felt more dejected, more alone.

Rhonda is gone; flew the coop for Florida. She left a month ago and it wasn't a short month, as in *February.*

I feel my ol' soldier shrivel and droop from attention to parade rest, to, well, anything but an honorable discharge.

It seems Rhonda left me, even without actually splitting the sheets of our marriage. She skipped out to be with our firstborn daughter for my little girl's first birth giving. Wouldn't you know she'd have a girl. I could've lent my expertise to the occasion. Maybe then it wouldn't take a month that's several days longer than *Helluary,* but no. It's a setup; *mother's obligation.* No granddads allowed to gum up the coddling process. No hero worship for absenting myself by extortion, no glory whatsoever.

And now the grand finality befalls like a ton of iced over dog leavings. I gotta climb up on a puny roof and shovel snow until the next thaw. And if the old sourdoughs know how long that'll take, they ain't sharing.

Depression has settled in for the long haul. I sigh deeply, but no one hears, nobody cares. I shrug into my uniform of ignorance, scruffy shirt first, and then the outer, protective layers. I finish with rubber knee boots substituting for the customary calked (spike soled) logger boots.

I step out into the blinding blast of a midmorning snowstorm. Oh yeah. As a reminder tainted by a nip or two, my snow shovel waits where I propped it against the trailer and dismissed it. With a mittened paw, I grab said scoop. If slugs could fly, I'm on the wing. In the meantime, my dreaded onus stacks up a few hundred more pounds. If I don't reverse the trend the roof will be the floor and the *Great Beyond* will be the roof.

With rheumy eyes, I blink, squint, and stagger-plow, squeaking and stumbling through maybe three feet of snow. I stop in contemplation near the built-on ladder astern. I'm about to become just another unsung hero. I aim for the roof and sling the shovel. It hits tin and bounces back. I dodge, but the renegade scoop is out for blood. It clangs off my forehead with an abhorrent vibration. I fling it again. It sproings back. This time I manage to dodge its want to dent my face. That cursed animated/inanimate object!

Normally I'm more kicked back than the mild-mannered *Clark Kent*. I don't usually lose it over the small stuff, but lord have mercy. This stress without letup has overcome my pressure relief valve. I rear back, set to launch the shovel the length of the trailer and into orbit. But then this feeling comes over me. It's as if she's watching…and is she ever pee..issed! Besides, my slightly less than cherry pickup truck is parked out there. It's probably covered in snow and safe, but the windows are fair game. I sneak up a little closer; launch a hook shot. The shovel has a split personality. It decides to submit. It lands topside, probably playing possum, but I'll be on guard for its next psychotic episode.

I touch a mitten to my face, detect no blood. I'll deal with the dents in my head later, with a shot or two of *Doctor Mitch's Snake Oil*. And discretion being the better part of valor, I'll iron out those insignificant creases in the tinware before Rhonda notices… oh, I'm just fooling myself. She can't really be watching from faraway Florida. And keeping a semi-cool tool saved me a tool of another breed, plus brownie points for not littering outer space. For that, I'm proud, no matter if my dear wifey-mate lectures me with her, '*Pride goeth before a fall*,' crapola. God, I miss that woman, even after all the female know-it-all aggravation. Cold toes aside, a man's still left to do what a man's gotta. . . .

As I brush snow away, I notice, without licking them (as I once did the monkey bars in grade school, and won't ever do again) that the aluminum ladder rungs are frozen and slicker than the stuff in the bottom of a successful whale boat.

I'm not overly coordinated in mittens. The un-insulated cow-pie cutters freeze my toes to a deep ache. Snow blindness is compounded with throbs from my freshly wounded head. My jittering knees are no help…vertigo sets in during my first slip and catch. But King Kong style, I manage to cling on with those alien cold digits and frozen toes. Eventually, I blunder up the last rung, and belly-flop onto that flat, contemptible snow slathered roof. I remember to breathe just before I pass out.

I envision her standing in thigh-high snow, watching my misery with arms folded beneath her prized assets. I imagine I read her mind. She's thinking, *Diddler on the roof* instead of *Fiddler*. My lady fair is self-appointed queen of the sarcasm scene, oh hell yes.

My mood interlude in white-on-blue passes, interrupted by the chore I can no longer avoid. Reluctantly I do it to it long after doing it becomes rote. Without a teensy bit of brainwork, I bend and scoop and fling a pile of man-made frigidity. And when I'm done I spear the shovel in the middle of that off-white mound. Observing my handy-work, my head throbs pointedly, self-righteously.

Being a hero has devoured a lot of energy. And then I gotta climb down, which is cool, but hairy.

I lay on my belly. I squirm and wiggle my legs over the side. Legs are designed mostly for upright activity. And feet lack eyes. I blindly, precipitously, dangle said ambulation devices over the edge. My feet telegraph the notion that my boots have discovered a frozen rung. I experiment. I drop down, detect another foothold...and my heavy boots decide now would be an ideal moment to test *Newton's Law*.

I push off to avoid the chin-xylophone effect, thinking it's past time someone invented trailer roof deicers. Whoopee! I land in a pile of snow of my own making. But unfortunately, I've performed a backside down belly flop.

It takes some doing to dig out without panicking. So maybe I do, panic a little, I mean. But what's a thrash or two? Nobody could have seen me through my man-made whiteout, right? I rise to my stompers and bitch slap my ears until I can hear more than I understand. I blow packed snow free of my nose one nostril at a time until I can breathe.

I'm still basically unfrozen. My injuries are limited to my mate's derisive pride thing that goeth before a fall — in my case, after, but whose splitting hairs? Fortunately, I didn't lose a single boot and I'm dressed in my Yupik hockey goalie gear. The parka is purported by a certain discount store to be made of Siberian reindeer fleece — guaranteed not to rip, run, unravel or fade while washing. What more could a man ask?

After a series of grounded jumping-jacks, I've shed a few tons of snow. I then regain control of my newly acquired death-rattle. Next, I retrieve my broken handled shovel — how did that happen? On the spur of the moment I decide to burrow a hole under said recreational vehicle. In case the camp generator fails, I'll have a really keen outdoor fridge.

Since my woman abandoned me, and I exist in Elvis's northern annex of *Heartbreak Hotel*, I've had time to list the benefits of living in a camp trailer. Discounting freezing one's nipples rock-hard, doing bad time here is void of any other advantage. These drag-behind houses, I suspect are built by trolls with an attitude. There may be some benefit in taking a shower while sitting on the toilet lid… but that too escapes me. Come to think of it, since my woman abandoned me, I might be a little lax in enduring that particular form of self-torment.

That, and shaving at the micro-sink, which is accomplished left-handed (and just as seldom of late), with my right elbow wedged against the far wall. Yes, incarceration in a tiny tomb is mind-altering torture. The pain has elevated since the oppressing snow shut down all production. This once vibrant camp is now, virtually deserted, leaving me glacier blue. I'm so doggone gone I'm approaching the notion that my woman ordered the snow as a really sick gag.

After a heavy sigh, I reenter my bachelor pad. It seems as though no human has ever inhabited this hollow tube. Everything is gone but the sadness.

I shed my three-deep outer garments, and in my long-johns I pace the floor; an exercise in the lack thereof. From the bedroom to the kitchen is a journey of several inches. Everything is scaled down except the prevailing smell. My personal low is at an all-time high. My condition progresses into a chronic case of rectumitis (a shitty outlook on life complicated by simpering and whimpering side effects). *Rhonda, return to me!* But when the only road leading to the ferry terminal, and or airport, is under several feet of snow, I realize my dream is a physical impossibility, even though misery loves company...especially here, on a rock-hard, exceedingly remote promontory in a weird, suspiciously uncivilized microcosm, inhabited by misfits.

I gotta admit I'd spent the better part of last week trying to drown my sorrows in spirits that turn out to be dispirited. True, my choice of medication is an ill-conceived antidote. And on the face of it I suspect my demons are evolutionists equipped with survival gear and capable of ingesting large quantities of ever-popular antidotal poison. The little blue diggers must've learned the backstroke or more likely, an offshoot of the *Australian crawl*, some time back.

My mate has absented herself long enough for me to suspect she's fell for Florida, or worse; some other dude. I can almost hear a lonesome *whip-poor-will* sing a crestfallen melody in the background — the *whip-poor-will* sounds suspiciously like — me! Crap, I succumb to my lonely paranoia and slide ever deeper into the blues. I long to put all I feel into words, but cannot. Instead I borrow lyrics from Paul Simon's *Slip Slidin' Away* and silently sing myself into a rare form of insanity. In my estimation a real man could never rip open his chest and display a heart that bleeds for his woman. Not in this wild and woolly environment. Why? Because it's not *the* socially acceptable display of he-man style! So I take up pen and paper. I'll write the words I cannot say in the form of a letter...but there's no way to force my pen to scribe a single line in what would, in time, prove to be a sudden malady those in higher station might just refer to as the *vagina spanked syndrome*. Regardless of the condition's label, it is not the sort of thing the king of his tin castle could live down. Not in a lifetime.

I rise from my pitiful despondency. As I dump my cup of cold coffee into the sink, I watch the black liquid trickle down through strange spikes of bluish gray, hairy culture, growing out of the helter skelter pile of dirty dishes, pots, pans and unidentifiable objects. It's high-time to dung out my little den of iniquity, yes, and I'll get to it first thing, well, tomorrow. For the time being, I step, once again, into my stiffer than starched work pants and hump into a smelly shirt. I hunker into my religious mackinaw, and top it off with a checkered baseball cap with earflaps and chin ties. With my frozen knee boots propelling me, I shoulder the door open and out sumo-wrestle blasts of frigid winds that endeavor to lock me forever inside.

Spring has sprung, fall has fell. The camp is closed because the snow is deeper than usual this Thanksgiving — at least I hope the storm is an early event that will melt before I find myself ice skating on the River Styx.

The skeletal remains of this once animated place seem as desolate as my soul... The bunkhouses, *Jungle Jim's nightmare, the Ritz,* and the *Apothecary,* are winterized with plywood storm shutters nailed over the breezeways. The cook shack doors are chained and padlocked. Most of the home guards that dwell in one and two-wide manufactured homes have split for America on the last outbound ferry. Those live-in timber beasties and their related families will spend Thanksgiving, Christmas, and up until perhaps February, outside, someplace down in the world... But it would seem not quite everyone made their escape; I notice a sneaky sign of life: a faint rustle of a curtain in the fancy two-wide that looks down on our postage stamp spot. The town crier and the company controller recluse: Starvin' Marvin and his alter ego, the hatchet-faced, blabber mouthed missus. She gets off by spreading the *Harper Valley news* and playing peek-a-boo.

Existing in a logging camp is a micro-version of living in small-town America. Everyone knows everybody else's business better than their own. I think I'll just present the next-door tell-all-and-then-some, a little stuffing to go with her turkey. I'll drop my drawers and bless her creeper peepers with a full moon. We were looking for a job when we found this one, but don't need the experience. This ain't my first time out of the chute, not by a long shot, if you catch my drift. But then I remember an old saying: there are old loggers and there are bold loggers, but there ain't no old, bold loggers. So I think about the moon shot, laugh about it and forget about it, even though my wife and I are on a busman's holiday, so to speak. We started out to see the sights behind the façade; the hidey holes that are never gonna make the glossy pages of travel brochures.

I plow through the deep and bypass the snow-covered derelict crew buses (crummies), parked haphazardly as if abandoned to the whims of a natural catastrophe. With an ill-wind watering my eyes, I wander through the deserted trailers along the snow covered paths hiding hard-scrabble rock. I flounder to the commissary and post office beyond. The notices on the bulletin board authored by the creatively gifted in our gaggle of social misfits stand silent guard:

Lawns mowed $3.50 (see Alfred E Newman Stalag 17).

As of now, garbage cans will be picked up twice daily. The early arrival of adverse weather conditions has made the resident grizzlies unseasonably hungry. Satisfaction guaranteed or double your garbage (and bears) back.
Your resident bull cook Flunky Frank

Daily Flogging Will Continue Until Morale Improves
The Management

For a good time see Ilene (better known as Miss Ling Cod).
Anonymous.

Final notice to Amelia Earhart:

Taxi your plane off the runway, Amelia! You are blocking Air Force 1 and stymying FDR's arrival!

You don't suppose the guy who installed Amelia's compass is one of those jealous-hearted male chauvinist pig types and transposed the letters N, S, E, and W? Probably not. The landing strip is a fantasy. And speaking of Franklin D? Well, maybe some of the good ol' boys have been here a shade too long. As far as Amelia went, I can't imagine it was ever here. I guess she's still as lost as my wife. Don't give up the search.

In the worst of times (*now*) I couldn't stomach a good time with Ilene. I've seen old matter-eyed, Ilene. Ilene, with a solitary front tooth that those hornier than I'll ever be, claim to be able to wiggle with their tongue.

In the same masochistic train of thought, I suppose the company flogger packed up his cat-o-nine-tails and caught the last southbound floatplane out before the storm hit. I haven't seen a blade of grass since we'd come upon this dismal rock. I feel meaner than any grizzly I've encountered lately, and I'm not unduly concerned about sharing a meal with a bear, even if he could stomach my cooking. At least I'd have something to growl at.

The barometer on the wall does the dipsy-doodle. The weather is set to kick brittle ass with its neurotic, frozen whims. Another Arctic front is making like the North Pole Express. I'm gonna need that RV roof deicer!

I whimper under my breath — wipe the phlegm from my snot locker with my sleeve and make tracks for my tin shack on wheels — which doubles for a cryonic chamber. As if freezing my manhood stiff could cure my boo-hoo blues.

Ah, Thanksgiving. As I enter the tomb and slam the door, I assume we are both a little weird after all that's transpired. We, I mean, like wow. It seems like yesterday, or hopefully, tomorrow.

***

And yesteryear comes at me with a gunnysack full of horrors and delights...

We idle up a rise. Schizzy is driving. She's one of the Borden twins. Her sister's the one we call *Lizzy*. Their given names, Thelma and Velma lack the flair to righteously describe their personalities. Velma, the twitched-out Schizzy, wheelin' and dealin'. Thelma, the ax tongued Lizzy, deposited on the passenger seat, smacking an entire pack of bad smelling fruit gum and lipping off.

"*Slide it over.*" I gracefully flip from the backseat to the front to assume the shotgun seat. In the process, I employ Lizzy's freshly coiffed hair for a vaulting pad. The spray job is particularly sticky to my palm. The gunk so powerful, thick and spongy, I figure her do will spring back in shape like a well-oiled Slinky.

Did I mention that Lizzy is narrow-minded? Yup. And her elbows are noticeably sharp. She's well-versed in cuss words — if a combination logger/mule skinner/longshoreman is capable of swearing. At times her verbiage gets out of sequence however. At my early age I really have no idea what a "Bastardly, buffoonized, uncoordinated, insipid asshole," is. I don't ask. I fend off her wicked elbows as best I can — hunker down and pretend to be your garden variety dipshit.

Lizzy is to be a second set of eyes and ears for Schizzy, our getaway driver. I'm the last of our wild bunch to slip out into the black night.

At the top of a steep rise, Schizzy snuffs the engine and douses the headlights. We coast down the road unnoticeably building speed. Schizzy feathers the brakes and stage whispers "Now!" I tuck the gunnysack inside my shirt and exit the vehicle by stepping into a black abyss, colliding with an unusually hard place, and skittering, ass over teakettle down the gravel for approximately fifty-six feet, five and a half inches.

I settle to a stop upside down and straddle-legged, picking tiny hunks of meteorite shrapnel out of my knees, elbows and forehead while peering between my legs and watching the black void swallow my hotrod '54 Mercury hardtop.

Schizzy is purported to be the best female driver in the county, but I'm left to doubt her sense of night vision. Likewise she seems lacking in depth perception. Without the aid of a speedometer, Schizzy, I suspect, has no concept of speed.

Oxy Bob slips out of the brush and squats before me. He whispers something about my whimpering being loud enough *to wake the dead. Oh Ha.* My breathing might be a little raggedy. The cold air could have caused my nose to run and my eyes to water a trifle, but Oxy Bob, being more scared than he's ever been, has developed an exaggerated sense of hearing. Oxy is certainly no judge of character. His only claim to fame is his name. I didn't learn much in Ms. Hardbottom's English class. But certain phrases stick to the tongue. I remember what an oxymoron is. It's little short legged, long bodied, Oxy Bob long. Bob, as in bobbed off at the knees, Oxy, as in the long and short moron of 'im.

I have no time for a witty retort. Slats McGee comes sidling out of the night wondering what all the "*Moanin', keenin' and whining,*" is all about.

Oh brother. Obviously Slats suffers from undo panic also. His condition causes his senses to elevate disproportionately with the gnawing fear the night has set galloping through his irrational state of mind.

Oxy Bob and Slats McGee batch together. They exist in a boar's nest apartment with a one-eyed cat they call *Clitty*, gender unresearched. Oxy and Slats: the deuce of clubs, the nine of diamonds, rejects; definitely *not* a pair to draw to. Those two will be far removed from standouts in the pile of dog-eared discounts in the poker game of life.

I wonder where Rhonda ended up. I pray she's alright. Just envisioning her golden flecked brown eyes makes my heart go thump. And the excruciating pain stinging and burning through my gravel rash fades off into the dark.

If only I'd known she somehow reached her post at the Hoptoit (Hop-to-it) Farm fence and almost within reach, I'd have tried for a few more style points in performance of my death defying escape from the wildly speeding, insane and foul-mouthed Borden twins.

Rhonda *Cool* Carmelnjam is all the flavors in the Baskin Robbins arsenal and much, much more. Rhonda. She's to live hard and go ape for. And here she is, at the oak tree rendezvous. While I untangle the half-hitches in my body, she whispers, "Shut up you idiots. Ol' man Hoptoit ain't completely deaf and his mean German shepherd is far from it."

Luckily the Hoptoit farmhouse is a ways off and on the far side of the disquieting gurgle of Hoptoit Creek's muffled alien sounds. But I don't figure why Rhonda seems so agitated about a lazy old housedog. Rhonda, nicknamed *Cool* is queen of the extra patient, kicked back, *in crowd*. Thinking about her cool, takes me back to the first time we were gettin' it on. *Gettin' it on.* Now there's another subtle oxymoron. In truth we were taking it off, me bare to the waist, her, so close to *there* I'm freaking out. I work intently to shed her last article of upper clothing. I hit upon a snafu, the extremely delicate, but all-powerful safe-tumblers clasping her bra strap across her back. Rhonda sits in the pale moonlight in the backseat of my Merc, leaning slightly forward while I diligently yet blindly paw for the elusive key to udder paradise.

My breathing escalates and becomes a little ragged. With my lips nibbling her tender ear and my heart beating out of control, the intensity of my wheezing, raspy breath must surely sound like a gluttonous, asthmatic hog drowning at the trough, and drowning out the strains of the *Platters* softly harmonizing to *"That Magic Touch,"* on the radio.

Rhonda possesses an inner, unflappable calm. She sits there unperturbed while my fatigued, stubby fingers curl into traitorous nubs. With one hand, she reaches behind. Her long, graceful, yet nimble fingers unsnap those imposing stays, and in one fluid motion…unfortunately timed precisely with her folks' porch light flicking on and off, on and off, and *on.*

Rhonda proves not only to be ambidextrous; she's also agile. She slithers from my embrace and pushes me across the seat, flops the hinged front seat up, while in a blur, her free hand re-clasps those elusive hooks. She slips on her blouse before tripping it for the house, tucking her shirt in her jeans. She's standing on the porch before I suck in my next labored breath, finger combing her scrumptious blonde hair while her pouting lips blow me a plaintive kiss goodnight.

The beach Boys ride me hard that night. They put me away wet, while the tune of *Help Me Rhonda*, plays over and over in my unsated soul. And I will *never* get Rhonda out of my heart.

It's not the end of the story. Persistence pays dividends, and eventually, I conquer those confounding, miniature clasps. After Rhonda walks me through the procedure, the safe guarding ambrosia is a cinch to crack. It's the lower, grand prize vault protecting mystically sensual ecstasy Rhonda is never quite ready to release the mysterious entry code to.

It's all too many trials and tribulations, unfulfilled fondles and failed forays later and it's November, Thanksgiving week, circa mid-1960s. A coffee shop plot hatches from the dark recesses of small town bored and listless young adult minds. We the afore mentioned masterminds, the alumnus of Tide Flat High (Go Geoducks,(gooey ducks) you mighty mollusks) are gonna rescue a great white turkey from a life of misery and despair. This poor creature resides, you guessed it, on the Hoptoit Chicken ranch.

We case the joint for a week. The white turkey is a creature of habit. Little is known of its days, but when darkness falls, the big bird invariably returns to the Hoptoit Ranch to a perch on top of the over and under duplex chicken house.

Each night the turkey stands guard, only to drift off for a lengthy snooze. The Hoptoit rooster then relieves the night shift and wakes the entire farm with his obnoxious posturing, strutting and crowing. We figure by midnight, the police dog, ol' man Hoptoit, the egomaniac rooster, and the crepe-necked, red-headed tom will be cutting zzzz's like anything.

With the help of his criminal collaborators and the legs he traded a whooping crane for, six three, 137 pounds of crater faced Slats McGee will endeavor to crawl up under the peak of the steep-roofed roost. He will then grab the legs of the turkey and pass it down to me. I will strive to stuff the main course in a gunnysack to keep its wings from flapping and creating a ruckus loud enough to alert among the farm critters, ol' man Hoptoit and his surly German shepherd.

***

Rhonda holds the wire. She guides the three of us under the fence. We tiptoe over a footbridge spanning the dammed damned fish ponds. In a column of worms, we belly-crawl across a grassy meadow. This field is less than fifty feet from the Hoptoit farmhouse. The relief upon completing this leg of our mission is palpable.

We converge on the double storied chicken house and somehow avoid waking its occupants. I can all but taste the mood of fear turn to dissention and mutiny. If not for Rhonda, I might well go with that thing about discretion being the better part of valor. But sitting beside her, our backs against the Strain 'N' Lay Inn's thin wall, I feel her tremble. It's too late for a simple proposition known as logic to intervene. The Machismo syndrome sets in — overpowering any hint of common sense.

There follows an interlude of suspended breathing. The only sounds penetrating the night emanate from inside the cackle factory. I wonder if chickens sleep with their eyes open. Is the rustling of wings and the occasional "Cluck?" the anxiety of hundreds of enslaved birds having nightmares about orders for extra-large eggs?

I bravely set the example by crawling from safety. I stare into the sky until my eyes adjust to the moonless, starless void. Finally I discern the roof's ridgeline. A ghostly white wraith breaks the jagged line of shingles. My heart pounds. My veins surge pure adrenaline. There, swimming in my vision, our Thanksgiving dinner awaits the taking!

We silently assume our battle stations. Oxy and Rhonda, the shortest members of our strike force, brace themselves together with arms interlocked, to form a makeshift ladder. After a couple aborted attempts and muffled curses, I successfully attain the top rung. Balanced precariously on Oxy's shoulders, I cling to a rafter to steady the human pyramid. Long and skinny Slats McGee scales himself atop Rhonda's shoulders. Slats' climbing skills leave much to be desired. The bony knees he deploys for death grips along my torso are like turn-screw vises and I long to bellow out my agony, but hero that I am… He nearly tears an ear off. In his relentless ascent he manages to glom onto a fistful of my *Fabulous Fabian* look locks. He perches with one foot on my head. He waits for the pyramid to stop swaying. When things settle, he springs unto the slanted roof as the pyramid all but collapses. But I hold tight with all my might to a rafter that's still, after all these years, embedded with my fingerprints.

Slats disappears. The pall of night closes back in. I cautiously draw forth the gunnysack I'd wisely stuffed down my pants. We've progressed to the improvisational part of our mission. Without a live turkey there's no way to rehearse the next stage of our attack; with one, why bother? However there's something to be said about the best laid plans of mice, men, and hoodlums of both sexes going astray. Yet another *Catch 22* has reared its ugly head. Unfortunately, in our meticulous planning, we overlooked an important factor. That small detail becomes the singular component that causes the successful completion of our mission to slip most noisily away. The element in question turns out to be — in a proper form of speaking, *turkey shit*.

The old tom proves to be either a long-time resident or is afflicted with an endless string of diarrhea. The higher Slats slithers up the roof, the slicker the shingles become. The old parable relating to *one step forward, slide back two,* demands precedence. I listen to the sounds of stymied progress. Slats, I begrudgingly admit, is a gamer. But the creaking of the rafters signals his progress and lack thereof. The occupants inside are on to us. Rustling, wing flapping and clucking, increases with each pronounced thump on the roof. The racket is fast becoming unnerving. I whisper, "hurry the heck up," or words to that effect.

Slats lunges for the turkey's legs and all hell reaches an ominous crescendo. The rhythmic thumping beat of a man sliding down a shingled roof alone, is beyond description. Add to the weird percussions the intermingling syncopations, a chicken house erupting in chaos. Blend in shrill screams, shriller screams and a very surprised, unusually vociferous turkey, gobbling as if there's no tomorrow. In the background, the intense barking of a mature German shepherd elicits awful emphasis.

Our Thanksgiving dinner's attempts to gain altitude are hampered by a long skinny object attached to its legs. The pyramid collapses, but I'm momentarily spaced out. A strange UFO simultaneously flaps past my head as the pins are cut beneath my feet.

It doesn't go down as would a *Wile E. Coyote* cartoon. Although my legs churn, I do not remain suspended in midair. The lights in the Hoptoit house come on the exact moment Rhonda, Oxy and I forget about the damned dammed creek ponds we suddenly discover ourselves floundering in. And

Rhonda, Oxy Bob and I, find that it's impossible to walk on water. Even at full speed, it is futile to remain on top. However, even fully clothed, even without Jesus shoes, it's feasible to run across the bottom of a pond and up the other side.

Some fifty yards ahead, and at a right oblique, a white object flies low, and somewhat languidly, through the night. This apparition seems to gain altitude just as I hear the throaty resonance of my Merc's tailpipes. Competing with a hotrod wound to the max are more screams competing with shriller screams, shepherd snarls, bellowing cuss words compete with the rising cacophony, and the blast of a double barreled scattergun shatters all records of previous terror.

***

It takes many a moon to gather the pieces of the debacle and to bring it all to a sort of failed fruition. It comes down something like this.

Schizzy waits in the Merc at the pickup point, but cussy-faced Lizzy has deserted her lookout post. She squats at the back bumper appeasing her weak bladder. Schizzy, peering through the side window, spots the white turkey flying through the night. She claims she doesn't see Slats. Slats, dressed in the standard black burglars outfit, is there. He clings desperately to the turkey's legs. Schizzy witnesses the bird flying over the fence. She reacts. Schizzy is, up to this point, a team player. Her adrenaline rush maxes out. She's not about to watch our dinner get gone. She cranks up the Mercury, floors the foot-feed, and drops the clutch. Schizzy is intent on turkey fricassee. Previous accounts relate the fact that Schizzy is no Shirley Muldowney (Queen of the drag strips). She has also proven that she lacks night vision, and depth perception. Because of these faults, Schizzy misjudges the point of impact, and rather badly. Over the rapping of the hotrod engine, she hears what proves (by footprint dents) to be Slats McGee's feet stomping across my Merc's evidently not so hard, hardtop.

Schizzy then panics and bolts to the loud Ka-booms of a double barreled shotgun. She pulls a Benedict Arnold, rocking and rolling and leaving her twin sister Lizzy tipped over backwards and covered in dust and more. Lizzy is cut down in midstream. Some things are best served to remain ignorant of, but let it be said that Lizzy is engendered with conniption fits punctuated with raw expletives. Bypassing the shock of mixed metaphors, Lizzy claims to have made her escape in a wet and most undignified posture. For a lengthy period thereafter, she refuses to converse with her turncoat twin.

Meanwhile Slats, who falsely claims title to the unofficial world record for the hop-skip-and jump, open field track event, has in midair, let go his hold on the old tom, And there are those cheater, telltale dents in the roof of my wheels (which McGee absolutely refuses to take responsibility for).

The record he claims for the hop-skip-and jump title is totally bogus. Pardon the pun but a fowl foul disqualifies the attempt. And the leap is further aided by a shotgun blast, fear, desperado turkey and a particularly intent, large fanged dog.

Slats, upon crash landing in the opposite ditch, rescues Lizzy, not from wetting herself but at least from the dog, and more pointedly, from ol' man Hoptoit's double barrel. While hiking up her pants on a dead run, Lizzy joins Slats and the twosome hightail it down the road. Their escape is hidden in the dust cloud of the long-gone Mercury.

As for Oxy Bob Long, well, he takes to the woods and becomes lost for approximately ten days. No one reports him missing.

I snag my sweatshirt on the barbed wire fence. Bare to the waist, I leave it dangling. Rhonda shifts into *lose-guard-dog* gear and leaves me in her dust. I follow her well-defined cloud. She leads me in the opposite direction of our pre-planned escape route. I don't care. I catch up with her a couple miles down the road.

The moon breaks through the clouds to halo her image. She seems small and vulnerable as I sneak behind. She trots along, giggling insanely. I remember the German shepherd setting off her fear a lifetime ago. I can't resist. I mimic the guttural growl of a junkyard dog and grab a hunk of her tight tush.

Rhonda is not only agile; she's extremely fast out of the gate. Amazingly, however, her great stamina wanes. She easily surmounts the four minute mile barrier then slowly starves of oxygen. I catch up to her a scant two miles up the lane. I notice right off she is no longer giggling. She is quite happy to see me however. We embrace there on that old country road. Dissipating oxygen is replaced with passion. Our hearts beat wildly, but as one.

We find an old barn to hide out in. The barn has a hayloft full of loose hay. The hay still radiates a little heat. I wrestle out of my damp burglar gear. I don't stop there. Rhonda hangs back. She's shivering and embracing herself. Instinct tells me not to push her. I burrow under the hay and make little snuggly noises, snore a little — make myself look none too eager to get it on when I'm delirious with whatever ecstasy awaits beyond the X-rated books called *DESIRE*...

Rhonda finally acquiesces. Once she makes her decision she doesn't fool around. It's dark and I can't see much more than her silhouette. It's enough and it's erotic. The sweater, bra and blouse are bad and good enough, but the way she wiggles, jiggles or wriggles out of her wet, clingy jeans and undies makes my heart do a drum solo. She could be a pro stripper goin' *all the way*. But when she snuggles into the hay she's maybe three feet from my nest, and that's a little tepid, yet not; all aspects considered.

There's no stopping the subtle heat waves radiating — sorta abstractly yet perceptible — as though she wants to but her conscience is locked in a contest — moral code versus curiosity and desire.

Me, well, I'm something akin to Oxy Bob; also a living oxymoron: prone-erect. I will not make the first move and it's killin' me. I try to concentrate on her father. What it would be like to be shotgunned down. What would death be like? I imagine being buried in Mr. Carmelnjam's garden. Fertilizer? How rude! I sigh and roll over. Maybe I drift off. I doubt it possible. Regardless, it is there, in that hayloft with the moon shining shafts of lovelorn light through the open bay, with a dozen coyotes suddenly howling the *Lonesome Polecat Blues* from the distant hills, that I discover there's nothing turns my stomach quicker than a pair of warm breasts mashed against my back.

In hindsight, I give pause to admit our first coupling touched more on a ludicrous comedy show than a tender love scene as portrayed in the flicks.

We squirm, we wrestle, and we stir up hay motes. There's all that flesh everywhere but there. As I wonder why Mother Nature chooses to protect the passage to ecstasy beneath the camouflage of a bristly briar patch, the urge to sneeze comes over me. With one arm wrapped snugly around Rhonda's neck, afraid she might change her mind, my fingers pinch my nose to waylay the sneeze, charley horses seize the calves of my legs. Kicking and thrashing, nearly passing out from lack of air, a paradoxical rapture beyond anything I'd ever imagined, assails my being. Spasms initiated by my charley's are the driving force Rhonda's primal instincts naturally arch into.

Nonetheless, our first exploratory probe into the mysteries of sexual eroticism is not realistically compared with eating ice cream as if there's no tomorrow, although it is excruciatingly delicious. It is simply far beyond chocolate, and far, far better. Sex is in fact, the most unbearably joyous discovery in the universe! Why had we waited so long?

All too soon our rapture explodes in a dazzling eruption and light show. We cry, we giggle. We sneeze. The coyotes howl and the Charlie horses are assuaged. An old parable states: *If you don't get it right the first time, try, try, and try again.* With the vitality of youth we do…and we do and we, WOW!

It turns out Rhonda enjoys sex as much, or possibly…(not likely) more than I. But the two of us are products of a monogamous, long forgotten, moral standard. Never again will we follow the wayward paths of Bonnie and Clyde. Our lives of crime are past tense. We've initiate ourselves into the secret cult loosely described as *adulthood*.

After first light we set out for home by hitchhiking on a road with seemingly zero traffic. We hike for maybe five miles before we dogtrot past the Hoptoit Egg Factory. Who'd a thunk Ol' man Hoptoit would come rattling up the road in his archaic pickup truck. He throws out the anchor when he spots us, neighborly old cuss.

Great grampa Hoptoit is a wrinkled old boy. His beak touches his chin in conjunction with the turned down slash of his lipless mouth. He squints admiringly at Rhonda through recessed beady peepers. And he's duded up for a trip to town. He wears bib overalls under a fashionably tattered sport coat. On his shriveled head, he wears a plaid hunting hat with earflaps down and bill pointing straight up. The cap strings are bow-tied 'neath his neck waddle under a shrunken chin. I find it difficult to distinguish the old geezers profile from that of last night's aborted dinner.

The freeze-dried, rain-pruned sun-shrunken goober has a workout herding his rattle-trap pickup between chuckholes and drainage ditches as we carom in the general direction of town.

The old curmudgeon allows he's on a chicken feed run. He's hopping mad about *"Some godamm wuthless egg suckin', hen house rustler, who'd gone thataway and escaped his blazin' scattergun."* Hoptoit commences whistling *Davy Crocket* in ominous tones. My feet are practically pushing through the floorboards as we dodge past an oncoming truck on the off side of the road. And I wonder if he originated in England before the Revolutionary War. It's been said that ol' man Hoptoit has been around this neck o' the woods since before the *Dead Sea* took sick. I wonder if the old codger notices that I wear a girl's letterman sweater with nothing underneath. Rhonda's some smaller than I. The dry old fart might just be a victim of macular degeneration...not to wish bad on anyone — as I nearly pray that Hoptoit's German man-eater ate my sweatshirt as a consolation prize.

The old raptor lets us out at the feed store. We hoof it away from the immediate area at a high rate of speed breathing twin sighs of relief. We find my (our) Merc parked in front of the Oxy-Slats bachelor pad. We don't go in. The keys are in the ignition. We steal our car back from that traitorous Schizzy Borden.

Rhonda's dad is at work. Her mom is out rounding up a combination search party/lynch mob. Rhonda packs a suitcase, grabs some goodies out of her hope chest, and takes along her piggy bank full of her life savings. We thoughtfully leave her folks a note.

We are married in Reno the next day, and until forever ends I will remain unforgiven by Rhonda's Mother, Elvira, the not-so-sweet Mrs. Carmelnjam.

***

So here I sit all these years later, separated and stranded by a kazzilion miles of heartbreaking, logging camp blues, which should be a tearjerker song. Poor, pitiful me, with no psychic powers to draw from.

And still, there burns a pulse in Rhonda I can never put a finger on. Even after all our years as one, she is at times taken with melancholy. When this state of being overtakes her, her gorgeous eyes seem to travel off to a distant place so far away, I wonder if she's someone else. Does she fantasize a Camelot completely removed from the kingdom I have provided with my love for her? Am I, in her grand scheme of things, a mere accident of circumstance? In awful contemplation of permanently losing her, I wonder if she has occasion to silently sing that nostalgic second verse from *Paul Simon's Slip Slidin' Away,* while immersed in an entirely different desire.

And I think about things that might've been as I rise from my sorrowful musings to search the cupboards for a little shot of memory enhancement to spike my fresh pot of coffee. I take a pull straight from the frostbite remedy and feel it spread through my gut. Funny, the lonely trailer shrinks all the more. I envision that first Thanksgiving when we'd became as one; how much I loved her then, how that love blossomed to become the vitality that makes me tick.

The money in her piggy bank soon goes the way of the buffalo, as did my pittance of an unemployment check. I muse about that old tom turkey, and I also think about the way things might have gone. If we'd have made the grab, I'll bet my month's wages the ol' turkey would have been tougher and stringier than ol' man Hoptoit. And I tip back another shot of pain tonic and pour another half cup in my pre-spiked coffee. At least my cheeks are beginning to feel rosy.

We dined on bologna sandwiches in a cheap motel that first Thanksgiving. Come to think of it, I believe it was during that repast, I might possibly have committed a slight error in judgment.

As we reminisced about the turkey trot, I confessed to Rhonda that I was the mean dog that nipped her on her sweet spot that hairy, scary segment of a terror filled night.

Rhonda bestows on me her subtle, half lidded, cool and tempestuous gaze. An enigmatic quality, more intimidating than sensual exude live sparks from deep inside those beautiful orbs.

I discover there's more to Rhonda than passion, athleticism, and intelligence. Payback sneak attacks start with a bucket of water propped above the door. From that cold, cruel awakening forth, her elaborate gags and hoaxes turn into a cache of dirty tricks that will, over time, involve our offspring.

As I sip the truth serum, the memories become all the more vivid. Our first Rhonda clone, named Sierra, came uncannily close to nine months from the turkey trot. Our daughter is a win-win. Back then she deferrers me from the draft. Now she presents us with our first granddaughter. But wait a second. Time out for a jolt of liquid reality they call responsibility. And I knock it back straight from the neck. I have a family to feed. I need a job. Being from a family of loggers, I take to the woods — and the weather — and the insufferable workload. But if you don't know any other life, the sum of circumstance is not a reality, and you and yours are richer than the Rockefellers. So, to keep on truckin', I tip up the jug, and with Adam's apple bobbing, I watch cross-eyed, the bubbles rise.

With ear shattering screams, my second daughter, Cheyenne comes out swinging. Cheyenne might well have been *Cayenne*. But that's the way it goes, huh, first your money then your clothes. Just thinking back on those sleepless nights urges me to imbibe a double quaff. I'm beginning to see more than I understand.

She, being Rhonda, is pregnant soon. It seems Rhonda and I don't need a crystal ball to see. We're perpetuating in the usual, unusual fashion. Time draws near to become proponents of birth control, and that's worthy of a by-god toast.

Number three is the son of sons, Hap. Rhonda's prize is all dimples and grins; well, not to mention dirty diapers, snot, puke and the usual frogs, snails and a long, long row of questions, and experiments, that eventually leads to the discovery of the difference between Hap and girls. So here's to Hap, and viva la difference — and I drink to it!

The similarities between raising boys and girls are not always the same: as Yogi Berra might have said, but it will always weigh heavy that I did not show Hap the affection I openly display for my girls. I swallow a little dollop of antiseptic. Well, despite me and my archaic ways, my boy grew up to be a man's man. I'm gratified that he has more of his mother's personality and can publically display affection to most anyone but me. Growing up is toughest on me, and I will, you know, later...after another snort and more reminiscing. So here's to the third verse of Paul Simon's *Slip Slidin Away!*

As my children grow, so do the practical jokes. It's as if it all is somehow my fault that Rhonda fell for me instead of some rich cull who would sweep her off to yon Kasbah in the land of milk, honey and piles of money. Hey! I made a rhyme, and here's to that long ago crime! I drink to that.

In truth I can't fathom a life without my wife! All this reminiscing has left me choked up to say the least...I swallow a large dose of antiseptic — to clear my throat and my thoughts, you understand. But the dosage is too weak, and I fall back in it.

In the interim there are short sheets, shrunken sweaters, the wedgies and any one or two of her daily-dozen tricks. I retaliate with the ol' three-cup bra, and the crotch-less panties. I remember episodes involving gluing her tenny-runners to the floor. Along comes the bogus doggie do. And there is something about a fancy dress at a party and a leaky drinking glass during a toast that turns into a real gone crisis....

Lulls in the storms leave me leery. Dispirited palls can easily be faked. But when these low pressure centers hover over Rhonda, and hours turn to days of inactivity, I, in empathy, become lackadaisical. These periods sometimes last beyond her periods. And I, being ostracized from her favors convert into the perfect boor. Am I talking marriage here? I think I need a drink, and I don't mind if I do. . .

My little bride has her ways of dragging me kicking and thrashing out of my personal doldrums. And I relive a couple of unprintably unseemly tricks... These memories are dragging me down. I pour myself a shot of half kicker, half sleeper. I'm thinking my thinking is bassackwards, but I learn to open doors carefully. My instincts teach me to be aware of certain stages of the moon, Halloween, St. Patrick's Day and April 1st. But I can't win 'em all, no matter how sharpened my instincts become.

This infamous day is a beast. I forget to set the alarm. (*Or did I*)? I'm starting out behind. Suspiciously, I can't find my boots. And when I do, I break a lace. I'm even later after changing a flat tire, I discover the gas gauge is passed out on the empty peg. From there, things go tits up. I'm beginning to wax a little leery, but no, no one woman's brain could be devious enough to…no one would go so far to set up a… No. I forget about it.

The day perpetuates in the style it started. Hang dog and hung over, I drop my guard and watch morosely as her haymaker knocks me silly; me, with no white towel to wave in surrender.

Stoop-shouldered and beat, I enter my castle. Something is amiss. No greetings from woman or children, even after I shout. I search the house. I discover my wife and children in the far bedroom. They are bound and gagged, squirming on the floor. Out of the ol' periphery, I spot a madman pointing *my* shotgun at *my* head! I dive out the door as I hit the deck and crawl like a nitro fueled dragster back outside.

My hunting rifle is in my truck in the rack behind the seat. I don't remember doing the John Wayne theatrics. They, my family, explain to me how I dive through a window in an explosion of shattered glass, turn a somersault, do a roll and end up in a military style isosceles triangle, with rifle pointing at the homemade mannequin sitting in a chair. The dummy, visibly pointing my unloaded shotgun at the bedroom door, is, on close inspection, unrealistically pitiful.

I watch my family convulse in laughter — even man's best friend, the family dog laughs so hard he cries. Being the sport I am; I laugh with them although my yucking is strained through thoughts of vengeance.

So, the next day during lunch I catch a frog and temporarily transfer it to my nosebag (lunch bucket).

That night I sit innocently reading the paper while watching Rhonda on the sly. Finally, during her dishwashing ordeal, she opens my lunch pail. I wait for her to scream in terror...and nothing. No scream — no giant leap for womankind, no outward signs of uncontrolled terror. Damn. The frog must have somehow pulled a Harry Houdini. It's back to the ol' drawing board for me. The sex was great that night. The frog of course totally slipped my mind until I unwrapped my sandwich the next *High Noon*. The poor little feller. He's mashed flat. His buggy eyes stare up from one crust, his webbed feet sticking out beyond the lettuce on the other. I'm hungry but not starving.

It's hard to imagine Rhonda being capable of mashing a defenseless amphibian. She hadn't. The mutilated toad proves to be a party favor she'd stashed in her bag of miscellaneous newts and bats and hair of the salamander paraphernalia awaiting a favorable opportunity. The fake frog works. I lose my appetite and a temporary hunk of my self-esteem. But fortunately, over my married years I've found that self-worth grows back.

So I take a little slurp of liquid shock absorber and revisit the many times she caught me in the shower and instrumentalized the kitchen faucets to play me like a human calliope. And I relish the occasions when I catch her napping on the couch and immerse her arm in warm water...to my delight, she pees her panties every single time.

***

But y'know, in the end, I gotta conclude that Rhonda more than gets even for that sneaky little fake dog nip on the posterior in the dark of night all those years ago.

Being an early blooming high school cheerleader and prom queen, I can't imagine her having designs on a career in modeling… Not back then. The *Twiggy look* was in for chrissakes. Rhonda, with her Marilyn Monroe bod was and is, way over qualified. Perhaps at the time she was on the lookout for some tall, dark and debonair doctor or lawyer or the like to come riding in on a big white horse and sweep her off to the Kasbah. But by thee gods, I ain't such a bad catch. I don't chew snoose. I don't belch or scratch nor urinate in public. I'm still, after all these years, a semiliterate action man. I've taken her and the brats on a purty wild ride since 1965.

And I suppose my woman could have done much worse. Hell, she might've ended up with Oxy Bob, or Slats McGee. Nah! I can't force my brain to conjure up an image that depressing. It turns my stomach queasy just thinking about it. I ingest a couple of shots of internal salve cure-all.

My motor is hittin' on all eight! I feel ten feet tall! I grab my pen and tablet and commence composing my *little woman* a little letter. With the salutations all in place, I get right after the main body. I get the opening line all ciphered in when I hear a pensive knock on my castle door.

I'm a tad surprised to see ol' Starvin Marvin, the company controller, come a callin'. Starvin' Marvin worries over the ledgers and books so devoutly, I doubt he took time for his mother's funeral, let alone Thanksgiving and Christmas. Yet here he is standing on my fold-out stoop, all covered with snow and wringing his hands.

Like all bean counters, Marvin is a nervous sort. But his eyes seem shiftier than normal. I swear he's shivering up a sweat. I figure he spotted my light bulb burning in Alaska's excuse for broad daylight and it has his panties in a bunch. But I have my rights. I've got a letter to write by god, even if for some strange reason my eyes are not focusing properly. I'm on the verge of saying, "Shove it up Uranus," but it turns out it isn't the electricity I'm wasting that's turned his Skid Road beak red. No. Hell no.

Good ol' Marv stutters out something about receiving a radio patch from the fishing vessel, *FV Deep Six*. My main man Marv allows the signal was weak, but he's gathered that my wife is aboard her, and *Deep Six* is headed this way.

Holy Crowley! Somehow Rhonda Cool caught a flight, made it clean into Juneau, and has savoir faired the Deep Six skipper into piloting her across *Icy Strait!*

Next thing I hear is that my ol' buddy, Stuttering Marv, enlightens me to the fact that the radio patch said *FV Deep Six* is sailing past the log rafts and just a short distance from entering *Eagle Beak Boat Harbor. Perhaps* within the hour.

A sensation of great calm washes over me. Somehow, through the powers of Kinetic energy, pure thoughts of love and devotion imbued in *me* has drawn *her* across a continent or two!

The feeling of contentment doesn't stay with me for much more than a heartbeat. There are a few thousand household chores I've sort of let slide since Rhonda flew the coop for Florida. I waste little diplomacy on Starvin' Marvin. I suppose I nearly flatten his face with the slamming door as I hump into it.

What to do with that horrible glop of greenish-yellow slime growing angora hair peppered with coffee grounds living in the sink and lurking on the countertops?

There's little time for KP. I rummage around in the debris and find a couple empty beer boxes. I roll up my sleeves and begin the process of delusion. The crawl in tunnel I opened under the trailer after my derring-do backflip from the trailer roof will make a dandy, temporary hiding place for the dirty dishes. And my hollowing out this hole beforehand has got to be way beyond coincidence.

Yankee ingenuity and a box filled with tater peels, egg shells and unidentifiable sludge I toss in the garbage can will assist the completion of my instant fix.

I dart around like a one-winged bumblebee caroming off the ceiling and walls. The noise is intense enough to be an infernal internal drum. The alcohol treatment caused a partial paralysis, both in my motor skills, and as later determined, in my thought process. I flounder outside with the crated dirty dishes, slipping and sliding in snow. From the prone position, it doesn't take long to roll over, re-box unknown paraphernalia, and broken shards. From here it's easy to crawl under the trailer to shove the scuzzy mess out of sight.

When disturbed, the reek of ammonia and dry rot exuding from the pile of dirty work clothes overflowing the hamper and trying to slip under the bed, prove to be a little tough on my somewhat sensitive schnozz. I'm forced to employ both hands with thumbs and forefingers extended like robotized pincers working at arm's length. I gag some; howl some. Wyatt gurges but Earp is temporarily lodged in my throat. I swallow the fiery liquid erupting from below. My briefs and long johns seem to be fused together with scruffy wool sox and one another. They've formed a moldy ball, giving rise to an odor that, if not for the *Geneva Convention*, just might rival nerve gas as a biological weapon of war.

Stay down Earp. I bundle the long dead rigor mortised thing inside the confines of the dirty sheets. I scamper off to the company Laundromat. I stuff stiff wads of wool, cotton, denim indiscriminately into four machines. With the lids closed I breathe again. I will craftily sneak back with the laundry soap I'd forgotten. I turn the washers on and scurry back to the trailer for one quick, thorough pass with a broom. And with housekeeping accomplished, I beat cheeks for the boat harbor.

Waist-deep snow with no trail open toward the cove and the stiff-leg dock confront me. This dock is where my woman and I will be reunited. With the icy air biting my lungs, my bounding leaps falter to an agonizing crawl. Horizontal snow pelts my face. Frozen flakes originating from somewhere above Labrador sail in flapjack size flying saucers, homing in on my immediate surroundings. I envision her there, somewhere where the gunmetal gray sky collides with the frothy pewter of the raging sea.

Knowing her, I know she'll be cold. I rush back to the trailer and jack up the thermostat hoping the warm air will not give birth to anything odorously appalling.

I stagger back to the mouth of my trail just in time to witness an awesome spectacle. As if ordained, a knock-down-drag-out gust of wind brings a clearing sky. The snowstorm departs Alaska and whistle-whoops for America. Left behind is a sheen so vivid, that I'm struck dumb. And more than that. Actually, in my over-indulged state, it seems the dipshit factor has set in.

Squinting through watery eyes, I see the resident boats tethered in the harbor the home guards call Raven's Roost. And I can actually see beyond the hooked peninsula. I see no commercial craft anywhere near Raven's Roost boat harbor, but way outside, I spot a trim little schooner cutting proudly through the whitecaps. To her, the storm seems less than a nuisance.

The fishing boat sparks a need in me. I lunge ever onward until I can clearly see the logs chained end to end and lashed together to form the stiff-leg dock. The stringers extend beyond the ebb of the tide. The plank catwalk scabbed haphazardly on top the stiff-leg logs are slippery under the best conditions. The loppy walkway is extremely precarious with ice stealthily waiting beneath the deceiving blanket of snow.

I glance back at the vessel forging through the icy froth. It's not making much headway. I have plenty of time to return to our love cabana and trade my rubber boots for my stickery soled calk boots. I slither back up my meandering trail. Home again, I sit outside on the stoop to lace up my spike-soled knee-high dancing slippers and deepen my tracks toward the boat harbor. At the top of the rise, I pause to check the progress of the schooner that pilots my lady-love home to me. The fishing craft seems to be marking time. I slip off a glove to rub my chin in estimation of the distance the boat has gained since my last sighting. It's then that I become all too aware of the rough stubble gouging my hand.

Becoming sophisticated with age, Rhonda doesn't particularly enjoy whisker rash on certain areas of her creamy skin. There is no accounting for her notion of suave, but considering the rewards and recalculating her time of arrival, I turn back and beat a hasty retreat for the mini-bathroom. And wearing calked boots inside is taboo, so there's that unlacing ceremony to complete.

Eventually, I'm propped before that evil little mirror. The face staring back into mine tells an unconscionable tale of decadence. The whiskers are long and smattered with grisly white cactus spurs. The stranger's eyes are blurry, unfocused blobs rimmed in blood and tinged with black circles dissimilar to halos.

Oh, well. I splash scalding water at the target, and after slathering on shaving soap, I slash at the whiskers with a vengeance born of shame. The blood is thin. The razor cuts bleed well. I splash on liberally the eau de pew. I stem the blood-flow with tiny wads of toilet paper. The wads stick well to tender areas. Will I ever learn to shave left-handed? Well, maybe I should practice more often than once in a blue moon....

Outside I worm my feet back into my tall spiked boots. Evidently a glop of snow has loosened from the roof and made a direct hit down the mouth of my right boot. I notice the slush almost immediately after stuffing said foot inside. I ignore my quickly numbing toes and lopsidedly hit the trail with due haste.

I'm unpleasantly surprised by the fishing slab, and on my wife's progress. The tide must be running with the current and against the will of that old plank's skipper. I would endeavor to drive a stake in the snow to mark whether the Schooner is losing or gaining ground — had I a stake and a hammer. But I do believe the icy adventure is sharpening my somewhat alcohol-hampered motor skills. The jaws of those arctic blasts are biting clear through my holey Mackinaw. I run my tongue over my lips. They are cracked and dry. I work at wetting them, my raw tongue laboring like a windshield wiper in a dust storm.

I fantasize that first welcome home embrace. When warm kisses turn erotic…but what about my boozy breath? I got a little ahead of myself, somehow. It's gonna take more than a stiff brush to stampede the monkey herd that has taken residence in there. I scurry back to our little bungalow on wheels. I reverse the boot lacing ordeal once more. I run to the mini-bathroom, rediscover a bottle of mouthwash, and gargle while thinking about things better left unprinted. I spit the sludge, knock back a shot straight from the bottle, and belch sweetly. I don't let the door slam on my posterior as I sit on the fold-down stoop. I re-lace my knee-highs and spurt for the trail.

Finally the boat draws nearer. She's still a good distance from rounding the point, however. I pull up my coat sleeve to check my watch, simultaneously catching sight of my scruffy shirt. I unbutton my mackinaw and take a gander. The once blue and white striped hickory shirt might well have been with George and the Continentals at Valley Forge. It's time to make a return trip to the ol' miniature domicile. I figure I've got time to shower, slip into a pair of slacks, don a white shirt and sports coat and be there or be square. Man, does that hot water feel good! Upon examination the ensemble is quite stunning. Well, the skull cap pulled down over my ears might be less than a fashion statement. But staring in the mirror I find no real fault. Fact is the shower washed the toilet paper wads from my face, leaving me the debonair rascal look. I wink at my image, pull on my semi-dry wool sox, and head out to the stoop for the boot-pulling ordeal. Wouldn't you know I'd break a string! There's hardly time to thread a new one — if I could find one — I tie a knot below the lace hooks and crow-hop the trail high-half stepping. I envision Rhonda waiting on the stiff leg as I make my entrance replicating a mildly handicapped business executive late for an important engagement.

The vessel is no longer in sight. They must've slipped behind the point to make a leeward approach then shoot through the narrows with the waves breaking astern. I visualize Rhonda standing at the bow" a beautiful bowsprit, those half-lidded golden flecked fawn eyes gazing sensually, wanting for me in the most erotic way.

I hasten to the dock, kicking snow off the steps leading to the waterline. I inch my way along, feeling a little disoriented by the motion before me. The floating logs lashed together to form the stiff leg undulate ominously with the will of ground swells combing in from the green water outside the snug harbor.

I sense the last of my liquid courage evaporate as I kick snow into the bay and navigate with dizzying caution. Those Ice encrusted planks nailed haphazardly to form a walkway atop the logs, have, over time listed this way and that. As if a roller coaster slowly winding down, the logs heave sluggishly underfoot. It takes the better part of forever to ambulate my way to the first empty stall lashed at a right angle from the stiff leg.

Legs braced as if an old salt, I smooth the crease in my slacks, take on haughty airs, and wait for the schooner to deliver my beloved home to me.

I wait and wait. The frigid wind knifes through my slacks. Gusts embolden heavier gusts. The temperature drops. I suppose that's why a dog up in camp begins to bark. A dog barking brings to my numbing brain a certain nostalgia from days of yore recently rehashed. The sword begins to lethargically penetrate, the blade to ponderously twist inside my cold, sober skull. A dim light blinks on and slowly brightens. I've been sucker punched in the belly while my back's turned again!

I turn a graceful pirouette while curses die on my lips as a sneaker wave surges into the logs. I struggle like a high-wire walker, but I have no balance pole. I teeter on one leg and windmill, vainly fighting the dizzying pull of gravity. I hold my breath as the bay rushes up to make my acquaintance. Impolitely,

I twist away, colliding flat on my back with a great resounding splash and bellow. Surprisingly, the water feels warmer than the wicked wind. I recover my breath, if not my voice, in less than five minutes.

I splash the backstroke some. But my heavy boots pull me down. I roll over and try the sidestroke to no avail. Holding my breath, I jackknife down, kick away my partially unlaced boot and work frantically at the laces of the other. I'm seconds from drowning as I fight my way to the surface only to discover that I'm standing in waist-deep water.

Defeated, I retrieve my waterlogged boot. I wade ashore and hop-cripple my way home. Like used, abused and shifty eyed Starvin' Marvin, I too have shriveled and shivered more. And now I'm forced to seek what I know will be there to greet me.

***

She's tanned and fit and even more beautiful than ever. She stands statuesque in the doorway, a can of spray deodorizer in her hand. She stares into my eyes with a bemused, bewitched gleam in hers. Her eyelids settle to half-mast. But still, that spontaneous twinkle cannot be denied. She helps me out of my boot, and pairs it to the one in my frozen hand. She pries off my clingy, soaked clothes and steers me into a steamy, mini-shower.

She sits at the café booth-like table when I, shrouded in our last clean bath towel, reappear as if it's just another day.

She arrived on a fishing boat, no denying that fact. The boat brought her across the strait the day before today. She'd easily sneaked past me and stayed the night at Starvin' Marvin's digs, where she and good ol' Marv's dingbat ol' lady, Florri, cooked up their coldly brewed cauldron, my ego being the main ingredient in their cruel and tasteless vichyssoise.

Hindsight is often debilitating. I recall the rustling drapes over there this very morning. If I had only known Rhonda's was the silhouette behind that curtain… I relive the moon shot in my mind's eye, but it's fantasy, not even close to reality.

"I almost came running," Rhonda says, "When you fell from the roof and did that cute little circus act routine. I'm so happy I resisted. It was so adorable how you went up head first and came down, well, unusually, instead of feet first.

"It was cool how you piled the snow for a landing pad before you did that human catapult thingy. Maybe you can do it over. The snow's piling up again. I could video it if you promise not to dent up the trailer anymore — after you fix it.'

"I didn't fall, y'know," I improvise, "I was just foolin' around. I decided on the spur of the moment to make the deepest snow angel ever made. Sorry about the dents. They ain't gonna leak, though. Can't fix 'em till I get some Bondo…if we ever get out of here — back to civilization."

Her eyes smirk, but she lets the lies lie for another time. But it's the notion her and that nosy-body neighbor watching from the ringside seats that cause a yearning in my soul. They witnessed almost the entire pantomime unravel before their prying female eyes. And if that's not an invasion of privacy, well, there oughta be a law. The parrot and the fox even snuck out my trail to the boat harbor and witnessed my how-not-to demonstration in the shallow bottom of the bay. Luckily, there was no camcorder in the mix. I might, if I live to be 100, live it down. Personally, I need no picture shows to relive the rise and fall of my demise. It's written all over her face. Staring into my painfully chagrinned eyes, she finally surrenders to loud, obnoxious guffaws.

I focus on the dry bread sitting beside the unwrapped package of bologna on the table. The meat has turned a nefarious shade of green. Our traditional Thanksgiving dinner is prepared and ready to be served.

Rhonda is weak with offensive cackling. I go for the dessert first. Locked in her embrace, my roving hand creeps up and under her sweater. I'm yet again confounded. There's no break in the strap.

"It's a front hook," she whispers sexily. "Something I picked up in Key Largo, um, Bogey."

Her eyes hypnotize mine, and it's Braille with a reverse twist… And eventually, I lick it. Who says you can't teach an old salty dawg a new trick?

Later, as we embrace in sublime afterglow, she reaches beneath her pillow, and extracts, unfolds and reads the opening line of the unfinished letter I'd composed for her and carelessly left on our mini-table. Somehow, she finds my drunken chicken scratchings endearing.

My darling wife,
I'm so miserable without you it's almost as if you are still here.

It's a small victory, but at least a triumph. Or is it? I sigh and roll over. We are not getting any younger. We don't *Play it Again Sam*, as often as we'd like, but if we keep trying someday, we'll get it, um, transcendentally divine. Rapturously perfect. Incomparable. Infinitely sublime. Impeccably flawless. Excruciatingly delicious once more.

I think I drift off for a second. The approach of our resident grizzly brings me out of it. He growls as he attacks the baited sludge I deposited there earlier. The can is outside our bedroom window. The walls are thin. He picks through the defiled leavings from a month of bachelor's debauched eating habits.

The juvenile bear sounds quite ferocious. Maybe he's ungratefully finicky, but as noted earlier, there's nothing that turns my stomach quicker than a pair of soft, warm breasts mashed against my back!

And I'm stone positive we get it right this time. Rhonda moans in excruciatingly delicious sorrow as her tsunami washes over us. So, as the bear roars and wanders off for better pickings, she finally falls into an exhausted sleep. I find her pantyhose on the floor beside the bed. I stealthily tie the legs together in a tight, quite fitting granny knot. When I turn back to spoon to her, my churlish grin is captured in her eyes. She stares enigmatically through those beautiful, hooded, peepers. I sigh again. There will be a payback. It will come when least expected. For now, we sleep it off, although I drift away and the last verse in Paul Simon's Slip Slidin' Away lulls me to sleep.

Thanks go to The Beach Boys' Help Me Rhonda

The Platters The Magic Touch

Johnny Mercer and Bobby Darin's Lonesome Polecat

And especially Paul Simon's last forlorn, but ever compelling verse in Slip Slidin' Away

FOOL'S RUSH
Prior To Alaska

Pale headlights feebly probe the black wall of night. The truck pitches and sways on shocks that absorb little. As the rust-bucket launches headlong into an accursed tempest, the night driver's gnarly ride displays the style and grace of a tugboat floundering through heavy seas and gale-force winds.

Oncoming lights slash the black void. The abruptly alerted, bloodshot eyes of *Mitch Waters* squints into the lightning-like flashes bursting from a solitary set of halogen headlamps. His truck lunges at the invading high beams as if a sow grizzly protecting her cubs.

Startled, reacting subconsciously, Mitch steers hard a' starboard to physically break the sinister pull, the greedy grasp of the *Grim Reaper*. The truck swerves onto the soft shoulder, intent on a nosedive into a flooded ditch. Intuitively, he cranks the wheel and floors the foot-feed. Mitch's truck spins a 180, fishtails, slithers, rights itself and luckily, regains the blacktop unscathed.

Unaware, the man called Mitch, backtracks some 11 miles before he realizes that the taillights of the rig he was following belongs to the same vehicle that had recently blind-sided his truck. He woefully completes an elongated 360 degree turn.

A surge of electricity sends a jolt of adrenaline through his system. A few dog-tired brain cells ignite. That little adventure costs Waters 22 miles and 33 minutes he can ill-afford.

The man driving the truck imagines a camera's flashbulb catching the look on his face when the lights startle him awake. He wonders if his hair actually stood on end. His pits suddenly itch and his mind's eye envisions *her*. It's only natural. She is etched in him

She's a maverick, his Rhonda... one outrageously wild Irish rose. Her face would have convulsed with laughter at the look on his. Hell, her entire body would twitch out. The tears would blur those mischievous eyes and the spasmodic laughter would be infectious. The night-driver concentrates on the road with a hoot, and a threat of renewed vigor.

Incoming jazz Dear Rhonda! Get down an' howl! Your big dog's on the prowl!

The storm subtly closes back over the lonely two-lane. He swerves into the hairpin curves. His fatigued orbs are locked on the shiny snake's twisted blur: heinous yellow stripes strike out of a sea of black. His brain slides in and out of hallucinations, his sanity drifts into dizzying vertigo. His willpower clings to a cotton thread — strains to hold out a little longer, to conquer the enraged night — his thread of sanity reveals appalling signs of stranding.

The truck's radio has faded to static miles back, but an annoying/inspiring verse plays over and over in his echo chamber: *A long ways to go and a short time to get there.* Ol' Mitch holds tight to his obstinate need. He *has* to make it home.

*

The date: April 3rd, time: 9:23. His *little woman* had incited the scenario herself, sometime during the night of March 31st. Rhonda Cool committed devious transgressions while he lay spent and sleeping. The vixen slunk from her side of their bed, and padded silently through the house.

Ms. Waters' depraved side had taken her again. She'd tiptoed through the night and fast-forwarded his life by two full hours. Every clock, including the alarm beside him on the nightstand and his wristwatch alongside it, she'd sprung 120 life cycles ahead.

Mitch Waters faintly remembered his near comatose awakening to the obstinate shrilling of the windup alarm. He revisits his bleary morning rote, the happy exuberance in her eyes as she steered him towards a cruel awakening. She lip-mashes his yawn with a wet kiss that energizes his bedraggled start.

As he'd drove away, the news of his woman's mother, *Frau Ironhosen O'Toole's* upcoming departure waned to a puff of euphoria... a weary notion that mother-in-law was synonymous with holier-than-thou! The all-night DJ announced the *correct* time. His pointless reverie was shattered! It dawned that dawn's on schedule!

He came to a skidding stop. Reality breached his mindless cocoon. He no longer wondered at the Olympic sex of the night before. It was all part of his wife's intricate conspiracy!

He rehashed his feeling of chagrin; he's been had again... had, in more ways than one. She'll expect him to roar home and chase her down with a bucket of ice cold water...she perhaps sat giggling in anticipation of that, or some other form of malicious payback: theirs are wild and uninhibited foreplays, excruciatingly delicious ecstasies.

The man named Mitch, sat contemplating his lust for vengeance. And then, with fenders rattling, he slowly motored away. A mile beyond his turnoff to the woods, where he cut timber, his truck and his laboring brain gathered speed.

He drives 500 miles north. Clear to Bellingham, Washington where he spends the lost interim in near sleepless secrecy, visiting with an old friend by day, reuniting with sticky, vengeful plots by night.

Somewhere inside that mischievous Irish side of Rhonda's brain resides a weak spot: animism, superstition: lingering fear of the unknown.

He plays on his woman's primal instinct for those two days while chilling-out. His mate, his on-again-off-again kindred spirit will be frantic by now. Her vivid imagination will have her poor man carried off into a macabre time warp, a twilight zone born of the inventions of her own anxious mind.

Hee-hee! Paybacks are only a gnarly bitch for those marked in spring-loaded anticipation. Time is now of the essence. He hopes he hasn't lost his edge to the storm. The pickup shudders and gains momentum. He accelerates down and out of the off-cambered *S* curves. The truck's light rear-end side-slips, rights itself, and boogies into slanted, dimly illuminated rain.

The driver's side wiper crow-hops across the windshield, skipping brusquely over zones of beaded water; the blur is nearly impossible to see through. Its unsynchronized counterpart begins screaming *CHIA--pet-CHIA--pet*, with each absurd slap at the incessant deluge.

Bony knuckles rub busy stinging eyes, heavy-lidded orbs dart from the brazenly beaded side of the windshield, back to the opaque.

Narcosis has returned. Squinting into nothingness, the night rider's mind becomes a picture show of virtual reality.

As usual, his mate is the star. The accompanying song accuses: *You Always Hurt The One You Love*. He has. He's mashed Rhonda's spirit flatter than the opossum road kill he' has just *thump-thumped* over.

Mitch's' sleep-psychosis re-creates Snidely Whiplash. Mitch himself becomes the yellow bellied black-hearted villain. He knows deep down he's committed a dastardly foul. The payback wanes to hallucination. Yellow flag! Game forfeited! Breach of etiquette! Brain tampering!

Mitch white-knuckles the wheel of the only vehicle on the road. His pickup careens through the storm to impale a burrow. The tunnel turns out to be the storm-thrashed Henry B. Van Doozer Forest Corridor. The towering, slashing trees are old growth Douglas firs. It seems to Waters' sleep-deprived mind he's been sucked into the wrath of a herd of enraged rogue elephants engaged in a frenzied trunk thrapping contest.

Mitch clings to a dying ember of sanity, and as a horse smells the barn, he senses home and the woman he loves so fiercely. It has come to this: his journey is reduced to a caroming pinball with only a slim chance of survival. No one would be moronic enough to venture through this tumultuous sea of fir needles and windswept broken boughs unless like him: threatened species: lovesick lemming *obsessed* with dire need.

Mitch sees beguiling hurt in Rhonda's intuitive eyes. His vision of her records the shame reflected in her wild id. He envisions her shoulders slumped in worry, fear and anxiety. And he loves her more.

He's crossed the line, gone too far this time. She will never forgive him. He thinks about turning back. There's no place to run. No place to hide from himself: *Dumb to the quick! Insipid over-re-acting selfish S.O.B!*

Miraculously he escapes the precariously swaying trees, the hazardous limbs of spear-point death. The fir needles, cones and alder leaves are left to cavitate in his wake.

*

Waters turns at the country store, creeps across the old red bridge, and eventually his feeble headlights faintly illuminate the meandering lane, which is little more than a causeway over a swamp; a drawbridge before his side-hill castle.

He hits the lights and idles beyond the muskeg and up the mound where stands his and Rhonda's daylight basement abode. The roaring wind will muffle the motor's purr. The black night will hide his clandestine approach.

Mitch twists the key and kills the engine. He coasts to a stop behind the shop. He remembers not to press his foot on the brake pedal and ignite his presence in fluorescent red.

His dilated pupils gather the lights that splash from the house. The shimmering shadows dance wildly through maple boughs. A yellow hue glows dim, yet bravely through closed drapes.

He's set his plot to action—maybe it's just practice, his covert exercises are performed perhaps in painful finality. He pauses in mid-step... the busybody frogs are calling his wife to arms with aid from afar! *WyattEarp! WyattEarp—wyattearp-wyattearrp?* Fortunately, all remains deathly quiet in the inner sanctums of Tombstone...he continues his stealthy closing with the house. The amber glow filtered through the blinds ignite cold silver darts arrowing out of nowhere. Luminous dollops softly impact, then percolate from the concrete walk.

Waters glances at his reset watch. In a singular thump of his heartbeat, the frog posse goes silent. It's as though the amphibians are capable of mental telepathy — are the little croakers attuned to the drumbeats of his heart? The Benedict Arnold SOB in his chest pounds louder than a bass drum!

Rhonda will not have heard the silence. She is an enigma. Her spirit is defined in paradox. The ancestry of strict German logic from *Frau Ironhosen's* genes, at times, dominate the wild leprechaun side inherited from her father. Weird as it seems, his woman is imbued with perverse disciplines...Her nightly showers almost invariably begin at quarter past 11.

**

Waters slips his key in the door, silently wedges it open a crack... All clear!!! He slithers inside. Her bizarre regimen hasn't failed him.

The shower is his gift to her. Multiple outlets aiming pressurized steamy water from six heads stationed strategically on three tiled walls. The sound of pressurized water escaping needle-sized apertures is alive. The hydraulic pressure roars and hisses. Her flume-plumbed shower is more noisome than the storm outside.

He sneaks through the house, creeps along the hall, and slips inside the utility room next to their favorite bath. His breath catches as he envisioned her beautiful face tilted back, welcoming the mesmerizing ecstasy of pulsating force. Her cobalt eyes close in rapture, her yellow hair a slick, flaxen sheen flowing from her scalp – golden ringlets sliding in sudsy spirals halfway down her bowed back. Her lithe fingers stroking her soapy cheeks hiding those mischievous dimples… And beside her elbows, the soap slickened breasts standing with nipples sensually erect. Her supple hips thrust forward, welcoming the powerful pulsing surge… Mitch feels isolated warmth, sudden pressing need!

But wait … there's that *little flaw* in the mechanical-hydraulic workings of the shower: with the culmination of such a tremendous volume of water focused on one area….

Sometimes, even when it's fourth down and forever, a man's gotta go for it – he hardly hesitates. Of course he can't resist! He abruptly opens the valve on the hot water faucet in the utility room sink.

Her scream is harsh: an icy shrill! An electric banshee soprano!

He shuts the tap and she winds down from the vortex of his long overdue avenging of her ornery April fools gags.

Chocking back guffaws, Mitch thinks about experimenting. He tries to imagine her caterwauling, her kangaroo-like bounding leaps; her wild levitations if he were to…to play Ms. Rhonda like a human calliope! Oh, he is a proud maestro, a born again legend in his own mind… but then…Mitch is not really a musician – isn't that deep. Besides, he has that *other* performance playing on his mind…

Looking back, he just might have wanted for a mirror. But at the time he is all too ready to make something happen. And he does.

Mitch busily machinates his own destiny! He scrambles out of his clothes and he comes to her.

Suffice to note the condition he deploys would best be described as bedraggled and unshaven: eyes, bleary and bloodshot

– accentuated by puffy black circles: Dull orbs glazed in carnal want. His below waist extremity is on the rise. He wears lust, along with a triumphant Cheshire-cat grin.

Her image is sexily distorted by the frosted glass shower door; his heart pounding, appendage at attention, he expels a distinctly unique version of a villainous chuckle, something he may have remembered from a bad French movie....

Mitch pops open the door and shouts above the roar: *HONEY I'm HO––* and swiftly, so startled, she jump-pivots!

The physical similarities between Rhonda and the Woman-Hitler abruptly ends at the larynx! Without benefit of the camo make-up and her clothes, the doused cat matriarch is a ghastly sight to behold! Reaction time is recorded in nanoseconds!

Her scream of terror blends with his! He leaps, and in midair, performs an outlandish, gravity defying pirouette! And with legs and arms flailing, hair again standing on end, aforementioned protuberance wilted, he takes note of another's presence!

A hearty cackle explodes from the fully dressed hedonist blocking his escape! She's braced herself in the doorframe – somehow manages a momentary stay of convulsions.

The flashbulb explodes! The exaggerated shock frozen on his face seemed magnified – is indeed recorded for album posterity on the film behind the blinding yellow flash!

Only then, did Rhonda's uniquely wild laughter become outrageous – eventually... contagious.

Later, much later, Mitch lay staring into the night–listening, listening. Listening to Rhonda giggle herself to sleep... *Dirty double triple damn HELL! Daylight Savings Time starts in the morn – ARGH!!!*

*****

DOG DAZE

Ya gotta make allowances for Mitch. He is growing older if not wiser. His brain has been thoroughly washed, wrung out and hung up to dry. The results are a touch bizarre....

A fine fall day

Eager footfalls crush delicate crystals of frozen stalagmites. It's autumn's first exploratory nibble. The asparagus-like heads of hoarfrost will soon dissolve under the ruby orb's assuaging warmth. Other than the crunching sound and the telltale tracks of man and beast, little harm is wrought on mother earth's rugged outer crust.

Light smoke hangs suspended in the valleys, and stains the jagged fir ridges a majestic shade of purple. White clouds dot the rump of the awakening day.

An appaloosa morning, Mitch breathes deeply. *Seldom witnessed and that's a fact.* The atmosphere is a balm to the senses of both man and beast.

The hardwoods acknowledge their surrender, if not their modesty. A majority of leaves cling stubbornly to branches, and are just beginning to weep individual shades of bloodstained death throes. There's an ill-defined passion, a hidden drama attached to summer's inevitable demise, Mitch opines. Has he walked this earth before? Was his previous id that of a dog that lived for this kind of partnership? Or is his thought process blasting off for outer space again? His woman, Rhonda says she's never met a man with such a wild and vivid imagination.

She could be right — if women saw the world through the eyes of a man... Or did females present their perceptions in the light shards of a colorless kaleidoscope? He would never know — unless reincarnation in the form of a female is in his cards, and that seems just *unjust*. Would a woman, blinded by practicality, see the family pet as being charged with extra-sensory perceptions? Would a woman, so pragmatically inclined, describe patches of blue in cloudy skies as *sucker holes*, luring the unwary outside for a thorough soaking? Mitch thinks not.

Can a woman, such as Rhonda, see magic in an autumn morning?

"Yeah, probably," Mitch sighs. "A woman is not only cunning and canny; she's nimble of thought process...as ambidextrous as a switch hitter's eye, or a fox on a nefarious mission... Only women's brains are twice as cunning, calculating, and God almighty, ambidextrous if I ain't mistaken! And that's part of a woman's mystique... And hey! If you don't believe women are a different species than man, just go shopping with one. And that's enough said about *Venus* and *Mars* circling the same orbit, by god! Hey! I believe I just solved one of the great mysteries of life."

The dog pays no mind to his master's off-the-wall musings or the crisp beauty surrounding him. He's beside himself with the moist scents of fall's lusty animal arousals. He is a born hunter. His breeding and instincts tell him so. Even though he's juvenile, he's near as big as a fifty-five gallon barrel with legs. His first hunt and he hasn't a clue as to what precisely he should be hunting.

Mitch, the man behind the twelve gauge shotgun, doesn't believe in training his big Lab to do what will prove to be ingrained in his retriever. Like Mitch himself, the dog knows only the bare fundamentals of discipline. But the dog, Mitch knows, is on the verge of becoming as one with his *pack leader*. They've become part-time kindred spirits — of the same soul, of the same purpose.

The dog is agog with the pictures entering his brain through his keen sense of smell. He actually howls with delight, his nose leading him on a trail so twisted and confused it seems to defy any semblance of logic.

With tail propelling, the eager dog dives into the willow tangles causing a covey of quail to explode in a blur of buzzing wings — an outrage of startled chirps.

The shotgun is up, butt piece pocketed into Mitch's shoulder. The safety is thumbed off and the muzzle sweeps out to lead the covey.

But Mitch doesn't squeeze the trigger. He isn't sure the dog is looking where the gun points. Mitch knows he has to get it right, especially this first time. He lowers the scattergun, just as a loner caroms out of the brambles as if a wayward rocket, keening to catch up.

The report of the 12-guage startles the dog, but watches as the bird loses its attitude of flight to tumble through the air, while a few feathers dance in the sky. The dog is on the bird almost immediately, but the quail thrashes in its death throes and the bird dog is bewildered — until he hears the familiar words of his master sing out: "Atta boy. Bring the bi-rird. Bring 'im here, boy."

And the dog reacts to one of the few disciplines it knows and enjoys beyond the veiled conceptions of the human mind. He nuzzles the bird over, and picks it gently from the bush, carrying it with tender care as the bird flutters its last.

As the dog lays the bird before Mitch, a partnership is consummated — an unbreakable bond between man and beast.

That union is to last seven happy seasons, and all the waiting times between the quail, the pheasants and chukars, the ducks and the geese. The connection is formed out of a love like no other. Mitch alludes to the nostalgia, the primitive nature locked in his soul; that his profound love for the dog is not like the special, fierce, yet tender and passionate love he feels for his wife. And not like the depthless and protective love he feels for his daughters. Not like the almost consuming love a man secretly wishes he could share with his son, but as a verse in the song, *Slip* Slidin' Away, relates — cannot.

No, the connection between man and beast holds no bounds of a reassuring maintenance factor, no restraints of fear, guilt, jealousy or reprisal. The trust is simple and boundless. And with that thought his governing force, Mitch believes the bonded discipline is shared in perhaps the purest form of love.

AUTUMN, 1997

Mitch is living a nightmare. Driving the crooked country road to the veterinary clinic is a hallucinatory chore; a sweeping dichotomy of emotions erasing any sense of concentration. The dog mysteriously has fallen or jumped from the bed of the pickup, and most surely run over by the rear wheels. Mitch is beside himself with shoulda done this-or-that hindsight, belly churning befuddlement and gut buckets of grief. A picture book whirly-gig sails out of the past and takes shape before him. At first the images are of a fuzzy little yellow ball separating itself from a wiggling, pulsating glob of like objects. The venturous ball seems driven by a happily wagging blond tail propeller. The fuzzy thing wobbles across a mirror-polished linoleum floor on humungous webbed feet attached to unsteady legs.

That's the one." Mitch's wife Rhonda submits. That chubby little guy has a personality all its own."

"I dunno," Mitch, the cautious, cynic airs, "he appears slow, short legged and clumsy. I think his feet are pink. Can't have a sore-footed dog a laimin' up and ruinin the evening hunts."

The fuzzy animal seems to sense criticism. He tilts his head and stares at Mitch with sad fawn eyes. The puppy lets go a shrill bark and squats to pee.

There's no denying the dog's sense of timing. Mitch decides the legs are not so short. Could be the pup's belly is over-full of rich mother's milk. Those tender lookin' paddle-feet will surely toughen up.

Mitch's eyes blur. The pickup swerves onto the soft gravel shoulder. He envisions those inquisitive brown eyes exploring its new home, seeking out obscure places to relieve himself and leave behind cold or sticky surprises for bare or stocking feet to discover in the dark of night.

Rhonda is the first to rebel as she's the agile, barefooted moonlight traveler shriekingly levitated — and to add insult to chagrin — chosen to clean up the puddles, and the worse.

Rhonda, most often stuck with cleanup detail names the dog after a comic strip character. His nose is rubbed in the crass liberties of his own making. He's unceremoniously and repeatedly tossed outside until he eventually learns to scratch at the door, not only to whine his way back inside, but to save his dignity indoors and search out places outdoors to slyly conceal land mines.

The dog grows to immense proportions. He's soon permanently ostracized from the confines of the inner sanctum. His needlelike teeth graduate from shredding socks, pant legs, and the hems of dresses. He chews on wooden furniture, shreds curtains and drapes. He has discovered a taste for the upholstery on kitchen chair seats.

The dog senses the last days of comforts near home and hearth. Sometime during his final day, he slips into the master bedroom and leaves forget-me-not deposit on the bedspread over the pillow on Rhonda's side of the bed. Of course there'll be no reprieve from his final expulsion until the coldest days of winter; and then only for short warming periods — affectionate interludes. By then, the dog's acclimated to the great outdoors. He's grown thick with coat and feels uncomfortable inside, so it's a win-win…more or less.

Still the beast has never lost sight of his unique sociability. He craves affection and receives large dollops from every member of the family. He moans in ecstatic pleasure when his head and ears are massaged — when his hide is stroked, his belly scratched — even by neighbors.

Mitch chuckles, though his eyes water in memory of the dog's late-night habit of charging along the side of the house, rubbing his sides on the board 'n' bat siding. The unusual habit tends to scare the bejesus out of first-time overnight guests. Rocket propels them from deep, peaceful sleep. Awakens them abruptly to wide-eyed, spine chilling racket — as if an earthquake and thunder has combined to roll out of hell — or some unknown form of unnatural phenomenon — a prelude to the apoplectic end of everything.

Mitch laughs hoarsely. His laughter turns to anguish and pain. His pain seeks solace in a myriad of memories. Unfortunately he can no longer separate the bitter from the sweet.

Mitch envisions the dog's handsome blocked head, how the dog sits with noble bearing in the back of the truck, posing for passer-by. The unusual beast seems possessed with intuitions bordering on paranormal. A strange occurrence at a drive-up window at an ice cream parlor comes to him... The Asian lady serving cones is totally enraptured with the dog's posture. She offers a no-strings-attached ice cream cone to the dog that resides atop his throne on the toolbox behind the pickup cab. The dog has an insatiable fondness for vanilla ice cream, but evidently has read the Vietnamese cookbook, *Forty Ways to Wok your Dog*. The beast with ingrained friendliness, strikes a pose of dignity, if not pomposity, and with a snobbish air, refuses the offer without so much as looking down his nose or a thump of his extra-thick tail. Miraculously, he's refrained from drooling or licking his chops.

*

But that's in better days. Now the dog lying in the pickup bed suffers indignity and possibly pain beyond the pale. Mitch feels the dog's agony as if his own — because it is. And now Mitch's worries are compounded by the fact that a veterinarian is waiting in the wings to examine the dog's injuries. The dog distrusts the alien aura of veterinarians and their clinics — along with certain breeds of uniformed authority figures.

And then this episode comes to Mitch... The dog appoints himself guardian of the garbage cans. When Mitch loads the cans in the truck and deposits them at the end of the long, meandering drive, the dog appoints himself guardian of the empties throughout the day — as though there lies immense value within. It's early spring. The sun's migration route has reached out to warm the blacktop... At the house, a note from the county dogcatcher is tacked to the door:

"Mr. Waters, your yellow Lab has taken to sleeping in the road. He is causing traffic mayhem. He refuses to yield to oncoming vehicles. But when I arrive, the dog alerts. He runs away and hides in the brush until I leave. He seems to know that I represent the law!!!

Please contain your pets behind a fence, or tether them by chain or leash. This is a lawful written warning. Be advised! If this violation recurs there <u>will</u> be a citation and a court summons forthcoming.

Sincerely,
A.K. Moore
Animal Control Officer.

*

Mitch lets go a heavy sigh. The dog seems to read the message over his shoulder, and grimaces. The loose skin on that great face collaborates with those sad brown eyes. He's woebegone, embarrassed, and guilty as charged.

Mitch says nary a word, but the dog refrains from napping on the blacktop from that day forward.

Yeah, but the dog simply trades one vice for another. Bored, he's taken up the habit of visiting the neighbors — playing the role of a hobo.

After toiling hard one sultry afternoon, Mitch stops at a backwoods watering hole, the *Old Fort Tavern*, just to moisten his parched throat.

Ol' one-eyed Pete, the proprietor, bartender, head-sweeper and bottle washer, unintentionally rats out the dog: Mitch's noble beast makes his rounds often, passing the pleasantries of the day with the customers. The regulars habitually set the dog up with a few pie tins of Rainbier Beer, and the dog always laps the tins dry before continuing on his rounds.

Mitch can't figure how his dog developed a taste for *Rainbier*. He swears to prefer a gallon of stagnant stump juice before a jigger of *Rainbier* brew.

The dog spends a lot of time developing his contacts, and that's not all; Mitch comes upon the dog swimming across the Limber River with a brood of pups of a suspiciously similar shape and color lined out in his wake.

One of the regulars at the Old Fort, a chef who practices his grease rendering skills in town, tells of saving T-bone scraps and other meaty tidbits for the big, friendly beast.

Mitch shakes off hundreds of whys. Even though the dog is always home at night to greet Mitch and Rhonda, there's no doubt that the big sop is lead dog of his own mutual admiration society. When this is over, his injured body will be collecting a goodly share of sympathy. Authority figures exempted!

The veterinary clinic is coming in sight. Mitch breathes a sigh of relief. The dog has never visited this particular clinic. It's off the main track, but the only place within a hundred miles that has X-ray equipment for large animals.

Mitch motors up close to the door, stops and reassures the dog: "Stay. Rest easy, boy. It won't be long now. You can trust these guys. You have my word."

The dog looks at Mitch beneath furrowed brows, lifts an ear as if to say, "This is the first time you've fed me a crock of it, ol buddy. If I wasn't so sore, maybe I'd be a little miffed." The dog takes a slow, raggedy breath, and closes his eyes. His last visit to a vet garnered him a week of quarantine.

Mitch is left to wonder. Are dogs capable of clairvoyance?

*

The pretty little thing poured into blue jeans with a tight tee stretched over her youthful torso looks up from her computer screen behind the counter. As if being pestered by a fly, she says, "We've been expecting you, Mr. Waters. Just leave the dog's file on the counter and bring him in."

Mitch shows a touch of agitation. He curtly replies "It ain't gonna be all that simple Missy. My dog is not on a social call. He's some busted up, I c'n tell, 'sides the fact he'd outweigh you by a bit more than I'd wager you could carry."

The sweet young thing sighs, and rises from her battle station. Torn between her electronic billing process and a pestering reality, she says, "Drive around back. I'll have the door unlocked."

Miffed, Mitch wordlessly obeys. True to her word the greatly put-upon veterinary assistant's assistant stand by at the large animal service bay.

Her attitude takes a quick turn when she sees the noble head of the great beast perk up. "My! What a beautiful dog…and so proud." Her empathy is revealed through a thin disguise as she hugs herself beneath her breasts, and softly adds, "Poor boy."

And the great beast assumes no distrust! Thumps his tail several smacks against the bed, and incredulously, stands! Weak and gingerly, he manages to limp to the open tailgate.

The gal Friday whispers in awe, "I'll get the doctor, his assistant and a gurney."

No," Mitch says, "He made it this far without losin' it. He doesn't think much of white coats. I'll pack 'im."

"But he's so huge."

Mitch remembers the song and whispers, "He's not heavy. He's like a brother to me."

All concern now, the receptionist says, "You said he feared doctors. Will we need a muzzle?"

"Girly, this dog ain't ever bit anybody in his entire put-togethers. He ain't gonna start now."

With that off his chest, Mitch gently lifts the huge creature from the tailgate. Blinded by great furry mass, Mitch gingerly feels his way up the stairs, through the bay and into a cold concrete room. A stainless steel cell just bigger than the patient, waits ominously. There's but a single layer of newsprint between dog and cold, cruel concrete.

The dog shows fear now, real fear. Mitch swallows a lump of regrets. With illogical strength, he levitates his friend into the cell. He whispers, "Stay." But so torn by emotion Mitch turns away.

The female veterinary assistant comes on the scene. She explains the procedure to follow: "We'll tranquilize him and stabilize the areas to be X-rayed. We have your cell number, Mr. Waters. The doctor will call. It'll be about four hours."

Mitch is dismissed. He wonders if prisoners of war are treated so aloofly. Waters is left to his own devices, his mind unrelieved of worry, his body and soul, stranded in a little dairy town propped alongside a manure pile on the shady side of a pasture.

*

The village seems as cold and as hard as an old maid's parlor. From the rank smell that burns the follicles inside his nostrils, Mitch decides the townspeople hang wet, dirty diapers on clotheslines and burn the remains for firewood. But that's just idle speculation.

Even without the aid of his injured sniffer, Mitch searches out the local saloon. There, he'll wait out the three and some hours that seem like three eternities. He bellies up to the bar and orders a draft. It comes minus a head. It's warm. He wonders if the local microbrewery is titled *The Skunk Works.* But that too is idle conjecture.

The jukebox butts in on Mitch's agony. The time-worn gadget is getting down on local hits to include *I Got Tears in my Ears From a Layin' on my Back in Bed While I Cry Over You.* And *She's Got Freckles on her But She is Nice.* Mitch is sure his dog would cock an ear over that little ditty.

While absorbing the all-time polka hit, *She's Too Fat For Me,* Mitch's ears tune in the conversations of the good ol' boys in bib overalls, blue denim shirts and knee boots. In essence the milk barons lament the price of feed compared to the governin' o' the milk commodities that stand stationary. The talk is so invigorating, Mitch finds himself humming along to the tune of *Only a Logger Stirs His Coffee with His Thumb.*

But somehow, every song blaring from the box (including the nasal sobs about the best buddy, who ran off with my ol' lady an' had the gall to leave the redheaded stepson 'n' take my last can of snoose and then had the nerve to come back fer the truck too, Final Indignity Blues) register in a brain consumed with pity, anguish and remorse...that and the problem of the housefly count compared to the number of holes in the nicotine-stained ceiling tile. Mitch cannot come up with a total of that essential bit of information. He's sure he counted one particularly obnoxious death defying blue tailed aero-bat twelve times more than two thousand and twenty-three. Visions of the last look on the big beast's loose furry face keeps messing up the final added and subtracted adjustment of the gross factor pertaining to the immobile final quadrant of the lost equation. And Mitch feels as though he's been shot at and narrowly missed

*

Mitch believes everyone in the joint jumps when his cell phone rings — he, possibly a foot higher than the average farm hand.

The veterinarian sounds sad, as if he's impersonating Dr. Kavorkian. Or maybe Mitch is the eternal pessimist and can't admit it. The animal Doc's words echoing through Mitch's ears. Is the Vet speaking through a galvanized culvert?

"The break in your dog's front foreleg is quite severe, Mr. Waters. The ulna is absolutely shattered. The break in the radius has allowed the bones to pass their alignment, shortening the dog's leg by about three inches. A pinning procedure would be required to hold the leg in place... If indeed there was a bone strong enough to hold a pin. I have never seen a fracture as complex. Also the dog's joints are so ravaged by arthritis; I'm truly amazed that the animal could even stand the pressure of everyday life."

'Good grief!" Mitch exclaims. "He never complains. He's a little slow gettin' around in the mornin's, but he's such a happy guy. I figure he was gettin' a little stiff in his old age. Maybe I shoulda been feedin' 'im a couple aspirin ever day."

"There is no accounting for the stoic perseverance of a dedicated animal, Mr. Waters. The dog evidently had more important things to do than focus on his pain.

"Now Mr. Waters, we can send your pet to a bone specialist in Portland. I'm almost sure the leg could be pinned, but I'm reluctant to advise putting the dog through an expensive surgery that would only escalate his debilitating arthritic condition.

"We could simply splint the leg, however it would be shortened by the aforementioned three inches...the dog would suffer the more for it...and there again, rises the arthritic factor.

"I hadn't taken the liberty of X-raying the dog's hind quarters. It's the hips, Mr. Waters where arthritis strikes most severely in a dog. There is a great likelihood that the hip joints are more eaten away than the front shoulder and foreleg joints.

"Now Mr. Waters there is always the option of euthanasia. If you'd like some time to decide…."

Mitch's voice breaks. Maybe he looks and sounds like a sissy, but he doesn't give a damn if every organic Frisbee launcher in cow pucky county is staring at him. He manages to blurt, "I'll have to call my wife. I'll get back to you."

As Mitch folds the phone, he knows instinctively that this will prove to be his hardest, loneliest day since his good friend died while Mitch himself had administered hours of mouth-to-mouth artificial respirations.

Rhonda, aside from her psychotic need to pull practical jokes on Mitch, has the instincts of a compassionate humanitarian and a not too shabby psychologist. But this is godawful sudden. Too close to the heart. She loses it on the phone. She manages to blurt an anguished, "I'm with you all the way hon, but it's your call." She wails loudly and hangs up.

Since they'd left Alaska, sold the bar in Texas, and Mitch retired from bull riding, and moved back home to Oregon, Rhonda might just be losing her edge. Actually becoming a shade demure? Nahh!

No gettin' around it. The time has come when a man had to do what a man has to do. He calls the clinic. "I'll be there to pick up my dog in ten minutes. It's better if I do it myself."

"Most folks prefer the alternative," the vet replies. Certainly the decision is up to you, Mr. Waters. We charge a minimal fee for performing the service. The procedure is quite painless. The animal will simply go to sleep…" Now the tinny voice is one with Dr. Mengle!

Again, Mitch folds the phone. He orders a fresh stale beer, and he contemplates the dichotomy of a strange dilemma. He knows he's weaseling out and despises himself. He shudders as he chugs the stale beer, and in the process, his manhood shrivels. And through his pores, a yellow tinge escapes the confines of his soul.

Mitch again calls the clinic, and with the farm-hands staring like *Far Side* scientists, mentally dissecting an alien brain, he woefully orders the in-house euthanasia.

*

Mitch backs his truck up tight to the backside loading bay. The dog lies within the confines of that cold, stainless steel jail. He is stretched out as far as possible in those tight quarters. His chin pillowed on his good right paw. He looks relaxed, and other than his unusual posture, might be asleep. Mitch swallows a lump of self-disgust. He walks to the front with the receptionist to settle the bill.

The girl relates her philosophy of the job: the greatest in the world except for this, the big hurt... "But you made the right decision, Mr. Waters, by not doing the, um, you know...the euthanasia yourself."

"You don't understand," Mitch begins, and an all too familiar effervescent sensation stings his nose. Bitter bile rises from his belly to block the swallow of spit in his throat. Tears come of their own volition. His voice again cracks.

"This place was hell for him. He must've felt like a Jew waiting naked for a shower in an extermination camp. The dog, like the Jew, had a purty good notion he wasn't here for a de-lousin'. Last time I saw him alive his eyes shone like an embarrassed wolf caught in a trap. He was beyond chagrinned. He trembled in fear.

"I would have taken him up in the mountains he loved. He trusted me. The dog was far from stupid. His nose knew more than all our inept senses combined. He would have smelled love and freedom, sensed the essence of the hunt. He would have rested in the warmth of the noonday sun... and when everything was right with him and with me, I would've done what I had to do. Instead he got this," Mitch snarl curls his lips, wrinkles his nose and sweeps his arms around the sterile scene.

The girl's eyes too, well with tears. With her throat constricted, she replies, "I'm very, very deeply touched. I'm so sorry. I never thought of it like that. If there's any consolation, he never woke up from the anesthetic we administered to X-ray his leg."

Mitch wipes his nose with his sleeve, manages a reassuring nod. Christ! It ain't her fault. He's pot-shootin; shadows, lashin' out like a spoilt kid. They were all compassionate, caring souls here, for God's sake!

He gathers up his friend, and in death's interim, his brother has become a very heavy load. Mitch staggers outside, blinded by fur. With soft hand attached to strong arms, he lays his awful burden gently down, in the bed of the pickup.

*

Mitch has no recall of driving home. But the speedometer gives in somewhere along the whoop-tee-doo roller-coaster straights before the endless string of sharp curves he partially straightened.

As he intercepts his driveway, the sun races him to its summit. Mitch slides to a stop before his shop doors. There he gathers a tarp, a pick and shovel and a few more tools. He will fold a shroud around his dog. He will bury him deep, although high; as nearest the highest point of the mountainous family tree farm as is practical.

How will he tell the little tow-headed ones, the wee people who are his grandchildren? They love the dog probably as much as he and Rhonda.

"Well," Mitch opines out loud "If ya run from one problem, yer damn sure to run into a hellish load more." That is a fact made painfully clear over seasons past. He'll tell 'em head-on. They're tough little ankle-bitin heathens. His offspring come from resilient pioneer stock.

Mitch starts the truck. But wait a minute… The old semi-automatic shotgun has a badly pitted barrel; has a busted spring in the firing mechanism. When one squeezes the trigger, the gun will like as not shoot its entire load in one fell swoop. The scattergun's become a fitful, sometimes fully automatic weapon. Dangerous as hell, especially with the grandsons at that full-on curious age they'll never get beyond.

Mitch will remove the game-legalizing plug from the tubular magazine. He then will load five live rounds in said magazine and one in the firing chamber. He will wire the gun's trigger to the dog's funeral shroud…leave the safety off. If any coyotes or bears try to dig up the dog — BOOM! BOOM! Maybe five or six loud BOOMS!

Besides, Mitch recalls, when the dog saw the gun the association was like turnin' on a switch of pure delight. The beast loved the gun; loved the scent of cleaning oil, the sharp smell of gunpowder. The scattergun represented the beast's contagious anticipation of autumn's primal lusts. Who says you can't take it with you?

Aww, what the hell. The birdshot might blind or cripple one of the wild critters. Needless to say, Mitch can't picture himself being so cruel and inhumane, especially twice in one day.

Mitch finds a box of .12 gauge birdshot. He takes his jackknife and he carefully pries open the crimped end of six shells. With the sharp point of the knife, he digs out the wadding. Mitch pours out the decimating loads of shot, and then stuffs the empty casings full of harmless cotton.

The cartridges are now, for all intents and purposes, rendered impotent. But rest assured the blanks would be something more than a moot point. The shock in itself would be loud enough to scare any predator into the next county. Oh you betcha!

*

On a whim, Mitch makes a sliding stop at the old country store. There's no accounting for the dog's taste. Mitch shivers at the thought of drinking even one stubby of Rainbier microbrew. He purchases a box anyway. He will saturate the grave with beer! A sort of symbolic bon voyage oblation for the sultry, tedious days of summer. Dog days!

It's nearing 2:00 when Mitch and his precious cargo reach the high mountain cirque overlooking the smoky valley. Down in the flats below, squirms the winding Limber River, wriggling as though a long, crookedy blue serpent, magically tapering to a trickle, miles away. Out in the west lies the big, peaceful pond, the majestic and mighty Pacific. Is the tranquil sea a mirror image of the heavens above?

Off to the east, Mitch can see a hazy gray and white teepee-shaped outline rising above the horizon, the early snows paint Mt. Hood like a hot fudge Sundae. And through the shimmering heat-risers, stands majestic Mt. Jefferson.

Mitch thinks about the great man the mountain was named for. The man who coined the phrase, *The pursuit of happiness.* By thee gods, or if his Indian friends are right, by the demigods creators of the earth itself, the dog's spirit will rise to the happy hunting grounds and the pursuit of happiness will be joyously fulfilled!

Mitch picks his burial spot. A place where the sun will warm the fur, and there is shade, and the sweet smells of the wilderness. Those pleasantries are right here! Here for the dog's spirit to roll in the cool dirt, enjoy the sun's providing life…for family and friends to find a kind of closure…later, when the time is right.

Mitch pats the dog's noble head, and still feeling the burdensome pain of deep remorse, unloads the pick and shovel. And there in early autumn's still blazing light, begins to dig.

*

Mother Earth accepts the spade's sharp bit cordially. Mitch is making good time…until he breaks through the topsoil and hits the marbled red and yellow shale.

And the sun bears down with each shovel of dirt, each swing of the pick. Mitch sheds his shirt then his long-john top. The dog seems to be looking on with approval, and Mitch is alone with himself except for a reflective glint on the mountain to the east… Deer hunters scoping out a clear-cut.

Mitch resumes the dig with great enthusiasm. Visions of *Dog Days* prod him on. He envisions the dog leaping high in the grouse brush, his ears flapping, his big head swiveling about, before disappearing again, swallowed by the thicket. The dog hunts hard, but keeps his bearing by checking on Mitch's progress. It's comical to watch; as if the big galoot is traversing the impossible while riding a pogo stick.

Mitch laughs out loud. But the laugh is panged with guilt, broken mirror shards of trust; kaleidoscopic divisions of shattered self-perceptions. And once again his voice cracks and hot, salty tears stream down his face. The hot tears track through the dirt, the yellow and red shale powder and merge with sweat.

A raven swoops into the boughs of a tall fir, west of the dig. Mitch recalls the time the dog came upon a raven lying dead in a cut alfalfa field. The dog sniffed the bird and let go a strange, mournful, wolf-like howl.

Mitch's tortured brain flashes back to his elementary school days on the Grand Ronde Indian Reservation. Though labeled Catholics by the early-day, bigoted missionaries, the Indians are animists. They never truly mainstream or assimilate into a society they will never fully trust. Or worship a God that's so suspiciously similar to their Caucasoid tormentors — the aboriginals pretend very well.

Mitch's copper-skinned friends hold to the belief that all things living or dead possess a soul. The would-be braves he grew up with know that ravens are the reincarnations of revered spirits.

The raven in the nearby tree takes up a mischievous falsetto "*Kakhoo*," reminding Mitch of a little furry bundle's first brave yapping barks.

And Mitch admits to himself that he believes in the Native American lore! He shovels harder, barking back at the raven, imitating the dog's maturing voice when the sobs will let him.

The raven imitates the dog's barks near perfectly, and the sobs and tears are a kind of expectant joy...and the sounds echo! Mingle with Mitch's anguished screams, the yapping wild barks! And the sounds reverberating from the canyon walls became as one with a tribal nation's uprising from hell!

All the while the dirt and rocks fly from the grave! Mitch is streaked in sweat and tears and rivulets of mud; something like an Indian painted up brown as earth, bloody as death wounds. 'n' pallid; painted up yellow for high-mourning...dyed up good 'n' fancy for a High-Chief's funeral party!

Mitch examines the dig with a critical eye. All is ready. He places the dog on the shroud, folds his compadre in, just so. He carries the shrouded beast with great care; and Mitch lowers a loved one's carcass into a hole that seems so similar to a human grave; long, narrow and deep.

Mitch retrieves the shotgun from his truck. He stands over the grave, the scattergun is held high over his head for all the predators to see!

And Mitch screams his first Indian chant, and Mitch trips the light fantastic in full circles of the dig.

Round 'n' round! Arms and legs akimbo, intimidating the sky with the shotgun. And when the time is right with the thunder gods, Mitch hops gingerly into the grave to unfold the top layer of heavy tarpaulin.

He lays the gun with the beast, muzzle above that great, furry head. He wires the trigger to a tarp eyelet, and very carefully releases the safety.

Mitch pops out of the grave. He kicks off his pants and undershorts. Throws them into his pickup window — utilizes the long-john top and work shirt as loincloth flaps — ties two of the sleeves together and ties the spare sleeves tight around his waist.

The raven barks his approval and falls silent. Mitch grunts and labors to fill the grave.

And finally, the grave is mounded. The chants begin again in earnest! Mitch leaps and hop-skips around the mound, chanting, shrieking, yawping, screaming, barking, and bawling his funeral dirge. He waves the shovel threateningly at the festering sun.

Mitch grabs the stubby bottles of Rainbier and pours them over the grave. Over his head. The beer stings his reddened eyes the more, but the warm beer tastes good when it runs down his cheeks and into his bellowing mouth. He dances in place while he chugs a full bottle. And when the beer is gone, Mitch again, takes up his crazed chant.

And over the howling cacophony, Mitch waves his spade at the spirits on high! And the dog grins down through the raven's eyes, and the dog-raven giggles fiendishly!

And Mitch is forgiven his trespasses.

*

And then the game warden and the trainee, an ex-animal control officer named Moore, come charging full bore out of a thicket to the east.

The officers are brandishing firearms. They point large-bore pistols at Mitch. The meaty one has binoculars dangling from his neck. The slender one tries, mostly in vain, to steady a camcorder that's also tethered 'round his neck.

Oh yeah! Now Mitch recalls the glint of binoculars reflecting off yon hillside…

"Drop the shovel, creep! Then take three steps forward."

Mitch peers down the black holes in the muzzles of their hog-legs. His eyes dilate and a certain area of his anatomy shrivels while another part of him puckers. He obeys.

"Flop on yer belly an' git'cher hands behind yer back. Do it now!"

Again Mitch obeys. He feels handcuffs click tight and cold around his perspirin' wrists. And the big, sweaty, out of breath one in charge, jerks Mitch to his feet. "Wanna tell me who yer a burryin' there asshole?"

"It's Andy," Mitch begins… "I —"

"Don't say another word, slime-ball! We'll damn straight use it against you! Moore, escort this pre-vert to his truck, an' cuff 'im tight to his steerin' wheel. Then go git our rig from the spur down yonder. Call it in. Don't forget to push the press-to-talk button this time! Looks like we got ourselves a righteous bust! Caught ourselves a pre-vert serial killer with his shats down! Move it Moore! Go! Go! I'll guard this creep till ya bring our truck 'n' shovels up. Might jis be yer daughter, Andrea, in that hole all raped 'n' wrapped all tidy like, huh, A.K., hee-hee!"

Mitch can smell an adrenal high over bad garlicky breath, sense a hyperbole of stimulated energy. Mitch is marched to his truck. He's ordered to back up to his door. He turns around as commanded. The trainee threads a second pair of handcuffs through Mitch's outside door handle and locks those cuffs through the chain of the pair that subdue Mitch.

Standing on his tiptoes, Mitch silently opines, *Andy* may have been part of a poor choice of words, but who the hell do those two think they are? Rooster Cogburn and Dudley Do-right? This is gonna be good. Mitch bites his lip to keep from giggling, but the game enforcement officer spots the weird gleam lighting up Mitch's eyes.

The long arm of the law thinks Mitch is a stark-raving maniac! Mitch recalls the dog's aversion to self-important men in uniform, and he chuckles with the raven, which is now spiraling overhead. And the dog approves.

The game warden mutters, "Crazy bastard, psycho sumbich! Knock off that insane gigglin'! Wipe that silly smirk off'n yer face!"

Mitch cannot stop giggling, and when he tries, his voice ranges from soprano to baritone.

The would-be Sherlock Holmes is about to take the law a step farther and pistol whip his prisoner into submission. Deputy Do-righty, in the guise of A.K. Moore, comes bounding into sight riding herd on the official white game warden Bronco. The all-terrain vehicle's headlights alternately blink on and off. The light bars above the cab pirouettes from blue to red.

Somehow Moore refrains from sounding the siren, or maybe he hasn't figured out how to turn it on. Come to think of it, A.K. Moore, alias Dudley Do-right, is sort of a living caricature of…Barney Fife!

Mitch's giggle escalates into a parched cackle, and slobber runs unmolested down his cracked lips; along his dirty, whiskery chin. Those two are definitely a pair to draw to — as long as jokers are wild!

"Holy Jesus!" Moore exclaims, "The guy's rabid! He's foaming from the mouth, and his mean, beady eyes are blood-red!"

"Yeah, I know," Rooster acknowledges. "He's bad to the bone aw'right. Freakin' blanket-ass albino injun, run amuck! Drunker'n a peach orchard boar, 'e is. Bear bait. Smells like a cross betwixt a road kill skunk an' Grampa's outhouse. Filthy sumbich buried the murder weapon along with 'is latest victim.

"Set the camcorder up on 'is hood an' we'll dig up the corpus delecti. We better git 'er all on tape. There'll be movie rights 'n' commendations to consider. TV commercials… Oprah! Hee-hee."

And Mitch, and the raven-dog too, chuckle insanely.

Mitch packed the earth firmly around his beloved dog. The digging won't be all that easy. Especially for someone as robustly out of shape as ol' Rooster. As for Barney, well, he's too light to stomp a spade to its hilt. But the soon-to-be keystone kops are on a mission. Their faces glisten with sweat, and those khaki uniforms are soon drenched a filthy dark brown.

They dig with much grunting; a fury unrestrained. They'll be famous lawmen before this balmy, humid, Indian summer day is through!

And finally they're better than waist deep in the hole. Mitch can no longer mark their progress. A lifetime passes until he hears Rooster holler "Bingo!"

A couple of shovels spring from the dig. There follows a long, pregnant silence followed by Rooster's obnoxious chuckling "Peek-A-Bo - —" cut off by the muffled booming of an old worn-out shotgun blazing its final half-dozen reports.

Mitch has never seen two earthly beings suspended over a grave before. Never witnessed anyone so beefy and thick, *lightly touch down*. Never actually saw a dancin' twosome fold their arms tightly around their heads, collide in mid-air and perform the foxtrot in opposin' directions. And with such high, exaggerated steps!

As the dust settles, A.K. Moore remains mostly exposed; head down, rear end up, peekin' from behind a trembling huckleberry bush. Moore, alias Dudley Do-right and Barney Fife, had performed a rather stylish variation of the Fossberry Flop, and in the process, cleared the tall bush quite handily.

Rooster actually out-does Do-right. He climaxed his rout in a uniquely clever vanishing act. Mitch wonders of it all; how such a lawman so broad across the beam could actually disappear behind such a disproportionately skinny tree!

Mitch laughs so hard he shakes his pickup. The camcorder slides off the hood, hits a berm of dirt, and then rolls under the truck's chassis.

Time pauses because that's what time does during certain situations. But eventually the keepers of peace traverse a strangely herky-jerky tip-toed sneak back to the edge of the grave. Here, Mitch gives Rooster and Do-right a little credit. Though quavering in their Engineer boots, they remember to un-cock the hammers on those .44 caliber hog legs before they slip the pistols back in their fancy hip holsters.

"Aw shit, Moore! Looky what you up 'n' done! Goddamn greenhorn idjit! It's only a damn ol' dog! Git the cuffs off that silly sumbich and let's boogie! We got us a posse to head off!

*

In less than a dozen heartbeats and so much dust, they're gone. But not before Mitch turns his backside to the escaping Bronco, flips his makeshift breechclout up and moons the police a not-so-fond farewell. It's from that questionably moral posture he spots the long forgotten camcorder under his pickup truck.

***

Mitch brings his family and a choosing of the dog's friends up to the crime scene the next day. Mitch and the boys take turns with the three shovels to refill the grave. At the head of the grave, Mitch sledgehammers the pointed wooden cross into the tough mountain terrain. Everyone speaks their eulogies in turn. The mourners have special memories of an eccentric character that was just possibly more human than dog.

They write, with black magic marker their farewells on the stem and crosspiece of the grave marker.

In the process, the leastest ones, the precious little granddaughters and still mostly innocent grandsons learn there's no redeemable coupon attached to a consumin' obligation known as love.

In time, Mitch believes the children of his children will recall a valued truth learned by loving a dog. A love without sin, with no holds barred.

For now, there are no hang-ups chaining anyone's grievous passion. It simply had been good knowing that happy-go-lucky beast.

On the crosspiece the crudely carved letters read:

ANDY CAPP WATERS
1986-1997
HAPPY TRAILS TO YOU

Epilogue

Halloween

The family and friends, to include one-eyed Pete, and Tommy the chef, greatly enjoy the video's premier showing. Tommy the chef, suggests sending a copy off to *America's Favorite Home Videos,* but in truth, the unedited tape is a trifle too X-rated for a syndicated family show.

Mitch, being shy and reserved, is embarrassed to be the star. The camera zoomed in on Mitch's bizarre chanting, cavorting, and nearly naked funeral dirge. And Mitch is yet to put his all in the show.

Not from where the game warden and his faithful sidekick first preempted a field glass surveillance sweep for poachers, but opening where the adrenaline pumped Rooster and Do-Right first sneaked through the pucker brush, hid, watched, and recorded.

In the film, Mitch is slightly removed from photogenic. He remains fish belly white below his leathery lined face, his sun-reddened neck. Streaked with muddy brown, rusty red, a sallow yellow seemed artfully blended with milky white that courses down his scarred and abused torso. The rippled mud streaks down his veiny, prickly haired, bony legs.

The clodhopper work boots worn under little else seem at odds with a rather unique fashion statement. However, the close-up of his wild, tear reddened eyes is the heinous, jump-startin' kicker.

The ending is anti-climactic. It's a dizzying, unfocused tumble from the truck hood to the ground, and a close-up of the undercarriage of an abused truck. Mitch's impromptu, tail wagging moon shot is not caught on film. But in the end, every word and every sound has been captured by the camera's state-of-the-art sound system.

The raven's eerie, mimicking barks, woofs, howls and yowls along with Mitch's echoing responses, are duly recorded. The animal sounds are hairy enough to scare the Halloween out of the leastest ones. The youngsters take a wide detour around their grampa, and do, for a spell thereafter. And when he encroaches into their space, grubby little fists grip tight to their mom's jeans and skirts. At first sighting of the patriarch, a silent alarm unleashes mayhem. The wee ones take cover. Gawkin' faced towheads with protrudin' lower lips drop dolls and toys, and swiftly, those innocent faces portray leery, furrowed brows of bewilderment.

For the young, most things come to pass. Grampa is also quick with bribery and a story from Grimm's Fairy Tales or the like. There are lessons inside — even for old fools.

And how about Rhonda? Is there a wedge of doubt pryin' open her closed mind? A shadow cast across her spiritual beliefs?

Andy would appreciate it if there is. Mitch never questions the truth he sees firsthand.

In the end, Rhonda is happy for Mitch. He got one over on the law. And dirty dealing paybacks did not nip her on the tush. Her husband better get his act down to the barbershop, however. His gray, unstyled hair is approaching something she'd describe as the *Wild Man from Borneo* look. Not fitting for an actor of his (scattergun) style.

THE LAST SONG

Mel Pelton's life is in a tailspin. The harder he pulls back on the yoke that is his brain, the more out of control his spin becomes. Sleep is as elusive as making sense of what he knows to be true. Running on the tumultuous edge of sanity for such a long period of time is an out-of-body experience. His truck is afloat on a sea of potholes. It's as though he sits stationary and the earth, in its perpetual orbit, rotates beneath his seat. Scenery in constant motion seems surreal: painted pale yellow by a moon that careens here and there, dodging from left to right, front and center, sometimes disappearing, often sneaking behind, but faithfully casting the shadowy light he drives through without the aid of headlights.

The night is warm. Pelton snakes around crookedy switchbacks with his windows down, the radio brashly pounding out moldy oldies. He is damp with perspiration. The pungent odor of the forest blends with his sweat and clings to his every pore, but Mel can no longer smell any more than he can feel, even though his bloodshot eyes sting through the blur of tears.

Visions of Margo flit through his soul to the tune of an old Gale Garnett song: "*We'll Sing in the Sunshine*" and as the song progresses to its terrible ending, Mel chuckles, laughs, guffaws hysterically and sobs pathetically—"And I'll be on my way."

Pelton grinds his teeth, cursing life in general and his business partner and ex-best friend in particular. And Mary Hopkin belts her brand of earthy nostalgia from the speakers, raking the smoldering coals: "*Those Were the Days.*"

Those days ended abruptly. He'd left Margo a cutesy little note Sunday morning stating he'd been called out on an emergency surgery. He had to dismember a tree for a friend. He'd be back in time for their luncheon date.

The tree in question happened to be growing near that scuzzy adult store located alongside the hot-sheet motel out on the seedy side of Sleaze Row. He spotted Margo's car and his partner's pickup parked out front. Mel checked it out. His partner and best buddy Harley Coldthrust, and Mel's wife Margo, were having a lusty old tryst before the sex toy counter. Harley was rooting around like a hog. He was wearing a pair of those Groucho glasses with the fake nose and eyebrows. Only the nose on this pair was a penis complete with testicles. Margo was dancing and laughing in paroxysms of pure delight. With the no-tell motel next door, Mel's imagination had little trouble filling in the blanks. He slunk away unseen.

From confidence supreme to emotional cripple. It seemed like a million years and less than a second ago—two days — maybe three? And how many nights? None that Mel Pelton slept through.

Through the cover of night, Mel wove a course through a mishmash maze of logging roads that haphazardly bind the Coast Range Mountains together: roads that twisted from ridgelines to streambeds — mountaintops to valley floors and back again. The hodge-podge network is a rough-terrain jigsaw puzzle beyond sanity to the inexperienced. There are hundreds of dead-end spurs for every mile of road that connects to another road that leads to another — mostly unmarked. Directional signs disappear as often as they're installed — destroyed by vandals, anarchists and terrorists. Anyone unfamiliar with the systems would be hopelessly lost and figuratively chasing one's tail. A compass would prove useless in such a complex labyrinth that blankets hundreds of miles.

Mel navigates by rote and instinct. It's no coincidence he carries a 55-gallon barrel supplied with extra fuel. Dead reckoning, he reckons he's within five-miles of the turnoff leading to his destination. The road is deserted. No one travels here in the middle of night — other than outlaws, eco-terrorists and their worthless ilk. On the radio, Kenny Rogers implores, *"Ruby, Don't Take Your Love to Town."*

Mel Pelton howls like a lovelorn timber wolf. "Sweet Jesus, Margo! Why did you do me like you did when you knew damn well what you did, did me wrong?"

The spur Mel seeks is practically grown over by a re-plantation. Boughs of ten-year old Douglas firs growing along either side stretch witch-like fingers towards the centerline, forming a darkened tunnel to drive and lose oneself from prying eyes. The old clear-cut is part of a crazy quilt pattern of industrial proportions — a topsy-turvy checkerboard of replants and standing timber in 40 acre squares, clinging to a mountain range.

Pelton flicks on his dims, splashes through a mud-hole and snakes through the reproduction. Tree limbs brush the sides of his truck, rattle the antenna. His all-terrain tires crunch loose gravel. The radio wails torchy deceit — Lenny Welch's, "Since I Fell for You," and tears stream down in red-rimmed misery.

A mile later, Lenny has crooned his last. Mel sobs in relief, pauses to rub hot eyes with gnarled knuckles and ventures on, picking up a little speed. He's beyond the crazy quilts and back under the sea of tall, stately timber. Pelton figures it's safe to run with headlights the three or four remaining miles to his destination — and as the radio, in some predetermined anti-climaxing conspiracy, goes to commercial, he's at the end of the road. Looming before his swollen eyes stands a root wad in the shape of a prehistoric octopus-like creature — as big as the side of a barn. As formidable as a sleeping monster: the end of this stage of his journey.

He flicks off the lights. His eyes adjust. The voice on the radio says, "Get your tickets ready. The talking head forecasts a single winner in this Wednesday's Power Ball Lottery. Some lucky soul out there is about to become a millionaire sixty-seven times over. Those lucky, lucky numbers will be broadcast after these important messages."

Way his luck is running he hasn't a snowball's chance in hell. But Melvin Pelton digs his lottery ticket out of his wallet while another contrived voice extols the use of a greatly improved hemorrhoid ointment complete with Magic Finger Applicator. A soft drink and a dietary aid later… the robotic voice announces the numbers. And Mel finger traces the prolonged drama beneath his dome light. He cannot believe his ears or his bloodshot peepers! Row-B on his four-dollar ticket is an exact match including the power ball!

He extracts a pen from a holder on the sun visor—signs and addresses the ticket with all the care he can muster. He folds the ticket and places it in his shirt pocket and buttons the flap. Sixty-seven million images flash through his fractured brain; every vision is heartache on heartache. What good is money? Money can't make it all go away. Margo has broken her vows and forsaken Mel forever. Come morning, she will arrive home from graveyard shift at the hospital to read the numbers he copied off the ticket and entered into their PC.

Margo Pelton, registered nurse: compassion extraordinaire. Mel howls like a sick coyote, and his howl traverses the endless black void to die alone in the black of night. The firs deaden the sounds. Nocturnal beasts don't give a damn about any lottery. He and Harley had always dreamed of winning, vowing to split the pot… the picture show in his mind's eye takes him back to the *last living moments of Harley Coldthrust.*

It was early that morning when Mel and Harley arrived on the jobsite. Pelton and Coldthrust were contract timber cutters. They worked alone (single jacking) cutting marked units of timber for a private logging contractor employed by a large timber products corporation. Yeah, Harley and Mel, the best of the best. Two buddies working side-by-side on the steep slopes of faraway mountains, laughing at danger, spitting in the eye of the Grim Reaper. But that was before Harley forsook what Mel considered the most sacred trust of all.

Mel recalled standing on the edge of creation, urinating on God's panorama. And Harley...shameless Harley had hiked himself up onto the open tailgate and began lacing up his calked (spike-soled) boots. Harley had had the gall to say,

"Hey, Red-Eye, why the silent treatment? Got laryngitis? Sleepin' too close to a crack? You keep raggin' the way ya have the last few days, you're gonna deserve yer birthday present."

Deserve was the go word for Mel. He tucked in, zipped up and marched up close to Harley. He drew his .22 High Standard pistol from his shoulder holster and said, "And you're gonna get what *you* deserve six months before *your* birthday, you back-bitin' rattlesnake, womanizin' sumbich."

Mel didn't give Harley a chance to respond. Harley was, after all, Mel's best friend. They'd been to hell and back together. Harley certainly deserved to die quick. Melvin Pelton shot Harley Coldthrust in the forehead and shoved his dead body into the bed of the pickup in one fell swoop.

It took a while to cut enough firewood to cover the corpse. Mel hardly remembers tucking the tarp around Harley, let alone cutting the wood. Daylight comes early in June. Now the eleventh hour is minutes away. Time to dispose of the remains.

Pelton retrieves a chainsaw power head from the box. He attaches a five-foot bar and machine-sharpened chain to the motor. Then Pelton fills the saw's tanks with mixed gas and chain lubricating oil. He takes a minute to size up the windfall. The tree is an old-growth fir. At the trunk where he will make the cut, the stem is some seven feet in diameter, thicker than the chainsaw blade is long, but being a professional feller/bucker, Mel will have no problem slicing stump from stem.

The tree has fallen alongside the road. The top is angled uphill. When the cut is complete, gravity will take over. The stem will drop six feet to the earth and the hundred-ton stump portion will upend back into the crater of its beginning, possibly six-hundred years before that damn Harley seduced Mel's lady fair.

"Yep," when Mel gets through, there will no longer be a tree attached to the stump. Harley's carcass will be dead centered and mashed flatter than a fritter beneath tons of root-ball: a burial cairn as big as a barn. No one will ever lay eyes on Mr. Coldthrust again.

Pelton remembers to trade his baseball cap for his halogen headlamp before striking off. He unloads the firewood exposing the corpse wrapped in a tarp. He flops Coldthrust out on the road. The godawful sound makes the hair on his arms dance. He grunts "And love brings such misery and pain." He sucks it up, grabs fistfuls of tarp and skids Harley to the edge of the crater. Mel remembers snippets of a line from some obscure song. He mutters, "Leaves will wither. Roots will die. I'll be forsaken and never, for chrissakes, know why. Ashes to ashes *ol' pard.*" Melvin Pelton squats almost reverently and barrel-rolls the carcass, tarp and all, into the crater.

Harley obediently flops to the deepest point—almost dead center in the huge divot, face-up and freed of the tarp. The reflections in his spiritless eyes shine white-hot in pale moon glow.

Pelton wonders about the birthday present Harley spoke of, but cannot dwell on it. He steps out of his body; does not allow himself to twitch out. He turns away and retrieves the saw; he flips the motor over his shoulder, balances the long cutting attachment with his right arm, and guides the heavy saw like the prow of a boat. He strides purposely along the tapering stem of the downed tree until its diameter is slender enough to mount. He climbs up and onto the stem.

Mel marches back down the tree, a pygmy on an elephant, until he's near the giant root-ball. He props the saw across the log. He flicks the switch, presses the compression release, thumb-pumps the plastic primer until the bulb is full. Mel pulls brusquely on the starter rope. On the forth pull, the motor comes to life with a resonate bellow. The saw is a Husqvarna model 3220, one of the largest chainsaws in production. It is loud. Its reverberations shatter the night, setting Mel on edge. He lets the saw chuckle for as long as he can stand warming up the beast. Not long, but long enough for a soon-to-be millionaire.

Mel clicks on the headlamp, illuminating the immediate area in a pallid splash of light. He starts his cut. Making sure he's square with the stem and as plumb as can be. He gooses the throttle, sets the dogs (metal spurs that hold the saw in position) and the saw swiftly cuts into the tree. Pelton eases the saw over the side, burying the length of the bar through thick bark and into the soft wood, first squatting then lying on his belly, maneuvering the saw lower and lower.

Even with the headlamp, it's too far around to see if he's cutting clear under the stem. He must be sure not to leave a strap of holding wood. He pulls the saw back up, shuts it off and retraces his route back to the ground and back to the roots. He restarts the motor, eases the tip of the bar into the precut line and undercuts as far as he can reach through the bottom and up the far side. Satisfied, he returns to the point of beginning. Mel works the cut around the remaining side of the stem, slowly descending while he cuts — until he can slither to the ground on the off-side. He repositions the saw to match his undercut and finishes the job braced a good two feet away from imminent danger.

Mel cuts the remaining strap of wood with the tip of the bar. The stem drops, "Thud!" The ground shakes. But in some insane defiance of either gravity or physics, the root wad refuses to tip up and fall back on Harley, mashing him to oblivion.

"Huh." It's not the first time, Mel thinks to himself. Sometimes the smallest of underground roots will have the strength of steel cables — even though those roots will weaken a lot quicker than wire rope.

"Damn the luck." Shutting off the headlamp, hefting the saw on his shoulder, and skirting a wide birth around the root ball, Mel works his way back to the truck.

"The stump has gotta set up," he mutters, "or I have to retrieve Harley and find another windfall, but how? I daren't crawl in after him and I can't leave him there."

Melvin Pelton thinks about lassoing Harley's head with a length of chainsaw starter cord taken from a maintenance spool stored in the truck. It's a passing thought. He couldn't sling a loop around anything except Harley's nose. He pictures the scenario and giggles at the absurdity. The giggle turns into a sob that becomes hysterical. He almost chokes himself to death in a coughing fit.

Feeling giddy, Pelton squats before the crater, and stares into the shadowy hole, concentrating on the silvery light reflecting from Harley's dead eyes. If it wasn't for being an instant millionaire…if not for visions of Margo floating in his conscience, he might find himself hypnotized by those unblinking eyes.

Mel wonders what went wrong with his conception of marriage. What turned Margo into a tawdry cheat, Harley an instant Judas? He thinks he hears someone singing Van Morrison's *"Brown Eyed Girl* — or did he leave the radio on? Mel blubbers like a baby.

He stares into his partner's unblinking eyes while convoluted visions of the past flit through his conscience in no particular order. Reality is so far gone, it's beyond recapturing. He hears a faraway roar. It's as if he's holding a conch shell to his ear.

Actually the tide has changed, and the westerly wind is hurtling in with the incoming. The windfall succumbed to the east winds of autumn. Now the westerly's of spring batter the wall of roots as if the stump were the mainsail on the sloop *"John B."*

Apart from the Beach Boys singing and oblivious to the wind, he hears a strangled, babbling voice. The voice pleads for forgiveness…is the voice his or Harley's? "Only one way to find out." Mel feels an irresistible urge to place his ear just above Harley's lips.

He slithers pell-mell into the crater: stretches out full length on top of Harley, places his left ear over Harley's mouth and listens. He hears something. It sounds like loose dirt trickling down an embankment. From the radio he thinks he hears the lyrics of *The Last Song*, by the *Edward Bear Trio*. And then Harley says, "Happy birthday, you dumb muth…"

And the dark shadow quakes, and looms over Mel Pelton.

*****

MANHUNT
For a Son-in-law

The call is received on line one. At the com center at the local slammer line one is the only line. The call is taken by Chief Al Barjinn's head bailiff. The chief bailiff says to the Chief of police, "It's for you."

Tone of voice and facial expression are tells of the bailiff's disdain for her boss, and incidentally, her husband. It's midmorning. The top cop is only half in the bag. He's up for the call. Or will be, shortly after he inspects his uniform. With a few grains in the hourglass remaining, perfection is achieved. The head-brass gravitates to within a hairsbreadth of fogging his personal looking glass. The image he sees from every conceivable angle is, of course, his face. The ever-critical chief checks for reflective flaws by staring into his special, three-dimensional, brightly lit, thousand-watt mirror. He arrives at the conclusion that he is far more handsome than Matt Dillon, and twice the lawman. Chief Al's outer ensemble consists of patent leather riding boots and khaki jodhpurs. He customarily wears starched pleated blue shirts He brandishes a quirt when (infrequently) in ambulation. Twin holstered pearl handled revolvers ride low on his hips. Gold star clusters encircled by a rope braid adorn the epaulets over his broad shoulders. A rakishly angled purple beret covers his hidebound head. When behind the wheel of his squad car, a white silk scarf often trails in the breeze. The silver, six-pointed star pinned to his jutting chest takes nothing from his cyan blue eyes, his aquiline nose, or his case-hardened lantern jaw.

Into the blinding looking glass, he smiles his peculiar smile. The gold star and crescent moon imbedded in his chisel-like incisors reflect much about his disposition. If not for protecting the gold, it is said that the chief could easily chisel down trees far faster than a particularly eager beaver. The chief is reputed to be capable of tracking a single raindrop down a swollen stream. His life is a legend manifested by his cast of hero-worshipping, easily swayed wannabees. But a consensus of those who know him best, swear the town cop has mastered eerie instincts. Insiders have often witnessed the lawman stalk a faraway whiff of Jack Daniel's straight to its source. Still he has an Achilles heel. Astonishingly, that soft spot in his armor plagues his self-mastery from within his very loins. And it is she whom calls....

"Hello?... You don't say." But apparently the complainant does say. After a lengthy one-sided conversation, the chief, now sporting a beet-red ear, cradles the phone's receiver. And the hunt is on.

The apprehension of the offenders is no less bizarre than their wanton spree. Eye contact is absolute verification. But a blind man, feeling his way along on a Moped might easily overtake either of the getaway cars by simply homing in on the fender clatter and the sporadic hammering of cooling fans clanging into crumpled radiator shrouds. The fugitives, though unseasoned, are classified as public menaces, and highly dangerous, if mostly to themselves.

In final analysis, the collars result from low-speed chases in opposing directions. Perp number one is taken without a struggle six miles north of town. Master criminal number two is nabbed a couple hours later, sixteen miles south on Highway 101. (101 is the only escape route available).

The arresting officer in both of those related affairs is chief of police Al Barjinn. Barjinn, the lawman, conveys a name that brings conceptions of old timey cattle ranches, bawling calves, the sizzle of red hot branding irons and burnt biscuits. (When they're smokin' they're cookin', when they're black they're done). There follows envisions of cold beans, and the sound and fury of distant thunder storms, stampedes and the ominous squeak of swinging saloon doors. Litanies of rumor mongers constantly envision themselves riding shotgun with their one-man posse. But it is he,

Chief Barjinn alone whom brings the soon-to-be felons to the bailiff for booking.

The prisoners are hobbled together ankle to ankle, and rope-cinched belly to belly in the tried and true, Barjinn manner. This restraining measure is a unique, highly effective control device. The downside is finding comfort in transport. Rain falls, and the chief finds it difficult to see over the prisoners he has lashed to the hood of his squad car. The cantankerous cop's mood exacerbates as he is forced at times, to drive with his face poked out his side window. Stinging pellets of rain splatter his grimacing and glistening, well-defined incisors, tarnishing the shine. And that is a hardship the chief will long remember, even though vengeance is right there, lumped before his squinting eyes.

Despite the rain slickened highway, and somehow becoming lost, the tin star eventually makes his return. Al Barjinn, the cold local heat with an id the townsfolk relate to Tombstone Territory, a classic character named Quick Draw McGraw, forests of saguaro cacti, handle bar mustaches, the OK Corral and a face scrimshawed from the stump of what was, until recently, the world's oldest living bristle cone pine.

The lawman's hogtied, totally drenched captives appear to be involved in an unusual ritualistic sun dance, as they are unsympathetically prodded belly to belly to the booking room. This is the first stop inside the dank and austere jail.

The police chief is also the village magistrate, and the self-appointed judge, jury and hangman: the purveyor of typical small town justice. He has, figuratively speaking, dumped the spoils of victory in the ample lap of his turnkey (and wife) Ms. Bedida Crackower-Lancefling-Barjinn With the braying siren grating on the lady jailer's nerves, the dedicated cop speeds off in twin rooster tails of grimy grit. Barjinn's aim is to complete his investigation by fetching his number one witness and lodger of the complaint, (coincidentally, his poor misunderstood darlin' daughter).

Upon delivery to the turnkey, the prisoners are unshackled. Captive number two, squirmily crossing and uncrossing his skinny legs, pleads nature's call. Left to his own devices, he promptly escapes through a latrine vent a ferret couldn't squeeze through. As he gains slightly fresher air, he cheerily sings the first prophetic verse of Hank William's *"Jambalaya!" Over and over*

Me oh my-oh — even though no one named Joe is in the vicinity — the jailer (and little missus) fail to take chase. *The turnkey/jailer-matron* is a little miffed by the interruption of her intellectual and religious pursuits divined from within the pages of the *National Enquirer*. She quickly decides that thing about a bird in hand being worthier than… whatever. She puts off radioing the news to her beloved in the squad car until it suits her schedule.

The fugitive escapee is last seen exiting town in the questionable company of a boxcar load of pigs. The pigs, and lately the felon, are riding a one-way-ticket to the big-house called *Hormel*, thousands of miles east.

The turnkey's alarm call an hour after the fact amounts to an insincere, one-point bulletin: *"Jeez Chrize. Gawd almighty! I cain't do ever damn thang a-round heah."* The radio patch is as close to sacrifice, as the bailiff/turnkey will suffer – other than another belt from the jar of self-inflicting flu she keeps in her top right-hand desk drawer.

It is not known at this writing why Ms. Bedida (rhymes with Ida) goes by her maiden name, although casting shadows over petty nepotism, (hiring practice based on family ties) is strongly suspected by a jealous-hearted few.

The gargantuan jailer lady is a chip off an old growth Louisville Slugger. She, in due time, finishes her warm-ups in the on deck circle and is ready to commence with batting practice. Ms. Deputy Bedida is proud to be meaner than Godzilla with a hangover, and at least as fascinatingly attractive. It is speculated by the remaining perp that the Amazon-Yeti cross suffers PMS on top of her moonshine inflicted headache, still banging and vibrating from a few too many wine cooler chasers.

Ms. Bedida poises at the ready over her keyboard. She directs her first line-booking inquiry at the remaining accused... *"Name?"*

Over the ocean's roar, raising hell in his ears, the doused perp can hear that fast freight a comin' round the bend. Or is it Ms. Bedida's antifreeze over pickled pig's feet breath chug, chug, chuggin'; building steam? The interviewee glances about his surroundings: A dank, double occupancy cage with the earmarks of a medieval torture chamber complete with bars on the door and a postage stamp window. He shivers cold fear while noting rusty lattice steel bunks without mattresses. The leg shackle rings imbedded in the concrete floor brings heebee jeebees crawling up his spine. And what's that rack thingy over yonder with motorized winches on either end?

As the suspect senses the stealthy approach of danger, he doesn't too studiously linger on his sudden change of environment, nor does he find cheer in it — he just shuts down.

The immense face under the scowl is beginning to glow purple from an onrush of blood. As she approaches critical mass, her lip curls, her mascara crumbles. Her whiskey tenor voice curdles to a guttural growl more animal than human: *"Cat gotcher tongue Sugah? If it has, I'll stomp lil' Sylvester on down yer throat, through yer gullet an' outcher rectal cavity."*

The perp feels trapped between a paving machine and a steamroller. He is tarred if he answers, asphalt if he doesn't. *Government Health Care's just some other words for nothin' left to loose*, he dimly recalls hearing somewhere.

"Wolf H. Nero," he squeamishly replies, bracing for the ire of Ms. Bedida's ever building wrath.

Ominous sounds rumble. Ms. Bedida's personality is reminding Wolf of his last meal three days ago at a road kill on a hairpin curve in the middle of god knows where. The meal before that repast was served at a radioactive chili diner called Saint

Helen's Cauldron. *"So,"* she erupts and interrupts, dry fire blowing cayenne pepper, volcano ash, skunky alcohol and garlicky embers in his face, *"If I enters your name in the cop computer, last name first, it will read back Nero, Wolf H. If this is correct, the file will match that ha-ha name to a social security number. If there is no match, don't make me put on my rubber gloves. If I put on my rubber gloves I will touch you. And coincidentally, I wear brass knuckles under my gloves. Now, shall we re-punch your dance-card?"*

"It's the truth, *I swear to Christ,"* Wolf interjects. *"Mom thought she was the abandoned sister of Goldie Hahn. My father is an Osage shaman the tribe called 'Nero.' Therefore I lack Mom's blond features. The comedian in Mom brought on the marriage to my ol' man. She couldn't wait to name her first-born Wolf. I was lucky to be born the male mom affectionately called Lupus. You don't wanna know my little sister's story."*

The turnkey shakes her mane, rolls her evil eyes. Looks almost sympathetic until her glance catches the headlines on her weekly copy of the tabloid, *The Star: 'Wolf Raises Infant To'*..."I ain't gonna ask. No sir, I ain't."

Suddenly, the chief's only patrol car skids to a stop after caroming off the side of the inhospitable concrete pod. The building withstands the blow without a quiver. The event is strangely coincidental with the gut of the story. *Rooster Cogburn to the rescue,* Wolf giggles nervously to himself, noting the suspicious nature of red-smeared rubber gloves on the desk of the socially reserved Ms. Bedida. The booking process is thankfully put on hold when the complainant and Magistrate's daughter, sweet Sue Nami, a name society will not attach any particular stigma to, enters the building. The chief with a name that elicits images of cattle barons, breathless beauty in the mornin' sun and a far wilder west, swaggers in behind Sweet Sue. She, doing a semi-straight line variation of the mamba, a mix of the rumba, the cha-cha with an extra cha and something quite possibly carnal. Sweet Sue is indeed triple X...not in the physical stature of her folks, but in status, as in marital, thrice removed. Sweet Sue has been d-i-v-o-r-c-e-d three times, the latter of which by putting the asunder to Mr. Nami, the *"mentally cruel"* monster of Oriental persuasion.

In consequence of Sweet Sue's abbreviated marital bliss's, the threesome of her offspring each has a different father: One of Spanish origins, one Native American, and the youngest, decidedly an almond eyed descendant of the Japanese Isles. The only thing her exes have in common is *little* hidden inadequacies and to a man, they are child support deadbeats. It is a remarkable coincidence that each of the divorcees had, prior to marital commitment, done time in the local slammer; Chief Daddy, and Ms. Bedida presiding. Sweet Sue is atypical of her parents. She is slim and not entirely homely. With her well-proportioned rack and that fluidity of motion, sweet Sue doesn't appear to be six feet tall. And she flaunts a sensual, though furtive look in her pale blue eyes. With a little dental work and a professional makeover, Sue Nami would be cocked, loaded and primed. And she already possesses *the walk*. She could, with those afore mentioned improvements, own a sexpot persona.

Sweet Sue is dressed in faded raggedy blues with American flag, wild daisy and peace sign insignia patches sewn over the tattered rips in thighs, knees, pockets, and buttocks. A fuzzy cutoff sweater festooned with gold stars, baubles, bangles and beads stretches across her most endearing features. A diamond stone twinkles from her navel: the central attraction is set off by a hypnotist's bulls-eye tattoo. She wears three gaudy wedding rings on the fingers of her right hand, has studs in her pierced nostrils. Trashy, pendulous earrings offset her lustrous yellow locks. Flip-flops slap rhythmically, the heels of her number twelve's.

She bops up close and personal to Mr. Wolf H. Nero (H, for Had) inspects him as though a spider might a succulent fly caught in her web.

"*That's one of 'em,*" Sue proclaims between gum smacks. "*He was at the counter. I was checkin' his groceries. Three Snickers bars* an' two a them 64 oz. Cans a beer the flatlanders call Harley mufflers. I was about to add on the Bull Durham when I hear a loud crash in the parkin' lot out front of the 7-11. The other alleged perp comes drivin' in, crashes into the side of this dude's ol' car, backs off and hits it again and again! Like holy shit! This dude just stands there lookin' at the sack I'd put 'is beer in like he's one a them desert dromedaries run dry."

Sweet Sue likes to expand her vocabulary by watching the Discovery Channel during her night shift, moonlighting as a turnkey, once again raising the ugly, somewhat disguised head of nepotism…however when rearing three hungry boys without a man, a woman's gonna do, well, what a woman's gonna do….

Sweet Sue Nami is thirty; Wolf eighteen. Chronologically speaking, a perfect… Sweet Sue eyes Wolf as if an electromagnet attracted to steel beneath flaking rust: Wolf H. Nero, who, even in his cleanest dirty tank-top, his Hawaiian Bermudans and once white tuxedo jacket complete with black bow tie and once pink carnation, looks like he's arisen from a Dempsey Dumpster to wallow in a pig-sty, before inserting his head up the intake of a *corn* husking machine.

"So I go, 'did you see that? That dude out there just hit your car, backed up and ran into it twice more again.'

"This dude just goes 'uh,' pays for his stash and like totally spaces out the dude that just banged up his wheels. They like practically collide at the door, without sayin' 'poop,' 'Happy New Year,' or 'take an aerial intercourse at a rotating pastry.'"

Sue Nami has an admirable knack for the arcane. But this time her words register in Wolf's utterly deranged sense of humor. The accused and his accuser share an almost feline furtive glance, and the perp cackles like a hen laying an extra-large.

"Anyway," sweet Sue continues, "this dudely hops in his beater three hole Buick Fairlane. He backs out to the street and tears a new one back into the lot and smashes into the side of the other dude's like, totally dented in Ford Coupe Deville Sedan.

"Alleged victim number two's still back at the beer coolers mashin' his face into the Micro Brew display case. He's frenchin' the glass an' doin' his subtle pocket-pool, change countin' routine. I'm like totally stunned for a tad. I don't even scream till the third loud crash bongs me. The second dude's slithers up to settle his cheapoid six-pack bill. I hear another loud crash an' I'm like torn while the runaway dudely forks over an assortment of nickels, dimes an' pennies. The hippy don't appear to take no notice of his destroyed wheels, but I'm like too intense, like totally wigged. I watch 'em split north an' south... like Hi-oh-Silver, rattle, crash, boom A-way, twinnish tin terrors of highway 101. But both are y'know, like blown off the cuckoo's nest. They're like too rad for words. An' that's why I turn nark. I dimed up Mom to like, relay on to you, Daddy."

*

And it's Chief Al who brings on the dog, a Rottweiler named Diatribe... Al Barjinn, whose last name portrays tumbling tumbleweeds, purple sage and the Chisholm Trail, plus that fella with an eye patch; fat boy with a bottle problem, big guy named Rooster, or somethin' along those lines.

"Well, well" says magistrate AL Barjinn, "Mister Nero, seems yew gotcher ass caught up the ol' creek in a bottomless canoe without oarlocks or related pro-pulsion de-vices. Yer charged with attemptin' to E-lude an officer of the court. Seems MS. Bedida wrote in Vehicular mayhem... Disorderly conduct... Drivin' whilst suspended.... Harassin' flatlanders...an' parkin' lot mopery. Yer under investigation fer operatin' a motor vehicle on a closed beach; de-liberately crampin' said vehicles wheels whilst drivin' at a low rate o' speed an' rollin' yer automobile onto its top.... Oh yeah, add open container to this here scum sucker's rap sheet Ms. Bedida."

"Brack. Why me? Jeez H. Chrize! Do I haft'a do ever damn thang a-round heah? I got a head ache 'n' a belly ache."

The chief ignores his second dearest possession to stack more fodder on his case.

"Witnesses say yew enlisted the aid of passersby's to push said vehicle back on its wheels only to repeat the crime again an' again. Yew an' that digustin' toilet bowl floater were seen playin' chicken out on the causeway above the clam flats. Yew narrowly avoided head on collisions by veerin' by one another in respective left hand lanes at the last second. And this here's a far piece from England."

The man born of a past that takes folks back in time to picture shows featuring arroyos, plateaus and a rope with a whiskery noose slung over a limb on a parched white oak, pauses to dissect his victim. The crime fighting family senses previews of sieved bleeding.

"I ain't gonna ax yew to explain yer actions. They ain't no excuse for yer existence here on peaceable mother earth, other than a blatantly cruel mistake Mother Nature made. I otter jist beat yew to death with a shitty stick…then beat yer corpus delecti jist fer bein' shitty."

"The drivin' whilst suspended charge is bogus," Wolf interjects with a whine. Seems he has never actually acquired a license to operate a motor vehicle.

The law, just south of the 45th parallel, but way overextending his jurisdiction cocks a ham hock fist.

"Chill a skosh daddy!" exclaims sensual Sweet Sue Nami, working a half pack of tutti-frutti like there's no tomorrow while summing up her mood swing. *"He looks so… like pitiful… so wretchedly attractive. He may not be like hunkish, but I think he's like…kinda bitchin'."*

*

To Wolf, Al Barjinn's surname is showing ominous signs of the red hot end of a Bar-J cattle brand, a black shadow cast by a High Noon sun slanting through loppy saloon doors, and a jagged, do-it-yourself weapon fashioned by breaking a bottle of dust cutter over a solid oak countertop.

But father Al's is a false grizzly charge. The devoted cop is of the notion that same said Sol rises and sets exclusively for Sweet Sue Nami, his one and only, though thoroughly misunderstood, darlin' daughter.

The long arm of the law casts aside his quirt. The legendary prosecutor swallows an immense glop of snoose and takes up his gavel. Acting as town justice, the Magistrate is now known as JP, Alfonse Barjinn Esq. Alfonse Barjinn, ESQ., still wearing his silver star, sentences Wolf T. Nero to sixty hard. Twelve long on the single link chain gang, twelve short: evenings, retiring under the watchful eyes of the night matron, none other than Sweet Sue Nami.

Sweet Sue is to eventually bring to Nero's cell, a basin of water, a scrub brush, a bar of Grandma's Lye Soap, a pillow with slip, a comforter and an air mattress. She also fetches a blanket to cover the tiny barred window overlooking the dank cell…

Wolf T. Nero is released early, not because of leniency on the part of his screw (slang for jailer) but to establish credit at the local jewelry store — approved thanks to the strong-arm tactics of long arm Al. The chief's contrary demeanor puts the jeweler to envisioning rattlesnakes, dry gulch ambushes, rabid buffaloes, monitor lizards and Gila monsters with attitudes.

A purchase is made: a gaudy thumb/wedding ring, fitted for a size prerecorded three husbands and three freebees in the past.

Wolf T. Nero, on parole, yet studiously imagining the business end of a rubber hose, or worse, the nasty hole in the muzzle of a .38 Police Special, attends, with a slight shrug and a mumbles, somewhat audible, "I do," in his own spontaneous wedding.

*

The newlyweds take stock of *their* offspring born of Sue Nero's previous errors in judgment. The lineup consists of little

Jose Guevara Jr. and Running-He-Who-Walks-Under-Horse In-Rain, an indirect descendant of Chief DePoe. They are an American mixed bag…a family of undistinguished names. The leastest one, dressed only in a flannel diaper, peers from behind his protectors. Wee Cam is short For Kami Kazi.

Wee Cam, continuously trades the thumb in his mouth for the thumb in his belly button, playing automated solitary switch-'em for no apparent reason. Sweet Sue and Wolf, due to his Osage-oil-well heritage, has just possibly more wampum than God. Nero and Sweet Sue, are soon seen at a navel auction. There they acquire an obsolete submarine. They enjoy a mighty long honeymoon beneath the Pacific, while piloting their unique home, home. Hiring a large bulldozer, they, through a series of blocks and tackles and heavy steel cables, haul their sub atop a high hill (sand dune). After setting a foundation, installing power, lights and a makeshift septic system, they paint their naval operational, battle experienced, but mothballed, nearly-instant home, yellow. The sub is to become the family's residence on a nob (erected by drifting sand) overlooking the local vehicle-recycling center.

The owner/operator of the junkyard spends many hours staring longingly at his new neighbor's steel house.

And the harsh grating noises echo-screeching from the hydraulic vehicle-compactor are absorbed into the sub's hull. The clamorous racket sooths a malfunctioning chip in Wolf's bizarre soul. The rest of the family wears earplugs as naturally as breathing in and breathing out.

The boat and the nob are harmonious with Sweet Sue Nero's peculiar compulsions to reside in a flotation device, and to plant her feet above the highest recorded tsunami mark since the *really big one.*

As uncannily as the first three, the fourth and fifth offspring (twin boys) of sweet Sue Barjinn-Guevara, He-Who-Stands-Under-Horse-In–Rain, Nami-Nero are born a month premature. This proves to be an extraordinary event that exclusively occurs with Sweet Sue's first time pregnancies. After careful consideration, and remembering the words of his father-in-law, '*Su-weet mother of the un-blankin' real,*' Wolf's firstborn son is granted the names *Naugahyde: Naugahyde T. Nero. And to the second son, the one that howls unmercifully through the echo chambered night is granted the name, Hyperbole Nero, (no middle name or initial attached).*

*

Did Sweet Sue, like, lick the curse? Was the fourth and fifth rounds ringers? Well… Wolf takes time for Sweet Sue to tame and only of late, did Wolf figure out that Sweet Sue will only withhold her favors if he insists on driving the family remodeled garbage truck/caravan type passenger car. And there is the occasional blindside kazzilion decibel put down from Momma Bedida. Surprisingly however, Ms. Bedida takes early retirement to spend most of her leisure hours promoting, and basking in the many benefits gleaned from enjoying *"poor health."*

Wolf opines that his matriarch-in-law is still as healthy and contrary as a pickled Missouri Mule. That Ms. Bedida would rather go to a doctor than a picnic. But dear old dad-in-law keeps the playing field level by taking an active role in underling affairs.

In patriarch Al's six-gun eyes, Wolf will always be compared unfavorably to the only place under the corkscrew tail of a shoat that is <u>not</u> pork.

Wolf T. Nero, alias Lone Lupus or any other lame guise is, according to dearly beloved father-in-law, on his best day, a no-talent weirdwolf sumbich; contrarily however, with beaucoup bucks.

Wolf doesn't hold much stock in the *Super Cop* legends of dear old *Daddy-in-law*. He secretly envisions the patriarch as being an over-the-hill hump buster, a daughter doting pervert and a worn-out reprobate. To Wolf, Al is a gassy sanctimonious old sot, reeking of a combination of raw whiskey and a cud of tobacco reprocessed a third time. The second, being through a barroom urinal. Daddy-in-law is himself a fugitive from a douche bag who does not and never will know from jack about his daughter, or his grandsons.

Nero, taking the pen name, *Rend Steel,* brings home the week old bread by selling short stories. He dreams of becoming a songwriter and blues singer, but discovers he can't rhyme moon with anything profound. He is remiss and finds himself wanting to carry a tune. He can't pick for squat diddly or vice-versa and his voice is so tinny his brand of the Small town Jailhouse blues (his finest composition) is torture to the human ear. But oh, well. With all that oil revenue, what the hell?

Wolf has a talent for the written word however. The proof is in Rend Steel's jargon pudding. To a bizarre corner of the market; (flakes, moon worshipping nudist cults and animal rights activists) the author has a knack for fabricating far out and *very mysterious* fables

The man his mother nicknamed Lupus, turns out to be a more than adequate husband, at least for the hippyish Sweet Sue, who has an almost normal manner of calibrating the measure of men.

But there lies the usual downside. Wolf is disposed of an evolutionary backlash that unfortunately exudes out of the genes of his firstborn twins.

The fourth and fifth born sons of Sweet Sue Nero, during certain cycles of the moon, howl in their sleep. The twins are soon to develop a faraway yearning in their four unique, yellowish-brown eyes.

Wolf-like genetics aside, Naugahyde and Hyperbole finally split from their landlocked sub-home in abject boredom. The young adults enter the mainstream of society. They bum around the badlands of America jamming cars in destruction derbies at county fairs. The twins do college simultaneously by forging GI Bill papers. (I mean the rich never spend their own greenbacks).

At their dual weddings to twin big rawboned lonely-hearts correspondents from Siberia, Naugahyde and Hyperbole are reunited with their half-brothers. They are to form the law firm: Guevara, Naugahyde, Nami, Hyperbole, Rain, and Cam who has lately shrugged the thumb-to-mouth-to belly button switch-'em monkey that plagued him through Harvard Law).

The DC firm with close ties to a liberal organization specializes in immigration, civil rights, tribal law and disposing police brutality cases.

In his travels, Naugahyde will always remember his father's only prophetic message: Never shout your middle name in the bars of the Great Northwest – "*TIMBER!*"

Unlike his twin, Hyperbole has no middle name to cause him grief in the form of a tremendous bar bill. However, he still has a suppressed affinity for howling. He secretly longs for a quiet home high in the snow-clad mountains of Alaska, far from a derelict yellow submarine stranded on a sandy nob next to a vehicle recycling plant's *EXTREMELY* high decibel vehicle compacter.

******

HAPPY HOUR
An excerpt from an as yet unnamed, unpublished, manuscript written by Steve Herndon

We sail from Dutch Harbor on a following sea. What follows is the biting cold. The boat bucks and rolls like a rodeo bull, only there's no eight second end to the hammering. Battering waves slam us from stem to stern, from bulwark to bulwark. Constant spray turns to instant ice. The ice sticks to virtually everything including our raingear. It's like extra-thick glass. We shatter hunks of it from the ship's outer surfaces with rubber sledges. All hands are numb from toes to Rudolph-like noses. The next comber hits and sticks. We do what we've just done again, and again. . .

It's comparative to wiping one's keester on a hoop. There's no end in sight. But eventually the barometric pressure inch-worms up the glass. The seas lay down. The outside temperature rises from sub-zero into the low teens. A short lifetime later, we snub tight to a transit dock in Seattle, safe, and as sound as, well, ever.

*

Next thing this young deckhand does is crawl off the Alaskan king crabber, *AFTER GLOW DANCER*. I'm relieved until the next season of bucking into the roughest waters in Alaska and just possibly, on earth. . .

F/V After Glow Dancer is an *old* rock 'n' roller. It doesn't take long to become old in her occupation. She's in need of bottom-end maintenance, a complete cosmetics job, and her twin diesel mains pulled and replaced.. It's all about to go down at a shipyard in Seattle.

With time to fritter, and big bucks to spend, I purchase a pickup truck. I cut a shrewd deal with a snake-oil salesman who's slithered into the parking lot one street below Pike Street Market.

*

The late-model Ford is fire engine red. She's endowed with 4-wheel drive. According to her plates, she's just in from Idaho. How the hell could those Ida-whorian tater farmers hurt her hauling a few spuds to the Lay's factory? The truck is also equipped with four on the floor and a *Lucky Lager Beer* tap for a shifting nob. A little yellow hangman's noose hangs from her inside mirror. There's a diamond-tread-aluminum toolbox with a shed roof attached to the box. Even more importantly, she's got a crudely hand painted sign in white letters on her red tailgate that christens her <u>Ol' BLEW</u>.

She's four wheels of mojo, and she's got a certain reckless style. I couldn't resist her even if I didn't have a special fondness for hucksters, grifters and veteran pitchmen.

Turns out my new used truck is cherry: guaranteed to make it off the lot, and not to lose its flavor on the bedpost overnight. Who could ask for anything more? This dickering shit is all in the eye of the beholder anyhow. If you think you got yourself a good deal, then by god, you got yourself a good deal!

I turn a quick trip back to After Glow Dancer to load my worldly possessions in my old army duffle bag. I toss the duffle in the fancy box in the bed of *Ol'* Blew. My long guns are in padded carriers. With particular care, I stow 'em behind the seat.

A climb to the wheelhouse, a knuckle crushing handshake. A jolting punch on the shoulder from my favorite skipper, Capt. Gus Gustafson, and I'm as gone as long gone John from Bowling Green.

*

The icy roads are non-conducive to out-of-practice driving. Not to mention the fact that I lack talent in wheeling and dealing on ice. *Ol' Blew* frequently slips, slides and regains its tenuous foothold. Consequently, a certain area of my anatomy occasionally finds the need to pucker. Oh well. we seem to be the only vehicle on the road. *Total ignorance?*

On the far side of the Narrows Bridge however, we edge up behind a semi-tractor and trailer. Time and again the trailer swerves from the shoulder to cross the center line. Perhaps the trucker is taking a snooze. Maybe hitting the booze? Low air on one set of duals? Did the load shift? Possibly, as a precautionary measure, the big rig is simply hogging more than its share of the slippery, crookedy road. Or just as likely, I have no clue whatsoever.

Above the mud-flap on the left rear of the trailer, a sign catches my eye: *How's My Driving? Dial 1-800-EAT-SHIT…food for thought?*

An abysmal length of time later, "Yippy yay kye oh, get along little doggy!" Stiff-arming the wheel on a straightaway, I shift into *pass-large-truck* gear and cautiously allot *Blew* a touch more foot-feed. I glance out the side window. All I see is a set of giant, hungrily rotating tires about to recycle my truck and me into scrap iron, blood and guts and so much debris. I inch over a bit. As I nearly pinch the steering wheel in two, I steer a centimeter more to port.

Its' preordained, I guess. But somehow, we are synchronized with the semi's fishtailing. In slow-motion, we dart around the navigational hazard. Just a small example of the dangerous life I lead, I think to myself. Still, my relief is as palpable as the sweat dripping off my brow, the itch in my armpits. I can't see into the big rig's cab, but envision Alfred E Newman up there over steering, randomly grabbing gears, and grinning vacantly.

Ol' Blew and I are into each other's quirks. She'll shift smoothly if I feel her up until her gears mesh. I promise to stop riding her clutch if she'll refrain from her oblivious veering to starboard. Thanks to Alfred E., Ol' Blew and I are on our way to becoming intimate friends.

I hang a right oblique and head west and then south. When I reach the Highway 101 Junction, I follow a frozen road luring me toward Oregon. It's the long crookedy route—the ancient trade-trail. The skimpily modernized two-lane, leads me ever nearer the Oyster Shell Confederated Aboriginal Nation. That unlikely hunk of real estate is the place that had been my home through my orphaned childhood including puberty.

Reminiscing about tribal relatives and staring into the icy sheen, my conscience goes on a lunatic picture show journey. The lid pops off the spirit lore implanted in me. A few miles of daydreaming in delirium leads to obsessing about butterflies floating in gossamer splendor over sun-warmed verdant meadows. Savannas of summer's daisies comfort my soul…and there's *you* beneath … Ol' Blew meanders into a skid. I startle back to wakefulness. Back on track, I shut the heater down, open the vents and tune the radio to a heavy metal station, cranking up the sound.

I guess my shivering transfers from my hands to the wheel. Damned if we don't skid out on an off-camber curve. I guess my self-manufactured torture chamber tricks were on me. We slide sideways and take out a rural mailbox. Oh well, Blew. A minor ding, a minor annoyance.

That last skid jolts me into a spell of eye watering, teeth chattering, selfishly weird thinking. On my wheel watches, I drove a boat in a virtually empty ocean. 101 is much narrower than the briny deep. It's a slippery moray eel, twisting, shocking, switching back and striking danger on its frozen blind corners. I'm driven to distraction. Something is missing. My throat is parched. Excused and accepted by society, attitude adjustment, and stress level recalibration will soon descend. *Happy Hour* draws near. It's somewhere nearby, waiting impatiently for me and millions of like-minded consumers operating under the self-deception that alcohol is anything but a depressant.

It's a bay front, Hoquiam's, or thereabouts, where mind overwhelms matter. Or maybe it's the name of the establishment that attracts and excites the magnet in my brain. It's *the Lost Sea Turtle*. The Sea Turtle is a continent lost. It is so lost it's all but extinct. The bar is a seedy, grade B, unpainted, board 'n' batten dump. The rehydration joint rises above a pothole-cratered parking lot at the shore end of a plank and piling wharf. Ol' Blew and I slide sideways into the potholed parking lot. The place is, all but for a rusty old Buick listing heavily to port, void of human spoor.

The heavy-duty dock supports seafood cookeries and canneries. A few fishing boats bob along the wharf, waiting to offload their catch - or on-load fuel, bait and groceries. Blasts of sticky wind, scented with boiling crab, gum up the Sea Turtle's salt encrusted portholes. And as always, flocks of gulls squabble and mewl, competing for fish guts and other unappetizing scraps.

The smell of crab cooking makes my abused stomach growl. I ignore the rumbling even if the setting is right up my alley.

The bowels of the Lost Sea Turtle smell like someone has tracked in low tide then made a half-ass attempt to swab the muck off the plank floor with vomit-scented disinfectant.

The occasional whiff of dime store perfume drifts with stale, cigarette smoke through sticky, stagnant air. It's muggy-hot and drafty-cold in the same breath. The aromatic blend renders a homey touch. I feel a thousand sets of eyes cutting through me as soon as the shaft of light from the squeaky door squinches shut.

With a voice deadened in dampness, I shout, "Fight, fuck, or run a foot race, I'm your man." I hear a disparaging chuckle and the ka-ching of a cash register from where I surmise the bar lies in wait.

"Two-buck cover charge for ass blowin'," growls a whiskey-tenor.

I vice-grip my eyelids tight, wait ten seconds, and then pop 'em open. I'm alone with the form of what seems to be a woman or a giant-size fluorescent sack with a strikingly beautiful face sticking out above the purse strings. I shuffle closer. Miss Channel Scow of '63 in a muumuu—all five hundred pounds of her—hoves into view. It doesn't take a Dick Tracy to deduce who owns the port listing Buick out yonder.

"Hello! Boy, howdy! How ya doin?" I muster, wondering just how many decades I've slid back in time, and wondering if I should be speaking in some form of water people vernacular that I can't quite interpret…

And then the triple-X barkeep takes off, imparting a sequence of Lost Sea Turtle rules in a staccato burst of localized, um, English. "We reserve the right to refuse service to any motherfucker with bad breath, the clap or hoof and mouth. And any shit eatin' dog with a burr under his collar or in his shorts. If you got a hardon, the whorehouses are further down the wharf. I do sandwiches and grog. I ain't nobody's pissin' post, manhole, sugar titty or shoulder to cry on. The name's Annie. Take it like it comes or take a hike. If you're stayin', squat 'n' roost. Oh yeah, no dogs or sailors allowed."

I'm an ex-soldier boy. Soldiers are not on her list of culls. I obey. I hunker down on a stool, leaving a little running room between her and me and the row of draft taps lining the time-scarred, cigarette-branded, mahogany bar.

"Now what's your poison?"

Annie has no trouble enunciating her off-center words. She chews them off and spits them out like an auctioneer, and right out of that dainty mouth. Am I back in civilization? Or is civilization as lost as the Lost Sea Turtle?

"A schooner of dark, a dozen shooters and a double bourbon, neat, to slide down behind the oysters. Nice place you got here, um, Annie."

"You ain't no logger nor a timber beastie, the animal the rest of those shitheads call a bushelor. Ain't no suspender tracks in your hickory shirt, no sawdust in your ears. I see you're wearin' Romeos, however. You're either a deckhand or a longshoreman, eh, Blondie?"

Annie wrist-whips a schooner under the spigot, tilts the glass, pulls the tap and lets the suds trickle in.

I catch the schooner she slides down the bar and flinch when cool foam splashes my wrist. "You're right as rain. I work by the bushel. But I ain't wore stickery soled Aberdeen dancin' slippers since I was seventeen and forced by the criminal acts of government to lie about my age. However I sure could use a pair of those spiked boots when the deck tilts sideways. I don't wear stagged-off britches. No suspenders, and no tin lid anymore. I wear oilskins, hip boots, a sou'wester and long johns. I also yank a couple three sweatshirts over my bibs. I fish king crab out west, in the Bering Sea, kings and dungeness off the Trinities—Marlboro Country—beyond the south end of Kodiak Island."

I can tell by the way she looks down her nose, the barely perceptible nod, Annie's not the impressionable type.

The beer splashes my tonsils with fizzy delight. The unique taste of the raw oysters brings bittersweet memories I'm taken back a couple hundred miles and six growing up years south of here....

My blood brother, Snook, once told me that the taste of an oyster was an oxymoron. "Royally nasty 'n' ungodly good. It looks and feels like a loogie, but oh, man, once you beat it beyond your lips, it's like somewhere your mouth ain't never been."

I guess you were right, for once, Snook. So have a little intercourse with a hand-cranked pencil sharpener—my pencil-prick brother, my adopted kin. A blood brother by ceremony. The creed of commingling blood. The scar is a little, jagged white line on the inside of my right wrist. I stare at the pox magnified through the 80 proof in the thick shot glass and then knock back the poison in abject dismissal.

Heavyweight contender Jim Beam jolts me out of my painful reverie. "Glad to make your acquaintance, Annie. I'm Cowboy." I make conversation easily. I tell her, god's truth, how much she reminds me of a gal I'd met the first day I got into Kodiak.

"I didn't have a boat. I was fresh out of the army and green as my fast-fading olive-drab fatigues. But I've always been a lucky sumbich. Anyway, word had it that the Ships Bar was the closest thing to a hiring hall in a few thousand thousand cubic miles of ocean, so I brazen my way through the door.

"The music is so loud an elephant seal couldn't hear himself yodel, much less fart. There are two fistfights in bloody process. No one's watching. They're six-deep to the bar. A half-dozen bartenders are sliding pails of ale down cue sticks to the parched customers in the back rows.

"This tall woman sidles up and looks down at me. She's wearin' khaki pants, has hip boots folded down below her knees. Gal wears a matchin' khaki shirt; gotta be six-five if she's an inch. Easy face to look at, like yours, Annie. This Amazon has my undivided attention. She says, 'You just get in?'

"Any idiot with eyeballs and a workable beak can tell I am yet to be cured and hung out to dry by the salty dog process, so I admit it, coy as can be.

"She says, 'Let me buy you your first drink in this here miserable excuse for a town.' She elbows a hole through the sea of humanity and I find myself sittin' on a barstool next to her. She says her name is Big April. Says she's been on this 'fuckin' rock for ten years.'

"It was the first time I heard a woman utilize the F word in general conversation. The drinks come, and she pulls out a roll big enough to pay the interest on the national debt. She peels a hunert off the top and says to a harried barkeep, 'Lemme know when ol' Ben Franklin, there, has shot his wad.'

"She turns back to me, lights a Pall Mall King, and says, 'I'm the taxi driver in this burg. Picked up a fare out to the airport. Remember passin' by you hitchin' it into town.'

"I nod, tryin' not to look hangdog whilst silently admittin' to the fact that I'm more than a little strapped."

I learned to lie about money and virtually anything having to do with interfering with day-to-day survival, back home on the Oyster Shell.

"'Anyway,' Big April says, through twin clouds of smoke blowing through her nostrils, 'this rigging salesman says he wants to go to the best whorehouse in town. I pulls the cab over to the side of the road, turn around and say, 'Buddy, you're in it.'"

For such an exquisite little mouth, Annie possesses a natural guffaw. She likes being compared to Big April. Her eyes turn inward and soften. She's gone back to a better place to linger for a spell. Old times, the good along with the bad, are never far out of reach of the agile mind.

Annie shakes off the memories of slimmer times, bounces back for the next round and tips a couple Singapore Slings with me. Not everybody has a soft spot for a come-and-go pop-in. She's thick and tough as hippo hide in a tough business in a tough town. She senses that I am what I am, a stand-up guy from the old school with an abiding respect for lady salty dawgs.

We bullshit until the regulars wander in: loggers, fishermen longshoremen, and local waterfront talent of the opposite sex. The crowd begin the beguine of nightly arm bending calisthenics and hand-to-mouth resuscitation from the day's labors. 5:30 brings Happy Hour. Annie, begrudgingly, makes a token effort to brighten up the place. The electric meter outside will not spin itself off the wall.

I move to a booth outside the crossfire of alcohol-inflated egos. The pungent aroma of spruce sawdust flakes off the timber fellers (bushelors). The fishy odor exuding from the deck hands blends with Dime Store perfume. All sounds and odors compete with the god awful groans of Johnny Ray sobbing from the corner jukebox. From my quiet observation post, the end product seems both pleasant and a shade foreboding. A strange electricity tickles my *trouble* receptors. I should exit stage left, but baby it's godawful cold outside. As a precaution, I switch to Coke.

A draft age woodsman, who's almost on his lips, laments that he chases skirts like a dog chases cars. "Wouldn't have much more notion of what to do with one if I caught one than a Labrador retriever with a three on the tree, or a by god Dyna-flow Buick Roadmaster Deluxe."

The dude's grizzled bushelor companion strikes a match on his stubbly cheek and then sets the stinky end of a little black cigar afire. The timber beastie passes through a death rattle coughing fit before responding. "No matter how straight and tall a tree be, you can always find the lean, hence the lay. But a woman, she'll defy the plumb bob, the prevailin' winds, and the wedge, kid. Mebbe they's some key to the mystery…ask the bull-buck, I dunno."

A wheedling voice from across the floor butts in with sage advice using a fisherman's analogy, "A woman'll play yez like a fish, Skippy. She'll let yez nibble the bait for a while, but she'll hold the good stuff back till she can set the hook. Once she's got ya on the line, she'll play yez like a keeper. She'll cut yez a little slack from time to time, but remember she's got a grip on the pole. She'll wear yez down; tighten the drag and reel yez aboard. Swim shallow, son, and don't visit the same baited hole too regular."

Sounds like sound advice to me, so I drink to it. I scan the setting until I spot a love child wearing a tight oatmeal sweater with a capital V-neckline. My gaze zeros in on sensual cleavage and then lock on a pair of pointy little objects protruding from beneath the fabric. The young lady, under the scrutiny of all the male eyes within range, has obviously set herself free of the muzzling harness called a brassiere.

The looker snuggles tighter to her fish in a corner booth. I watch her slide her tongue around her sweet lips and hear her say, "Don't you believe a word of it Alvin. It's all a crock of shit."

I admire her subtle moves, the moist pouty lips, the thrusts and parries of her big guns, the sensual way she swivels those twin cannons. Hey, baby, I think to myself, nary a one of us could resist the subtle bait you cast. It's that old black magic and I don't have to wonder why blues, and torch singers, even sob sisters like Johnny Ray, will always make their jack.

"You tell 'em the way it is, honey," a more experienced woman says. "Tell 'em how the female gender, the intellectual side, operates. It ain't in the direction we lean, if ya know what I mean. And it ain't by hook or by god, crook."

Patsy Cline is appropriately belting out "Crazy" from the corner jukebox. A beer-bellied guy at the bar says, "Beg pardon, but I was purt'near an intellectual myself, a time 'r three."

The speaker, through a rudimentary form of parliamentary procedure, has taken the floor. I squint through the smoky gloom and read the message on a ratty tank top stretched tight over rolls of blubber. The backside reads: *EAT A BEAVER—SAVE A TREE*. From observing the half-hidden, vertical smile flashing above the guy's droopy jeans, I naturally assume he's not an environmental scientist.

He swivels his stool around and the message on the front of his stained shirt reads: *SAVE OUR HOUNDS—TREE AN ACTIVIST*. From his backwoods demeanor, I'm not surprised he's a proponent of the hounds. I am surprised, however, how still the atmosphere becomes as the red-faced, balding diplomat grabs his pitcher of beer by the handle, takes a horn directly from the mouth, wipes his dripping chin with a hairy forearm, and tucks the pitcher and what's left of its contents, between his stubby legs. That accomplished, he says, "The first time my brain surpassed genius levels I was laid up in the hospital. I was the victim of a sneak attack by a log what deliberately detached itself from its bed and, without provocation, up an' rolled clean over me.

"Or was it that time down in Mexico whenced I was runnin' that weird fever? They never did isolate that peculiar virus…still with me I guess. Makes me intolerable thirsty. Don't really matter. I think I was experiencin' what you lady friends describe as a feelin' called *pain*. Yas, I believe it was the log, by gawd.

"The surgeons had gathered up my body parts and sewed 'em back on, an' damn close to their original locations as I pictured 'em to be. Anyways, the ol' sawbones said I was experiencin' *'pain'* or something near it. His medical descriptions went beyond my immediate conceptions. Somethin' was mentioned about my screams bein' a little annoyin' to the rest of the ward, to the staff, to the visitors tryin' to enjoy a peaceful misery in the cafeteria, and to them other intellectuals tryin' to keep their intellects primed an' current in the liberry, a coupler miles down the road from the hospital.

"Oh I knowed it wasn't real pain. Not like poppin' out a kid, ner PMS. Nothin' that severe, fer sure, but the doc needed some placatin', so I let 'im shoot me full o' morphine.

"That's when my capacity for deep thinkin' began t' take root. Why, within just a few heartbeats, I'd solved the bugs in the quantum theory and moved on to higher math. After math got beyond infinity it got boring, so I took on the world's problems, an' by damn, I solved 'em all! I eliminated ever'thin' from poverty to pestilence. Then I went to curin' hunger…believe there was somethin' about developin' a taste fer sand in that one…then I initiated world peace.

"I topped 'er all whenced I puzzled out why the women-folk bunch up, and it takes 'em so long in the can. An' why they actually enjoy shoppin'. Then I studied out why they ain't a bounty on them ol' plucked hens what go thirty in the blind corners, then when yer lookin' t' pass, ream 'er up t' a hunert and twenty in the straight stretches. And I figured out why they slow 'er back down to twenny-five an' drive side-by-side in them passin' lanes.

"An' then I throwed in a bunch a other stuff, maybe even a coupler personal, well not problems persaktly...just leetle hang-ups, ya unnerstan'?

"I lost 'er all when my wounds healed up an' the sawbones held back the morphine stimulant, but it was a dimension I remember quite fondly. By damn, I knew 'er all from top t' bottom and sideways fer quite a passin' spell.

"I got me some o' them pills what's supposed t' rebuild yer memory capacitors. Maybe they'll bring 'er all back for me...if I could only remember to take 'em...."

As Droopy Drawers runs out of gas, I turn to watch the reaction from the female element. A woman down the bar grinds her cigarette into her ashtray as if the tray was the rotund guy's tongue. Twin blue-gray contrails jettison her flared nostrils, and she takes a heavy pull from her glass of refreshment. Her face seems to narrow as the glass hits the bar with a resounding thud!

Like a rattler without rattles, a soundless electric current coils the air. This would-be dissident is perhaps not the only person in the crowd taking exception to the previous speaker's little denigrations.

"Listen, Kegger Calloway, you disgusting sack, you're as far removed from brilliance as my first husband, Divot Minor. You're so fat you'd have to resort to an upside-down periscope to even see past your belly and detect your withered brain.

"Oh, an' by the by, Buzzard Breath, nary a one of you pansy-ass men know a whit about pain. Why a teensy cold will start the likes of you howling and whining for the wife or mother you so readily choose to turn a deaf ear to when you get well, or as well as you hypochondriacs hiding behind those macho images ever get.

"Why I wouldn't invest a quarter for the lot of you Curly, Larry, and Mo, butt-headed couch potatoes. You wimps are all a pain in my royal red rectum."

"Careful now," Annie says. "You know the rules. You can't get personal, and some of you are gettin' a little close to borderline. I don't wanna cut any of you fine, upstandin' consumers off."

"I'd just as soon cut somebody off," says a hatchet-faced woman. Her lips curl into a sneer of pure loathing and she stares poison ramrods into the fat dude, the guy called Kegger. Only she's staring directly at his partially exposed second smile.

"I'll drink to that," another woman shouts, and does, and deeply. "And speakin' of drivin', blubber butt, you couldn't drive chickens downstairs with a broom. Little wonder us good drivers don't want you passing to crash and burn in front of us—thereby leaving us true intellectuals destined to go down with your sorry ass."

I flashback to Alfred E. Newman in the long-hauler with his load of loose bowling balls. I don't know squat about women drivers, but I would venture, as a whole, women are more conscientious. However, I want no part of this debate, because looking back at Big April, I'm aware that life in general is a stacked deck, and women hold all the aces…not to mention the wild card…

"Not to change the direction this conversation is taking," a deep voice farther down the bar cuts in, "but the name's David, not Divot. Majors, not Minor like that prune-faced specimen yonder chooses to imply. She should know my name by heart. I'm her first husband, thrice removed.

"Sophie, there, said somethin' about clingin' to the quarters she earnt whilst layin' on her back countin' the holes in the ceiling tile. You owe a little more than a cheap shot to mankind, Soph. Even stingy as you are, after a hundred rides a man should be up for a medal or a least a two-bit rebate for gettin' it up beyond the call a duty, don'cha s'pose?"

Skinny dude sitting on the stool next to the woman called Sophie leaps off his stool and trips the light fantastic down the bar, confronting David, or Divot, whichever side of the rail one props his, or her heels.

The little guy assumes a John L. Sullivan bare-knuckle pugilistic pose, feigning and weaving, his fists performing an interesting variation of the hokey pokey. I presume the featherweight champ is Sophie's current squeeze. I can feel it coming. It's like pitching a bag of rotting, chopped herring bait over the rail. The milling gulls are about to launch a squealing, screeching feeding frenzy.

Divot, or David, takes on a quizzical expression, evidently confused by the little guy's fighting stance, but with a short, swift, experimental jab Mr. D pops the skinny guy flush on the beak. The little dude drops like a pole-axed steer, his nose gushing blood.

Screams and shouts of strange metaphoric obscenities ring out. Suddenly everyone in the joint is whaling away at the nearest semi-ambulatory target. Sophie is leaping up and down and shouting, "Hit the mutherfucker Wilbur! Hit the mutherfucker!" But Wilbur seems to find sitting on the floor and holding his wounded honker more to his liking.

The place is a blur of motion. A bearded dude, possibly a closet peacenik, is beating cheeks for the back door but makes an unscheduled course change due to a sudden impact with a flying chair to the back of his head. His legs turn rubbery; he veers off at a right angle and takes a header into the jukebox. Frank Sinatra croons, "I've got you under my skin—under my skin—under my skin—under my skin."

As I crouch and peer around the back of the booth, ashtrays, shot glasses, booze and ice cubes fly through the din in a veritable meteor shower.

Sophie is still coaching her man Wilbur while screaming obscenities at David, or Divot, and at motherhood in general.

Someone, who perhaps has a mother, launches Sophie into horizontal flight. Pin-wheeling through the smoke, she lands flat on her back on the shuffleboard table where she rockets along with impressive spin—if little English. Sophie, the human puck, loses momentum at the far end of the board where she appears to go limp—and oozes to the floor.

The liberated gal with the fine hooters squirms from beneath a tumbling, cursing dog-pile. I notice right off that her sweater has been refashioned into evening apparel. She wears it with one arm sleeveless, and the V-neck tucked under a delectable alabaster melon with a dark purple stem. Her face afire, she manages to arrow her arm back through the sleeve, but the sweater's neck is stretched into a large oval that hangs off the shoulder and down to just below those pointy objects of attention that were previously kept semi-covert.

Squealing melodramatically, she sprints for the ladies facilities pausing only when she spots Kegger Calloway crawling in high gear for safety.

The gal's anguish fades. Her brows furrow into a look that could be concern. The lady's intent is on enhancing Kegger's memory—at least to the feeling of pain. With her arms crossed in an X over her exposed assets, she places a swift kick. I decide she's gonna miss low, but nope. Her sharply pointed high heel penetrates exactly the target she's aiming for. . .

Kegger is infinitely brighter than Sophie claimed. He remembers pain. His screams are quite piercing and likely carry far enough to annoy the studious set, attending intellectual pursuits in the library a mile or so east of the Lost Sea Turtle.

The draftee, whose affliction for skirts started the debate, staggers free of the melee; Skippy's got a shit-eating grin plastered on his mug. Suave is not in his strange vernacular. Even so, young Skippy seems a tad more enterprising than he'd led Annie's regulars to believe.

Annie fires a large caliber six-shooter into the ceiling, signaling the end of Happy Hour. I leap a good six inches without outwardly moving a muscle. I reach over and unplug the jukebox cutting Frank Sinatra off at the "skin". For the blink of an eye, the Lost Sea Turtle is rendered deathly still.

A mutual consensus groan emanates from the patronage. Most of the contestants mutter under their breath and pack it in for another joint, possibly one with a longer interval set aside for attitude adjustment.

The girl with the exposed arsenal now covers her guns with her bloodied boyfriend's mackinaw. The coat is buttoned tight under her chin. Her face still beet red, she sobs loudly and takes her leave huddled under the comfort of one of her man's broad shoulders.

Annie alludes to the fact that her six-gun was shooting blanks, "Just like most of my regulars."

Kegger and his rather effeminate screams are conspicuously absent. I wonder if he has crawled off to die in the seclusion of the john. Wonder if Skippy, the draftee wearing the triumphant grin, ended up out on the street happily chasing three on the tree, Dyna-flow Buick's, or skirts. Alas and alack, military service will beckon all too soon.

The foulmouthed one named Sophie is snoring peacefully under the shuffleboard table. Her man is downing every drink left standing, motivated, perhaps, by the assumption that alcohol reduces swelling.

Wilbur stares through eyes swollen nearly closed, stares as he dabs at his noticeably off-center beak. Draining the last whiskey sour, Wilbur stares as David Majors revives his ex-wife, Sophie, thrice removed. And Wilbur stares dejectedly as man and ex hold each other semi-upright and stagger off into the frozen night.

Sophie may have been wrong in her assessment of Kegger's intelligence quotient, but her categorizing of David Majors is uncannily astute. In the pitching wedge of life, David Majors truly is a minor divot.

Couple longshoremen slip into heavy coats and head for the next joint down the waterfront, one of the two mumbling something about participating in better brawls at family reunions.

Annie sighs and sweeps the broken glass into a remarkably large dustpan before mopping up the blood and the beer. She keeps my glass filled. I reciprocate freely with the tips.

The jukebox is plugged back in, and the Lost Sea Turtle slowly refills with bar-hoppers from down the wharf. "The Battle of New Orleans" blares loud incentive. I slide my Coke aside and order up a schooner of draft Lucky Lager. Sadly, the new crowd seems lackadaisical. Nary a philosophical discussion evolves into pursuits of a physical nature.

Long about 10:30, Annie lumbers to my table. We're bar buddies, by now. Having borne witness to one of the more classically entertaining brawls to ever come aground on the west coast; we are comrades in arms, of sorts. Annie motions me to follow her through a black, EMPLOYEE ONLY door which is just wide enough to accommodate those remarkable jellyroll cheeks undulating beneath her psychedelic muumuu.

Behind the door, the room is filled with wine and whiskey cases. Annie drives home a deadbolt lock, turns a 160 and slides a row of empty boxes aside. The boxes partition off a hidey-hole with an old horseshoe booth sitting under a shaded light. The lamp, like the ones hanging over pool tables, casts its dim glow in the shape of an upside-down colander. My eyes drift past the light splaying on the booth and I follow my nose to two girls shadowed just beyond the colander, in front of a door leading to God, the girls and Annie knows where. The girls are gnawing their lips and hugging their breasts. They are totally out of their element. They look as nervous as prostitutes in choir practice.

The girls are too young to be in a bar. They're purported to be eighteen. If they are, I'm not a fisherman. I'm a jet aviator. The twosome wear near identical mini-skirts, hot tops under overall jackets, peroxide jobs and way too much foo-foo powder.

As a sideline, it seems Annie runs a quarter-ton, single-handed, clandestine operation—a flat-broke Underground Highway for wayward, waylaid daughters of darkness. Annie, after a brief educational spiel, introduces the girls as "Luann Swift and Elise Maul," from up the Coast.

"I'm Cowboy," I mumble. "Cowboy Heldig, from nowhere in particular. Mostly at large." Annie, motions the teens to slide in beside me. She waits till everyone's settled in, then cannonballs down across from me. The two girls trampoline into the air and come down where they weren't without changing expressions. It has to be one of those gender things Kegger failed so miserably to express.

The bumper car T-bone effect leaves me in one-cheek vertigo. Luann is glued to me. I'm asphyxiated with putrid waves of nickel-a-gallon perfume. Jesus H. She must've bathed in a cesspool of Eau De Essence of Fermenting Pee-u. I'll be delirious before my beak grows numb.

Annie says the girls need a ride to Coos Bay, Oregon where Annie's big sister, Aunt Mable, takes up the slack. I have trouble perceiving Aunt Mable. I'd give my left one to see anyone, living outside the confines of a carny freak show, heftier than Annie. Still, I want no part of the jailbait twins. Annie's eyes implore, as I try to puzzle out a story Elise tells with her hands covering her face.

She's sucking air as if she just dove into a pond full of ice-cold water. And I decipher a tale of stepfather molestation as told through deep soulful eyes hidden behind slut layers of mascara.

I'm a little leery of convenient stories, having recently survived the teen years more than a few owies over the limit. My eyes scan between mud-oozing tears and tally a different version of teen truth. The fine print says Elise has taken some liberties with the facts. More likely, she's gotten herself knocked-up by some long hair hippy, impressing the teen set with his dubious charms from cannery row. I opine to myself that she can't be more than six weeks along.

She's sitting across from me, and lighting up a Marlboro. Her hands are shaking. I see the pain and the humiliation coming unmasked in her eyes.

She's got nobody of family, nothing to cling to but the old survival instinct ingrained in her soul. I'm an orphan. I've felt the pangs; been lost inside the lonely blue labyrinth ... maybe I'm wrong about her. Hell, I'm no prophet, for chrissakes!

Sympathizing is tough to accomplish when I'm dying for a breath of air. Annie, without excusing herself, leaves me to fend for myself. She squeezes her flab beyond the black door and miraculously disappears. Elise locks the door behind that huge departing stern, terminating the hog auction on the far side, but leaving me wishing I were there with the crowd of lackadaisical ass-blowers.

Luann slides over a good two inches and says, "Oh Cowboy, thank you so, like, tremendously for coming to our aid. I'm so thrilled to make your acquaintance."

Her eyes are robin's eggs in shadow, but the kind that, if provoked, might just flare into acetylene torches. Her voice is a warbled rasp exuding sexuality from a hollow sugarcane stalk.

I admit she sparks the naughty in me. She's damn tasty looking— voluptuous, in her wild mane of white-hot hair, those dive in the incendiary twilight eyes—maybe little Miss Luann's hedonistic in the carnal sense? But then again, I'm slightly more than slightly inebriated. A dim memory of a single-toothed Tlingit princess passes through my cranium. In my state, Nikita Khrushchev's warty ol' lady would easily pass for Marylyn M.'s double.

With her blood-red stiletto fingernails, Luann extracts a coffin-nail from a sow's ear purse. She lights it with a Storm King Flame Thrower. She inhales and blows big, round smoke rings as nonchalantly as if she's been hooked on ciggies since first grade. I watch her eyeballing my half-drunk schooner. I haven't heard a sobbing confession to rival Lady Chatterley. I figure Luann, with the husky, very adult voice, is riding Elise's cannonball express for the thrills.

She looks too up, too easy and I've been there too. I'm an old cowboy at four 'n' twenty. I lay down the law. I tell the sexy little JDs I'm not looking for trouble. No contributing to minor bust. No statutory nooky sandwich jobs. No crybaby acts. No stops other than gas stations along the trail.

Lightheaded and tipsy as I am, I feel obligated and don't know why. Don't know why I decide to go along with the moron hemisphere of my warped brain, but I'll take 'em. Take the two wayward teens to Coos Bay, clear to Gracie's unimaginably big sister, Aunt Mable's front door. But first, they're going to listen to a story about me and my redskin blood brother, Snook, the day we ran off from the Oyster Shell thumbing rides to the carnival a few miles, a mountain range and a dozen insurmountable social gaps later. . .

The End of the Beginning

TORCHY BURNBAUM'S MOMENT OF TRUTH

In a wide spot along a forest corridor of towering Douglas firs, the old Rose Trellis Store clings tenaciously to existence. The sun, coasting on its downslope, gains momentum. The archaic Mom and Pop is engulfed in ominous shadows that grow to astronomical heights. A harbinger of evil, only detectable by creatures of darkness, whimpers. Old Sol is swallowed by the misnomered Pacific. The forest returns to nocturnal savagery.

Traffic is reduced to the occasional set of high beams that slash the night and zip by to swiftly disappear — a blinding flash — chased by mean rubescent eyes. Gas prices have soared to an all-time high in lows. Nobody is going anywhere anymore — not just for the hell of it, especially on a country two-lane leading to whatever misfortune may spring beyond that down-at-the-heels country store.

Outside lights are turned off in token protest of soaring electric bills. Neon beer signs attract moths and the occasional consumer in need of hydration. Perhaps the hypnotic illusion would be more tangible — in a flush economy. The store by night, morphs into a thirst quenching island oasis in an all-encompassing desert of tall timber.

*

Bernadette, *Torchy,* Burnbaum glares at the *Miller Time* clock suspended over the beer coolers. She curses, *Mutherfucker* under her breath. The hands seem glued to 8:28. She hasn't had a customer in over an hour. Closing time is 10:00 — at least a lifetime and a half in the distance of Torchy's ho-hum doldrums.

Torchy quits the clock to gaze unseeingly at the flitting characters on the mini-TV perched high on a corner shelf. The plot is at best sophomoronic. "*Happy Days* my miserable rerunning ass. My God," she mutters, "It's Tuesday to boot. A dollar to a frigging bottle of Diet Coke, that perverted creature, Harry Tooms, and his slobbering beasts will be moseying in one minute before ten. If *I* had my way I'd make sure Harry stood a public pee-pee thrapping. That dirty old man leaves me cold and disgusted. Maybe Mr. Tooms will stumble while crossing the White River Bridge...the railing will break and... fat fucking chance! Why does it always have to be me? When am I ever gonna catch a break?"

*

Four miles off and out of sight of the allure of neon beer signs, Harry Tooms sits on a swayback bench on his ramshackle porch. He patiently untangles the chain links on a pair of canine pinch collars. The business ends always latch onto anything and everything within grasp, including one another. Persistence eventually prevails and Tooms separates and attaches the collars to the strong, semi-obedient necks of his twin half Doberman, half Labrador retrievers, Thissy and Thatty. It's time for old Harry to head out for the much older Rose Trellis Country Store. As he snaps the leashes to the collars, Harry stares into Thissy's golden eyes. He truly believes his mischievous dogs often read his mind.

If his dogs were somehow capable of describing Harry, they might find him a muddle of contradictions...still the dogs are atavistically ingrained to follow their *pack leader*.

Harry Tooms has never heard the newfangled acronym, *PTSD*. He sees things in his mind's eye. Battles sometimes rage in a plate of scrambled eggs with ketchup. The scrape of his fork on his plate becomes a sneak attack consigned to oblivion. His thoughts are often erratic punctuations of a beleaguered past.

Memories spurt like the staccato chatter of machine guns. Shock waves infuse his nerve endings.

Harry is physically strong. His aged face is highlighted with a patch of unruly white hair. Bushy eyebrows guard pale blue eyes. His features seem scrimshawed out of an oak burl. His nose is bold. His lips present an affectation of a colorless, single line. His lantern jaw is highlighted by a chin cleaved down the middle.

Tooms' daily attire consists of cowboy boots, a set of bibs, and a checkered flannel shirt beneath a worn mackinaw. His apelike arms, his gnarly hands are built for extreme use.

Harry, though he doesn't acknowledge age, is 74 and change. He's an eighth grade graduate. In his prime, he was a Korean *Conflic*t soldier. After his war years, Harry became a five times National Rodeo Finalist: a bronc rider, a bull rider, a bulldogger, and calf roper. Tooms carries the aches, the sharp, electric jolts of pain associated with a hard playing, harder drinking past that has merged with his present lifestyle. Harry has recovered from multiple injuries; recuperated by performing rope tricks and a bullwhip act to subsidize his meager income.

Harry does not dwell on a reckless past, and probably doesn't recall much of what happened just yesterday. He is a social recluse existing on his meager government dole, his shack, an acre of hardscrabble, and all the wild game he can outlaw from the adjacent forest.

The half breed dogs are a gift from a daughter who at fortyfive, displays no lack of affection for a father that during her childhood and developing years, mostly neglected her.

*

Harry shrugs into his packsack. He and his exuberant dogs strike off for trouble. Harry isn't thinking straight. He's fixated on Torchy, down yonder. Little slut with an attitude, that one. Her and her plumber jeans suspended a hair above her hairline...navel stone that glitters seductively when she twitches that thing — her wicked spider in a web tattoo just above the crack of her ass — belly revealing, low cut half-shirt, a push-up bra accentuating soft cleavage, too much makeup, nose and eyebrow jewelry — an attitude for chrissakes.

If only Harry was still a teenage broncin' buck he'd show her attitude with a capital A.

Harry is so engrossed in what has never been, he doesn't notice that his whiptail dogs, Thissy and Thatty, are not darting thisaway and thataway, in front and behind him, to trip him up and cause a backlash a contortionist would have a tizzy untangling.

Perhaps Harry's dogs are indeed clairvoyant. They seem to sense danger. All Tooms can sense is his aroused manhood stimulated by a walking fantasy involving an uppity little sexaholic tease twitching her wares. Before he knows it, he's crossing the White Rapids Bridge. Although it's a moonless night, Harry carries no flashlight. He feels the planks, the limber stringers that gently undulate beneath his feet.

A mile north of perdition, Harry envisions kinky red hair a shade darker than the curly locks on her head: Bermuda Triangle disguising the pit of temptation.

Still oblivious of his dogs, his stride lengthens to that of a young buck in a hurry to latch onto a lion's share of trouble. Thissy and Thatty automatically match their master's pace, resigned to what lies in wait.

*

Torchy's ears perk. A car purrs into the parking lot. A live one? A box of beer and chips, she predicts. Maybe a pack of cancer sticks. *Big whoopee*! A door slams. Moments later the obnoxious buzzer above the entrance throws a mini-fit. Lonely, Lanky Jones strides confidently in. The handsome man takes a left at the second aisle. He's wearing mirrored sunglasses, a Smoky Bear hat, blue jodhpurs tucked into black shiny knee-highs, a tailored pleated shirt, a badge, a gun belt and big pistol. His holster is strapped to his leg; a quick-draw artist a century lost in time.

Miss Burnbaum does a quick fix, fluffs her hair, pulls the half-shirt down a tad, and *accidentally* bumps her labium against a drawer knob behind the counter, awakening things south of the border. Torchy just might be harboring visions of surrendering to the long arm of the law.

The lawman swaggers up to the counter. He has a bag of chips cradled in his arms, has a couple bottles of wine clenched by their necks. He sets his supplies on the counter and says, "Great to be off duty ma'am. Say, could you reach me a pack of those Winston's up there in the rack behind you? I guess that'll hold me till morning."

Torchy smiles seductively. "It's, like cool, to see a policeman stop by, especially like, just before closing."

The cop says nothing. Torchy forgoes the mechanical arm extender — turns, stretches on her tiptoes, hoping the officer is getting his eyes full — and in a flash of headlights sees Harry Tooms out of her periphery. Harry and his dogs are almost to the intersection with the highway, a hundred yards from the store. She snags the cigs, drops to the balls of her heals, and in mid-pivot begins, "Speak of the devil"…completes her swivel and goes mouth-to-mouth with a very large, very metallic, black hole — and Torchy is suddenly tongue-tied.

The cop has shed his mirrored sunglasses. His teeth are grinning, but not his eyes. Torchy sees madness therein. And he holds the pistol steadily. "You're under arrest. Ass flauntin' is a felony punishable by beheadin'… Yee Ha! Just kiddin', sweet lips. Now wiggle it out from behind the counter, but first, strip. Leave *all* your clothes back there."

Torchy knows she has little hope of staying alive. Comply or die. In a zombied state she does as she's told even if her strip lacks any semblance of a tease.

She moves from behind the counter in herky-jerky puppet fashion, using her hands to shield her privates. Her tear-blurred eyes can't help glancing down at the cop's crotch. It's standing at attention, but there's a large dark spot surrounding the area. A creep as screwed up as this bastard is not about to leave a witness behind. Torchy has never felt so humiliated, but knows her shame has hardly begun.

"Pretty little ugly thing," the rapist snarls, pushing Torchy's hand aside with the nasty end of the pistol. Now let's us lock the door and me and you find the electric panel. Closing time is runnin' a few minutes ahead of schedule."

*

The dogs whine in unison. Harry pushes against the locked door just as the beer signs die. The overhead fluorescent lights flicker out, but Harry sees what he sees and ducks down. What Harry sees scares the bejesus out of him. But his adrenaline rush is as crystal clear as a time in Korea. Old Harry seems to know what he has to do.

"The back door is blocked off with a mountain of cased beer. Everything's gotta come our way," He whispers to his crossbreed dogs. "I'm gonna undo your collars now. I'll have to use 'em and your leashes for grappling hooks. We're gonna play tug-o'-war. Thissy, you go high, Thatty, you go for the middle." The dogs softly whine, and thump their tails on the plank porch in anticipation.

"Hey, in there!" Harry pounds on the door and shouts in indignation, "Open, says me! It ain't ten yet. I walked four goddamned miles to get my supplies! I ain't leavin' till I get 'em. Open to hell up. I know you're in there Torchy. The lights went out just before I got to the door. Open up! Lazy little spoilt brat! I'll by god tell yer Aunt Fey ya closed early. She'll reshape yer pantaloons — kick ya where the law don't allow, you c'n bet your uppity ass on that!"

Harry stays crouched below the windows, continues his verbal assault while the dogs lie in ambush whining in apprehension of something dark and sinister — carnal.

*

The former rape artist and murderer, disguised as a state policeman, and turned desperado, nudges Torchy to the floor. He'd left his roll of duct tape in the stolen car thinking he wouldn't need it for a hayseed slash and dash. He whispers to Torchy to crawl-fetch duct tape from a shelf.

"They don't carry it in the store," Torchy lies in pleading tones. "But I swear I won't move or scream if you'll just go. I couldn't pick you out of a lineup if I had to. I'm too afraid to think. That's just old Harry Tooms out there. He's too feeble to fight back. Shoot him if you have to, to escape. I haven't even seen your car."

"Keep your hole shut and lemme think," the rapist barks. "I gotta get out of Sticksburg, yeah, and there's no Ollie, Ollie oxen free. I need a shield. It's your lucky day, bitch. You're it. Now stand up. I'm gonna stick tight to your filthy ass. This .38 Police Special wheel cannon is gonna bore a hole in your brainpan if you so much as sneeze, fart, tinkle or whine. Got it?"

Torchy manages to sob out a gurgled "Yes."

*

The dogs, squirming inside their skins, stop whining. Harry tenses. "Ain't never been a bull what can't be rode — a cowboy that ain't been throwed."

The immortal lament of many a hapless cowboy, Tooms thinks to himself, and wonders how those words apply to a dog leash attached to a heavy-duty pinch collar.

The alarm pitches a bitch. The door eases outward. The dogs and Harry, crouching behind it, stop breathing, stop squirming. The gunman stage whispers, "I know you're out there somewhere *old* man. You best give us free passage or the broad gets her brain scrambled."

The rapist/serial killer's nerves are fried, his heart racing like a trip hammer.

Harry smells two distinct odors — both being abject fear — the dogs have processed those individual scents for a while.

An eternity of stillness slides by, but the gunman is a coward with feet itching for the wheels parked just beyond the door. He makes his play, prodding Torchy off the stoop and out into the blackness. She lurches, creating a miniscule space between her head and jolting death.

There is no light; no way for Harry to spot the pistol — and a car zips by on the highway — light splashes momentarily on the revolver. Harry whips the leash. It's a little like flicking a bullwhip that changes into snagging salmon with a weighted treble hook. And Harry's done both.

The pinch collar is a dozen little grappling hooks. The hooks whip around the gunman's sleeved wrist and tangle together. Simultaneously, Harry hauls back hard on the leash — Thissy and Thatty are airborne — the pistol goes off KA-BOOM! Clatters to the ground — the rapist, the dogs, Harry and Torchy wallow around in the dark. The dogs play tug-o'-war with a pant leg and a sleeve of the fake cop's uniform. Torchy scrambles free of the melee, screaming like a banshee. Harry comes up with the pistol. He presses it to the rapist's nose.

The serial killer bellows, "Hold it! I'm a police officer. This is a drug bust and strip search! You're aiding and abetting the escape of a suspected…"

"Jesus Christ!" Torchy sobs, "if he was searching me it was with the eye in the head of his…"

"Just let me get to the two-way radio in my car," the gunman says, the desk seargent will vouch for me."

"No, I don't think so, Harry admonishes, gasping for breath. "Y'see I was peerin' in the window before the lights went out, an' what I saw says you ain't tellin' it like it is. Seems you was a might closer t' fact when you an' Torchy come out the door. Nope. We'll just go inside an' sort 'er all out.'

"Okay," the rapist/ serial murderer says, "so I'm not a cop. I was just havin' a little fun. No harm done. But I'm sorry anyway. I don't know what came over me. That little slut playin' peek-a-boo with her… It won't happen again. Just let me go. I promise it won't happen again."

"Oh, I agree." Harry is blowing so hard he turns soprano. "You ain't gonna hurt no more little girls, not ever again, no-how.

"Good job, Thissy and Thatty. Hang loose. We'll do our shoppin' and be on our way. Little lady, you go get dressed. Don't call the law or anybody. Just turn on one light. When you're all set. Me an' this bad seed, we'll come inside — do whatever's fair and just."

Harry seems disoriented. Regardless of determination, old age drains resolve. Torchy wastes no time making herself scarce. As she feels her way inside, Harry stops the prisoner's incessant pleading with a fierce command. He exerts more pressure on his captive's nose. For a lifetime, Harry waits for Torchy's signal. The pistol never wavers from the rapist's face.

At last a dim glow flushes through the windows. Tooms nudges his prisoner inside while the dogs lie on the plank-walk and pant as though there's no tomorrow.

Once inside, Harry seems to regain a measure of focus. And to her amazement, Torchy feels something bordering on amity towards Harry. Together they decide there's one more disgusting thing Ms. Burnbaum must endure. She must procure some of the stuff from the rapist's crotch and wipe it on her belly, and well, lower.

Torchy lets go another banshee scream, rakes her long nails down the sociopath's face and while the rapist screams curses just as loudly, she steps outside herself, unbuckles the gun belt, unzips his jodhpurs, jerks them and his underwear down around his knees, smirks and says, "Tiny little ugly thing." Torchy has granted herself the courage to do the rest.

"Now just turn your back a minute, girl, and I'll do what I gotta do."

"Oh Sweet Jesus!" The unconscionable one becomes aware of Harry's intent. He turns a few shades whiter, and cries, "You aren't going to execute me in cold blood! That's murder! I have my rights! You can't commit…"

"Yeah, I know," Harry whispers sadly, almost reverently. "You weren't gonna rape and murder that little girlie, now were ya, Slick? Trouble with this world is they's way too many do-gooders what feel bad about poor little sick puppies o' yer caliber an' think they c'n mend ya. That sort tend to turn people like you back on the street to repeat, repeat, repeat. But enough palaverin'. I could castrate ya, but that would just open another can o' worms. Nah, a man's gotta do what a man's gotta do, even when it's sincerely hard. Even for an old cowboy."

"NO!" the bad boy quivers and sobs — about to lose his bodily functions — Harry shifts the pistol to the criminal's forehead and squeezes the trigger.

*

When the pistol goes off, and the body flops lifeless to the floor, Torchy loses thought and motor control. It's as if she was the one slumped dead. But Torchy is a survivor and soon recovers.

Harry first associates the ringing in his ears as the pealing of the bells of St. Peter. But no, there was no repentance, no remorse in the sociopath's eyes. The stench of death is vile, overpowering.

Harry seems to have converted into a robot. He grabs and tears open a roll of paper towels from a nearby stack. With hands atremble, he wipes the pistol, and holding it with the towel, Harry wraps the dead things hands around the grip, finger on the trigger.

"Take hold of the barrel," Harry commands Torchy, "and then wrap your right hand around the pistol grip."

Torchy, on autopilot, obeys. "Now," Harry says, "shoot into the ceiling. All you have to do is pull the trigger." Again, Torchy subconsciously complies. The weapon clatters to the floor all but breaking her fingers.

"Good'n'," Harry compliments. "Now ya got powder burns on your hand in case the medical examiner does his job. Leave the pistol right there. Call 911," Tooms says through a voice box as diluted as skim milk. At least it seems that way to Torchy. Her ears ring. The putrid odor of death lingers with the stench of gunpowder. Her thoughts are disconnected with reality.

Harry tosses three crinkled one dollar bills on the counter. He walks back to the cooler and fetches his Diet Coke — returns as if a scholar deep in contemplation of a mathematical quandary. But in truth, the old cowboy is running low on go-juice.

"I wasn't here. Gal o' yer caliber won't have no trouble actin' hysterical. You'll know what to say. That fella cooked his own goose, impersonatin' an officer of the law. Best tidy up that burn hole in yer hair. See ya in three days, give or take."

Torchy is about to vomit. She knows she should thank Harry, knows she'll be forever grateful. The words won't come. She finds her bottle of water beneath the counter, somehow gets the lid unscrewed. She splashes the water on her hands, scrubbing fiercely, thinking she'll never be clean again. "Why do you drink so much Diet Coke, Mr. T-Tooms?"

"Goes good with diet rum." Harry slips the Diet Coke into his backpack, humps into it, ambles outside, leashes his dogs and drifts away. The night swallows the black dogs. Then the old man disappears into its maw.

Torchy wipes her hands on her pants, grabs her purse and follows Tooms out. She vomits up everything she's eaten of late. She sucks in a few drafts of fresh air, sloshes water around in her mouth, spits and sits in her beater. Under the map lights using little scissors, she jerkily trims the singed hair from the first bullet that sped by just a hairsbreadth from her scalp.

Torchy relives it a thousand times. Missing Harry, shivering up a sweat, thinking that car flashing by was more than a coincidence… Wanting to crawl off somewhere she can be by herself, curl into a fetal ball and sleep it away, never to return.

*

Time treats Torchy diabolically, yet benevolently. She has dream episodes so realistic she's sure she'll die of fright. Being a hero and national celebrity has its moments but it's not all it's cracked up to be. She feels fortunate to be a natural liar.

Just when her fame is about to burn out, an aristocratic type woman shows up at her folks' house. The high-society woman rides in in the backseat of a stretch limo. With the chauffeur's guidance she alights and introduces herself as, *Mrs. Eleanor Trueblood.* To Torchy, Mrs. Trueblood relates the story of her college age daughter, Edwina. Eleanor Trueblood's Edwina was not as fortunate as Torchy. Neither were a dozen other innocent young ladies.

The mad rapist was identified through DNA and forensics as, Percival Schultz, paroled sex offender. Percival raped and butchered his way from east to west — including slaying the policeman he stole the uniform from.

Thank God Torchy, in a life or death struggle, grabbed Schultz's pistol and shot the animal dead.

The conversation leads gently to Mrs. Trueblood presenting Torchy Burnbaum with a long-standing reward and then doubling it. Torchy is granted two certified checks, each for five-hundred grand.

*

The nightmares take a temporary sabbatical. Torchy resigns her position at the store. She acquires a new wardrobe, baubles, bangles, beads. She purchases a gas guzzler — buys an apartment in the big city. The nightmares return. She is nearly positive the flashbacks will dissolve if she could make herself split her reward with Harry Tooms. But Harry is such a pervy old letch, for fuck's sake. Creepy Harry and those slobbery dogs give poor Torchy the heebee jeebees. Besides, she knows what cowboys are like, she's watched more than her share of movies and TV shows. The old fool would just blow the dough on rum and Diet Cokes and high-priced teenage hookers… A while later it comes to her via a commercial on the background giant, flat screen, surround sound, super resolution TV! Her heart throbs with the emotion that her newfound generosity brings.

Torchy radiates an inner glow: a promise that will prove as untenable as the synthetic light that emits from those neon beer signs back there beyond the razor edge of insanity.

***

A couple-three days pass. Harry Tooms checks his mailbox stationed along the old county road. There's the usual batch of crap mail…and a flat package propped diagonal. It's addressed to Sir Harry Tooms Rural Route (etc.). No return address. Harry opens the mysterious box where he stands.

A sort of pictorial book appears. On the cover is Willie Nelson's picture, and fancy letters that say, *My Heroes Have Always Been Cowboys — Comes to you along with a Stampede of Willie's Greatest Hits!*

Inside the book, ensconced in a circular nest, there's a flat, round thing. Looks to be about four inches in diameter — a pygmy Frisbee? Harry thinks on it. He decides it might be one of them new-fangled gadgets…a record for a miniature nickelodeon, maybe… Tooms commands his dogs, Thissy and Thatty, to sit. After he sails the CD off into the underbrush, Harry gets to wondering: where did he meet Willie? *Albuquerque? Cheyenne? Mesquite? Pendleton? Calgary?* Rodeo arenas rumble through his mind like ominous thunder.

The bull is a macabre monster called, *Disjointed*. The chute flies open. Disjointed arches for the sky, rolls and twists, but Harry, outside himself and loaded with adrenaline and cocaine, is glued to the buckin' bull's back.

The rank bull has never been ridden for the required eight seconds. Disjointed has grown slyer with each draw. The desperado bull rears his tail end almost high enough to turn a somersault. Harry snaps forward at a colossal rate of speed. The bull whips his head back as Harry slams down.

The collision is brutal. Harry's hand is tangled in the bull rope. He's knocked unconscious and dragged around the arena like a rag doll. Disjointed pivots and gores. His hooves slash and stomp.

Harry's flashbacks are just as fearsome as the ride. His brain is jolted with a piercing white light. His knees buckle. The stroke is massive. Harry Tooms is dead before he hits the ground.

*****

DRAW THE LATCH
Maximum Security Homicide Ward Oregon State Hospital for the Criminally Insane

Moody undercurrents sent pangs through my gut. A pox on my conscience indicated the year 1976 had begun the process of dying. I tallied the months of my brother's imprisonment. His four seasons behind the harsh walls had turned three times. In that lost interim, both textbook criminology and the school of psychic voodoo have drawn blanks. There's no discovery of fact to indicate that Burl has the mind of a serial killer. Burl's volunteered little help to his keepers. His last spoken words were a tribute the Audubon society, a secret code or just plain gobbledygook. Those words however, led one particularly far-out brain shamus to promote a notion that sexual perversions associated somehow with Canadian honkers, play 'round and 'round in my brother's tortured cranium.

A panel of loftier-than-God psycho-babblers theorized and hypothesized until anatomies of Burl's heinous executions ranged from asinine to absurd to the aforementioned rock-bottom ridiculous. And finally to a consensus that my brother is indeed a sociopath. Hocus pocus diagnosis by committee: manic depressive with paranoid schizophrenia facilitating homicidal tendencies.

Psychological lingo is Greek to my twelfth grade and NCO school education. I had to consult a dictionary, but not before Taco Ruiz, a *no hable* Mexican farmhand stuck it in my belfry. Taco described Burl's condition in one clear, understandable phrase. Ruiz appeared on the scene while I was calling the law from a phone belonging to one of the objects of Burl's attention. Taco confronted Burl standing like a stone before his first victim. The Mexican National gawked at his boss man — reduced to a headless, grisly cadaver, then at my brother's maddened eyes — then at the blood spackling my brother's insane face. And Taco backpedaled from the room, his eyes perhaps a mirror reflection of mine as he whispered, *"Loco!"*

Three years under lock and key, and motive remained a pile of analytical pasture crap serving only to fertilize the guilt in my conscience. Burl created a hell on earth and clammed up like a giant gaper with lockjaw.

There were moments when, in my despair, I would bait her, and I would raise the sex-angle thing with Burl's wife, Elise. Her gaze was a cloudy sky denying rain, reminding me that I had forfeited my right to delve into my brother's psyche. Ironically, Elise longed for closure more than I dreaded it. But in the end, we both sensed that the system was as timeless as it was merciless. It would eventually smash Burl's shell, and likely ours. The only way out, at least for Burl, would be a tits up relocation to a much hotter climate.

Trouble comes in threes. I had spent three years running a warrior's gauntlet in the limbo of self-induced hell. I'd spent the next three, ignoring the fact that my brother's brain was on a slow freighter headed straight into a big blow. He converged with that typhoon in his mind's eye. Adrift in madness, Burl squeezed pitiless bars for those last three. I wished I'd been *kin* for him. Instead, I had betrayed a sacred trust. As far as sanity went, maybe we'd both had our one-way tickets punched. There was nothing like shame and guilt to tie the mind in tight knots of self-loathing. That was a certainty.

*

Dr. Margaret O'Riley, the latest in an endless string of charge psychiatrists, capitalized on my remorse, my self-reproach. Perhaps my need for contrition compelled me. In any case, I finally made a pact with my conscience. I had, with reluctance, agreed to see the stranger who had once been my brother; the only family I'd ever claimed.

As customary, the doctor was late. An orderly had solemnly ushered me to a sinister study area before rushing off to the klaxon call to some dire emergency. The orderly screwed up. The polarizing setting had to have been off limits to outsiders such as me. I was left to wonder if bearing witness to a day in the bowels of an insane asylum was the doctor's idea of bizarre shock therapy designed for my personal wake-up call.

Fidgeting in place, I tried to focus on the scene confronting me while keeping my mind detached. That proved to be an emotional impossibility — even for a rhino hide like mine.

The viewing windows were thick and cold. Staring through the wire crosshatch imbedded in the glass, I tried to catch a glimpse of my brother Burl. Instead I witnessed a cross-section of morbid humanity shuffling through a fog of cigarette smoke. The images portrayed seemed distended by some sardonic, deeply disturbing sorcery.

I wouldn't call them a group or a platoon. They were not a society, a fraternity, a group or a warren. They were not in any respect *as one*. They were lost souls moving about in a drug-induced stupor. They navigated muddled courses on separate Loran Systems transmitted from hell. Their eyes, though modified by color, seemed similarly disconnected from any semblance of spirit: the glassy eyes of *fish*.

The lost souls might just as well have been swimming about in a giant tank. They were suspended in animation together yet remained completely segregated. Once sharks, piranhas and crocs, they were all, in their own personal torment, reduced to flounder. They disassociated themselves from anything human, and one another, by degrees of madness.

I sensed the psychiatrist's aura as she drew near. It was eerie, uncanny, the way the current changed. The inmates began schooling, instinctively facing the glass as if *she* were the enigma waiting upstream. I never caught a single glimpse of Burl before the lady shrink's presence drew me away from my unsuccessful probe into something all too alien.

Sneaking a peek at that slender pied piper of insane impulse, I caught her in the act of performing oral sex on a long, hot, Chesterfield straight. She dragged ecstatically before wilting me with the ol' spider-to-the-fly look. As she exhaled, blowing lurid blue contrails from flared nostrils, I noted that the uniform du jour was a frumpy sweater buttoned tightly over a sixties, ankle length flowered dress, complete with couch potato wrinkles.

Her feet were incased in black and white Converse high-tops with fuzzy pink laces. Her hair, absent of curls, was fashioned into what might have been an Afro or perhaps a unique replication in dirty blond of Albert Einstein's do. I couldn't really define it, finally left her do, or not, as unusually smirkable. The lady head hunter was the epitome of bizarre... But who was I to nit-pick? In a world beyond Oz, the inmates probably doubled as fashion police.

Dr. O abruptly bent to an ashtray and mashed her lover half consummated. Presumably so she could dispense her full, microscopic attention on me. She tongue-spat a shred of the forsaken from her lip and examined me through spectacles with shot glass lenses that distorted her eye language. But I felt she dissected me as if a reincarnation of my third grade teacher. I wondered if there was a booger hanging from my nose and my fly was open.

I flashed back to that loosey-goosey ménage of lost souls suddenly swarming before her. I had to change my attitude. There was, after all, a spark of want, or need, bayonetting me forward... I subconsciously nicknamed her Radar — the handle wouldn't stick.

"Hello. I'm Doctor O'Riley. You'd be August Norwood? You look like him, your brother. Sweet Jesus. Four AM is an awful, ungodly time of day."

I'd made it plain a few weeks ago. The only time she could smoke the peace pipe with Burl would be at the crack of dawn. Burl had always been a son of the morning. One of the few times we were kicked back at first light at the fishing hole, he'd said, "The day is born at dawn. The process of dying begins with the birthing. If you don't have your jaws around a bone by daybreak, you'd just as well tuck your tail and crawl under the porch with the housedogs."

The couch skipper may have been earning her keep. By the clock over the cage doors it was 3:13 in the afternoon. And while I'd perceived a savoring of triumph in her voice, I decided by her superior bearing, the victory was hers first, for Burl only in some hidden context.

Imposing at six foot five, I looked down and through her with the ol' sanctimonious SOB stare. I assumed one of Burl's aggravating quirks; he had that annoying habit of mulling over his sentences before he lined them out. If a response wasn't evident, he could wait in silence until unease became unbearable and you'd blurt out some inanity, just to break the silence. I worked his style with ulterior motives. I figured an experienced bartender had seen more and knew more of life than any doctor in a fish bowl could ever begin to grasp.

She broke the silence. "Your brother is loony tunes. That's his excuse. I'm trying to be civil, but you choose hostility, *sir*. Your ignorance derives from the disdain of your false virtue, *Mr. Norwood*. The conceit in you rings as true as your inexcusably bigoted attitude."

She'd launched a surprise attack; caught me flatfooted. She jerked her glasses off. She postured like a squinty-eyed flyweight defending stinging jabs. She counter-punched where she could give more than she'd gotten. She slashed with her rapier tongue, her nicotine stained incisors gouging at the jugular.

I had a sudden urge to protect my kahonies. I turned as red as she before I grinned sheepishly. I said, "Touché, but is loony tunes your official diagnosis? I don't guess I've heard it used as a clinical term."

"I spoke extemporaneously," she countered. "I've worked this case every single day for endless weeks. I never missed a single morning. I've made your brother my life's focus far too long; long before he uttered an intelligible syllable. I won't repeat the process for one single second. Not for a fool relative trying nothing more than my patience, trying to goad my temper."

I needed to look up *extemporaneously*. For the time being, I contemplated the crux of her outburst. I wanted to point out that her string of '*singles*' hissed like shingles, but my temper started burning the wick. "What'd he say and where the hell is he?"

She softened down to a diamond-faced grinding stone. "He's down the corridor staring out the window where the sun first strikes over the east wing. He's there rain or shine. Every morning…except when it's foggy. When it's foggy, your brother burrows under his covers and refuses to move. What does fog have to do with his condition?"

"You'd have to ask him," I responded, my rancor disguised. "I never knew Burl to fear fog, or anything else for that matter."

"Homichlophobia," she spat, tilting her head back so she could look down her nose. "And now, since he heard you were coming, he's drawn inside himself. Drawn the latch. Aphasic. I haven't yet analyzed our previous conversations. Until I do, his words will remain *confidential*."

I have no more use for sanctimonious, self-important bureaucrats than for a two-bit palm reader. This was a state hospital in all its institutional glory. I knew enough about the system to know O'Riley was a short-changer — a trophy hunter stealthily spearing fish in a barrel — that she yearned to use Burl's sudden awakening to stiff her dues. That she, most likely, felt as averse to this ungodly place as I. It was her boot camp, but she was a fuckoff. She would flaunt Burl Norwood as a record-book trophy. She would swim out of the aquarium — onto an overstuffed leather couch practice to mollycoddle the socially acceptable malfunctioning sissies with the big bucks.

Through the crosshatch, I focused on a lumbering behemoth. The monster knuckle-traced imaginary wainscot: a red stripe separating shades of green. He wore his baseball cap sideways. His coveralls were unbuttoned, half his dirty orange collar tucked under, the other half flipped up. Slobber glistened on his hairless chest. The man-bear wasn't Burl, but he could have been because the message on his baseball cap read "Who gives a shit." I gnashed my teeth, watching the prototype of a human cabbage grin his toothless, private joke.

I wanted to ask O'Riley if Burl was still obsessed with tinkering, if there was any way to get him broken watches to fix. I wanted to inquire about mood-altering drugs, but I refused to give her the satisfaction of another put-down. I knew she would never let me in the tank to smell the decaying urine, the sour vomit, the fresh shit stinking up unwashed coveralls.

Bummed, I struck like a stupid sidewinder. "You ordered me here under false pretenses. Dipshit. Over-educated hippie bitch retread. Shove it where the sun never shines."

I whipped a 180, my mind's eye envisioning a liquor store a couple blocks beyond the hospital grounds. I would pick up a down-and-out old friend in a brown paper sack. We'd get bonged and sad, and sing the blues on the long trek back to the Basin.

*

I resented that familiar feminine voice pestering cruelly from afar. I begrudged my burning eyes squinting into cold rain sieved through high-beam colanders. I tried to fend off Burl's yellow Lab, Marilyn, licking vomit from my chest. Shivered my subconscious awareness of grass plastering my shirt to my back…giggled when my legs did the wet noodle boogie.

Elise, with some mysterious inner strength, levitated me to the semi-vertical, then propped me into her deceptively strong shoulder to stagger-steer me to her shelter from the storm.

*

I felt like a flounder behind the crosshatch, laboriously swimming towards consciousness in the strangely familiar surroundings of Elise's boudoir, she, feeling much warmer than my shirt had, stuck to my back. I tried to remember how I'd arrived here, at my brother's place, his wife, naked as I, beside me. But the lighting flashes, the thunder rattling through my head every time I tried to open my eyes was non-conducive to the power of reason.

I breathed lightly, just enough to keep the room from capsizing, and to stay alive. I broke the suction of her supple body. An eternity later, I slid my feet to the floor and sat on the side of her bed. I held my face in my palms while the room spun out of control. She came out of nowhere bearing aspirin, a glass of water and a tube of toothpaste along with her toothbrush. I unstuck my wounded tongue from the roof of my mouth, knocked back the aspirin and wistfully rubbed the monkey dung off my teeth. I watched her slip on her panties and bra. I wanted to hurt her, but knew I couldn't.

It was like the song says *"You always Hurt the one You Love."* I hated her and I hated me. All that was left was Burl, the one you shouldn't....

As I showered I could smell the coffee. My clothes were MIA. I wrapped a towel around me and followed my nose toward the caffeine. She stood before the range, her apron wrapped around sexy, black bikini undies. Forbidden fruit. I shut the stove burners down and nuzzled a dainty ear. I snapped the elastic opening to an assuaging sin while on the other hand my fingers feather-teased the fluff over her soft mound. She arched herself on tiptoes and clasped the back of my neck, but her knees went weak. I Fred Astaired her around. She's a lightweight.

Hung over as hell, blood hammering danger in my head, her legs tentacled around my waist, I backed our melded bodies into an armless, hardback chair.

We had breakfast after dessert. Over the second cup of coffee, she had to spoil it. It was inevitable but she didn't have to put it quite the way she did. "What about Burl? Did he talk to you, or the doctor? Did he get into that crazy, wild goose thing?"

I was born in the late forties to parents I imagined were descendants of the brutal slave-trader, Simon Legree. My folks could not conceive a future, would never have crawled out of the despair of the Great Depression. Elise was a post war/prewar 50's baby — the by-product of a wiener schnitzel/spaghetti union consummated in Oklahoma. After Americanizing so gorgeously in *y'all* country, she still had a touch of ancestral tactlessness lodged in her throat. She's grown accustomed to my evasive wanderings into the land of eternal deafness, however. I stared into her beautiful eyes. Those intensified orbs were as unreadable as the zinc gray of the autumn sky they were stolen from.

"The psychiatrist said Burl was 'Loony tunes.' Other than that, I haven't the *foggies*t notion."

*

Fall was swooping in on rattling boughs — windswept leaves. The geese were on their migratory route. Squadrons would descend on Elise and me all too soon. I remembered how intense Burl's had become that bright sunny day when he'd taken his 10 gauge double barreled goose-gun on an insane hunting expedition.

*

Burl had politely knocked on his neighbor's door. When it swung open, Burl let go a barrage at his handsome greeter, Jimmy Lee. The repercussions of that shot and Burl's next blast will echo through the Basin longer than the rest of my days. The scattergun's discharge plastered the far wall in a surreal, circular collage consisting of hunks of brain, bone, teeth, hair, goose shot and skin tissue. Jimmy had kicked and thrashed like a chicken with its head lopped. The living room bore witness to the bloody shambles of Jimmy's death throes. Pools of blood saturated Lee's remains and sopped up the morning paper Jimmy still gripped in his fist. Jimmy had a way with girls. The female of the gender would long lament his passing.

A field hand named Taco Ruiz fetched me, and then fell into shock. After the dust settled, Ruiz was discovered down the lane, walking tight circles around a pothole.

I spaced out until lights flashed, sirens screamed. The law came in a thunderous cloud of dust — a mechanical posse out of the Wild West. Fortunately the High Sheriff had a level head — or — perhaps unfortunately. I led him and a faltering group of his deputies into the room where Jimmy's current woman lay blown in two. Her legs and bits of her torso, imbedded with hunks of her clothes were in the doorway where Burl had caught her exiting her hiding place in the utility room. My brother had evidently fired both barrels from the hip. Jeanette's gutted upper portion lay over the washing machine. Her diamond navel stone was found intact with the shrapnel that had pierced the steel, caromed off the agitator and landed in the bottom of the washer's tub. It was my first prolonged look. The stench of her entrails would gag a buzzard. The cops had an excuse. They were country boys; unexposed to violence. The long-armed lawmen took turns vomiting their coffee and doughnuts. I'd seen worse, but in a world far removed from Burl's perplexing hell.

My brother Burl could squat and hug a 55-gallon barrel of diesel. He could straighten up with his 380-pound load and totter off for some 70 feet before taking a breather.

Before the law arrived that godawful day, Burl, with his bare hands, and without deploying a knee, had bent the scattergun's barrels int a U.

A few minutes later, Burl Norwood stood stoically while a deputy handcuffed those giant mitts behind his back. To his captive, the County Mounty stutter mumbled the standard Miranda spiel.

Burl's face was spattered with the young couple's coagulated blood, his demeanor, other than the strangeness in his eyes, soft and reassuring as he said, "I kill the wild goose no more."

Burl would not, for many a blue moon, utter another word.

Burl was a student of Native American history. He was rechanneling words first spoken by Joseph, chief of the Nez Pierce, who would *Fight no more*. Burl's and Joseph's words had parallel meaning, but no one could break Burl's illogical code. No one, up until the false prophet O'Riley, may have compelled *him* to break it.

Knowing his words were meant for me, I'd let the insanity plague my sleep. He'd lost me. After I retired from active duty, my brain could no longer condone, or fathom, violence as a problem solving discipline.

*

I envisioned O'Riley masturbating while playing a recording of the words of a madman. Perhaps the State Hospital was a breeding ground for Nurse Ratched clones… I conjured images of her as cold, calculating, hoping to derive power from dire sensationalism. I changed her nickname from Radar to Wretch. A chill coursed through my bloodstream. I was left to wonder if it was real or if Burl was feigning, aping the role of *Chief,* in Ken

Kesey's *One Flew Over the Cuckoo's Nest*, but hell, no one could be that resilient without being loony tunes, could anyone?

*

We received another shot of Indian summer. I had finished plowing the wheat stubble under, first on Burl's place then mine. I was down by the marshes where Burl and my goose blinds are still visible to the trained eye, where our inherited acreages bridges the narrows, the natural divide between the halved sections. To be honest about it, I was scanning the northern sky looking and listening for long black V formations.

Highlighted in the midday sun, I could see Elise coming downgrade for a quarter mile. She was driving Burl's farm truck; the same truck she'd driven to the deer meadow three and a half years ago. It seemed like yesterday, but it had started shortly after I'd mustered out of the corps.

I suffered still from flashbacks, even after coming home to a familiarly unfamiliar scenario beyond the pale of my imagination. Burl had mechanized the farm, but he'd married Elise while I was lost in military madness. She'd sparked a need, Elise; a sometimes wistful, ever-beautiful rose in the thorn bush in my head. Burl was indeed one lucky son-of-a- bitch. It was a strain to contain the desire hidden in the false front of my supposedly impenetrable demeanor.

Elise had moved here from Tulsa, here to the Klamath Basin with her folks after I'd had enough and hatted up. She had just graduated high school when I'd begun my second tour.

Burl, according to his letters, was following his obsessions. Over the objections of our self-centered, medieval parents, Burl had found contentment studying nights to become an automotive electrician. It was his meek rebel yell. He'd met and married Elise in a flash-fever — before she'd taken a real notion to sow a few wild oats of her own. From the pictures I'd received, I'd first decided that Burl was the lucky half of our brotherhood. Still, I never envied him the bad and the ugly.

It was long after Burl and Elise's wedding day — during my third tour — when our parents, the bad and the ugly twin gothic throwbacks, got themselves accordion slammed and char-broiled in a multi-collision of high-speed fog-stressed traffic on I-5.

Burl sent news clippings and pictures of fiery Destruction Derby decimation. Those scenes were from a world I wanted to forget. I never believed anyone so evil could truly be dead. I shrugged it off as another ploy instituted by Burl. I never bothered to go home for their planting.

My brother handled the burial of burnt offerings just fine. He'd also handled the splitting of the only thing our parents held dear: the farm they had themselves, inherited.

Burl petitioned the top brass nuts and I became the beneficiary of a hardship discharge, but the atrocities of war had turned me deeply inward. I'd mustered out wise and wary, jungle wise and street smart — as long as the street was Hayseed Way. If Burl had distanced himself from humanity, he wasn't the Lone Ranger. In my eyes, the only thing of any importance was me. I didn't much give a shit about anything beyond my day-to-day survival. I'd lived in a dog-eat-dog jungle too long to realize that the civilized female is ruled by subtler hungers. Elise's needs infiltrated my heart, catching me unawares. The wiles of that Old Black Magic snared — and bound us both in a web of deception — an insoluble dilemma that neither of us to this day, has found the will to escape....

*

She'd come to the deer meadow where I was fixing fence. It was summer. The Basin's hotter than the hubs of hell in summer. She'd looked cool in her black satin shorts and halter top. She'd carried a beach towel, a thermos of iced tea, some grapes and sandwiches in a plastic cooler.

She had rested her elbows on her knees. She hid her face in her hands. She talked to her painted toes. Beneath the shade of an apple tree, her downcast southern drawl told of some inner guilt eating away at Burl. The lonely days crept in, she said, some months before the folks met their foggy-bottomed Waterloo.

Burl had slowly isolated himself from her. They hadn't for some time, practiced what goes on between healthy young couples when the night softens to an idle. Burl had replaced her with a devil that tortured his soul, she said. She didn't know who that devil was, only that she'd been cast aside and left in bewildering torment.

My experience with the opposite sex was limited to barroom chippies, rice paddy bargaining and the quickie cribs in Saigon. I likened those journeyman angels to the way I liked my eggs — fried hard and fast — with a metallic taste and a little gristle on the bottom. In hell, there is no other kind.

Elise was soft — over easy — an enigma with a strawberry wine aftertaste I could not relate to. But I knew what she wanted when she shed her top, as big, salty tears flowed. As she stood and unzipped her shorts — her black panties a flag of pleading — an amateurish and awkward dime-novel seduction.

My morals had suddenly vaporized. I surrendered without a thought of Burl, without a twinge of conscience.

Black is for sin and mourning combined. We mourned for Burl some, after the sin. She had me hogtied. We were both bound by that notorious knot.

*

Fenders rattled, startling me back to reality. I watched the truck come before the dust cloud, thinking of train smoke. I muttered to myself, "She's still got you August. You're still tied to her." The only running I could muster then or now was on a squirrel cage in the circus in my mind's eye.

She looked just as delectable in her skin-tight jeans as she had while desire razed shame in sacrificial fire while she stood straight-backed defiant and proud...naked and crying.

The truck door creaked and sagged on worn hinges. She pushed up and swung it shut. There is steel beneath that soft, smooth flesh.

"That doctor, the one you call 'Wretch,' wants you to go up there to Salem again, August. Burl's talking. He wants to see you."

Where had I heard that crap before pray tell, or was it p-r-e-y tell? But what the hell. O'Riley too had me in her web; wound tight and bound by my own complicity.

I followed Elise's dust back to my forlorn modular palace. She loaded my AWOL bag in the back of my pickup. She stood before my window. I kissed her gently, as though she was made of fine porcelain.

"Auf Wieder sehen, mien schatz. Keep your powder dry and your assets covered. Oh, by the way, how do you say it in kraut lingo? *Ich leibe dich*? Lord have mercy I...I love you so."

Her tears got my face wet, and somehow burned *my* eyes. She blubbered and sobbed, getting sticky all over me. "I'm not sauerkraut. I'm a sweet little southern fried damn Yankee. I love you more!"

Those significant little declarations were the first for either of us. Sweet Jesus, I almost felt content. I put the blues tapes away and tuned in some ol' time rock 'n' roll. I set the cruise on 77. My mind was as free as an ocean breeze...until I spotted a flock of those high-flying, southbound mind marauders. They goosed me back to reality, but as always, it was an exercise in the shameful futility of wishing Burl was as literally deceased as he was apparently brain dead.

I envisioned the complete woman waiting in the wings. She was but a foxhole dream I could only hold until reality brought incoming fire. I replaced Elton John's *Jeremiah was a Bullfrog* with Mad Joe Funk and his *Bad Boy Blues*. How could this rig keep going 77 with my mind's heels digging in so hard?

Whoever wrote the line, *He Ain't Heavy, He's My Brother,* had a lot to learn. He was my hero, my big brother for oh so long. I was carrying a formidable load. It was spilling over. I'd just dumped half of it on Elise's delicate shoulders. It was new to me to admit loving anyone, let alone my brother's woman. I used to believe the angry coward in me that drove me to two bonus tours in Vietnam had it by a country mile, but having the time to mull it through, there was no emotion stronger than guilt, I swear to God!

*

Maple leaves slipped in the door with me. With my toe, I tickled them back outside. This was no place for man or beast. Wrong for anything as outstanding as a dead leaf. I found the elevator and rode it to high hell...the umpth degree on the Richter scale of *loony tunes.*

Doctor Wretch Frankenstein O'Riley met me at the gateway to Hades. She ground out the perpetual butt and we passed through the security system labyrinths of checkpoints and vault doors as if we ourselves, were normal and sane.

We passed through a staff area which was isolated from the inmates. The West wing had an institutional homey green touch. There were no bars on the windows, no lockups, no guards in the hallways.

By the time we had reached the cubbyhole she'd picked for Burl's and my reunion, I sensed she had nothing but gibberish from her star patient. Hell, she was treating me like I was one of the shirt and tie good ol' boys instead of a gross, long-haired fatigue shirted throwback from the freaked out drug-culture memory-lapsed decade of the seventies. I almost rubbed my palms together. She needed a go-between, and that missing link was me!

We waited for Burl to show without the inane chatter. It wouldn't have played. We were Lyndon B. Johnson and Ho Chi Minh trying to decipher a Polish menu written in Sanskrit for a restaurant in Paraguay. We were trying hard to avoid the ptomaine special, but we were very aware of one thing: the maître d' was gonna be *Loony Tunes*.

*

He came with a flourish. The doors opened and he loomed between two Charlie Atlas orderlies edged behind. He was manacled wrist and ankle with a log chain between. His beard was trimmed and neat; his long hair braided Indian style. He wore bright orange coveralls. His soft brown eyes sang out unspoken words. My brother was lonelier than Eleanor Rigby and Father McKenzie combined.

We were not by nature a huggy-kissy clan. I managed a slow wink before I glared at O'Riley. "I'm outta here," and started for the door blocked by the two butterfly netters.

O'Riley scrambled to her feet behind me. "Listen Mister, I have virtually broken my back to set this up. If you think for one second that —"

I towered over her. "Two choices. Take the twin goons away. Take the manacles off. Make yourself scarce, or take an aerial intercourse at a frozen rope."

She looked ugly when she was fully torqued. Her magnified eyes were afire. She looked as if someone had set an M-80 off in her hair. She wasn't Samson but she'd lost control and control was power.

Wretch shook her puny fist, waved her shot-glass spectacles and cussed like a street thug, but in the end, there was nothing for it. I cut her a little slack by agreeing to the tape recorder, if the twin monsters would wait *with* her in the next cubbyhole west.

I gotta hand it to Burl. His expression never changed. He never said a word until it was a done deal and we were alone with only the sound of the tape recorder whirring. When he offered his hand across the table and I shook it, it felt soft — devoid calluses. His grip was sincere, his face a study of contradictions. He swallowed a dozen times, making haste in his usual maddeningly slow manner

"Burl, Burl. You're a hard act to follow."

He finally cleared his throat and tried out his tongue by working it around in his mouth for maybe a half a minute that lasted a half an hour. His voice surprised him, as if it was coming from some forbidden hollow. Finally my brother began. He had a lot to say but he'd caught an ore train pulling a steep grade. Burl worked fourth his story just as slow, just as melancholy as that overloaded train....

I didn't know how to get you to come home. You hated them worse than I did. I remember you sayin' that the folks were so cold and cruel that they named me for a mutant growth on a dead tree. They just took the name of the month you were born in for you.

Pa could beat down my independence. His fists just drove yours deeper inside of you. Vietnam was your freedom...I couldn't break away, didn't have the gumption. They made sure I was deferred from the draft. 'Essential to the farm,' Pa said. Besides, I never had your fight in me, so I had to get you back or they would've plowed me under forevermore.

I thought about it and thought about it. It was an obsession that brought an idea. I went to night school to pursue my idea. Elise come along and I got distracted some, but I didn't like not havin' my idea. I never really knew how to be married y'know. She began to seem...almost repulsive when she got to wantin' it and I was thinkin' on my idea and didn't want any distractions.

I fixed up the folk's fancy car, I jump-wired the cruise. When the time was right, I would excite my circuits. I'd eliminate the manual

controls. But I didn't think about those poor innocent, unintentional victims. That was bad, August, real bad.

The folks, they were goin' up to Roseburg to visit Aunt Hattie. It got real foggy that day. And the fog didn't lift for the rest of that day and for maybe a week.

It was time y' unnerstan'. I set up my electric gizmo so the cruise would switch on after a bit. It would, in slow increments, build speed. I read an article in one o' them Popular Mechanics, or some other place about how fog is mesmerizing. It plays with your mind so you think you're goin' along on a slow cloud, sorta like. Only in real-time you might just be zingin' down the highway at a high rate of speed.

I pulled the fuse on the dash lights so Pa couldn't read the speedometer. I bypassed the foot-feed so he wouldn't notice it flexing on the hills an' such. I jimmied the brakes by puncturing a hydraulic line.

In other words I made pretty sure the folks were on their way to hell. And it worked, what with the fire burnin' up the evidence.

It took a long time, August. You finally came home. But then I got to worryin' about Jimmy. Jimmy. Jimmy was always comin' around. He poked his beak under Pa's hood a time or two when I was workin' on my idea. He probly knew my secret. I wondered when he was gonna use it against me. There was a long time there I couldn't get no sleep. And if I dozed off, I dreamt about Jimmy poppin' out of the bedroom closet t' accuse me. It niggled on me for a couple years.

I remember one day when you an' me were down in the goose blinds. The sky was black with flights. You brought down a big ol' gander. Marylyn fetched it, but the flock flew high an' we couldn't shoot any more. But that purty girl-goose kept flyin' around, lookin' for her mate. I could hardly stand the sound of her mournful callin'. It made me real sad that I couldn't help her nor put her out of her misery, so I made real sure with Jeanette, Jimmy's mate.

I had to pretend I was crazy. I didn't like thinkin' about that terrible mess. I don't know how you were man enough to be a Marine.

My head got to hurtin' real bad and I thought about killin' you too, August, for what you and Elise didn't know I knew about you *two. I might'a been able to too — if I could've killed Elise first. But I was afraid that if I killed Elise, I'd be too sick to kill you too. And then you would be as heartsick as that mama goose. Then after, when I was locked up I got to thinkin' about all those people that got killed, or maimed and lost their mates too. It wasn't such a good plan. In fact it was the worst thing in the world to cause... It all whirled along with Jimmy and Jeanette, 'round an' 'round in my head.*

It's time to stop all the reruns ever day. I had things shut down purty good — thought I did — but then that woman doctor hooked those electric coils to my head. Ain't that illegal? The convulsions from those shocks hurt so bad they woke up my conscience, and I got real lonely...just like when you ran away.

Dr. O'Riley, she seemed like the devil doin' the Lord's poetic justice. I had to talk it over with you, August. You tell Elise not to cry over me. Maybe she could forget the bad an' just remember the good about me, I dunno. But it was me that fetched you home for her, August.

Thanks for comin' to see me, for settin' me loose. Take good care of Marilyn but please don't shoot any more geese.

*

Burl rose like the wrath of Satan. His chair clattered to the floor as startling as a surprise attack with small-arms fire. He stood there for a flash to return my opening wink. Then Burl became a rogue elephant. His timing was perfect. He was quick as a cat, especially for a big man. He screamed like a terribly heartbroken banshee and he trampled down the locked door with 260 some pounds of insane fury inspiring him. Unfortunately, when the door imploded into the hall, O'Riley and her two circus freaks were slammed beneath.

I homed in on Burl's paper-clad footfalls as he shagged ass down the hall. An instant later, I heard the godawful sound of shattering glass. I knew Burl had dove through the corridor window and had plummeted to his death on the brick rialto six stories below.

There came the clamorous sound of an instant melee outside the cubicle. The Chesterfield protruding from her lips had become Shredded Wheat. The doctor looked even less appealing in the dying cockroach position — her dress above her pantaloons her hairy legs and goofy tennis shoes bicycling in the air.

Dr. O Wretch, spat hunks of soggy Chesterfield while struggling to her feet. The threesome regrouped and clattered over the splintered door, and off in the wake of Burl. The wing came alive. The melee turned into a full-scale brouhaha. I pushed the *Rewind* button on the reel-to-reel tape recorder. When Burl's voice stopped helium screeching, I pushed *Erase*. When the button popped back up, I pushed *Record*.

Not ten minutes later, I drove past the liquor store without a sideways glance. Somewhere South of Roseburg, when it felt right, I tossed my *Bad Boy Blues* tape out the window. Just beyond the Canyonville off ramp, I watched through the side-view mirror, the bong pipe shatter on the pavement. It was a long way home from God knows where, and it had been a long autumn day, Indian summer or no.

*

Time does not heal old wounds. The scars are left for a purpose: to bring back all and knock cockiness back on its ass. Fortunately, through self-taught self-hypnosis, I've cleansed my mind of grief and despair. I doubt if I'll ever shake dishonor. I used to think of time as a commodity, rather than a sneak thief that stole away everything except the guilty residue when I wasn't on guard. Time is more precious to me now. I nurture my allotment.

I look back on the day I came back from Burl's final statement. Even in my anguish and grief, the place finally felt like home. That was seven years ago. The windmills no longer batter me from deep inside. Hell, I've even found the confidence to stop worrying over old bones. There was so much a man couldn't know about the woman who shared his bed, but I no longer agonize over mind games about *Jimmy and Elise.* I seldom wonder if Burl was trying to excite a circuit in my brain in schizophrenic dreamscape hints with that *Jimmy suddenly appearing from a bedroom closet* line... Infrequent were my musings of the secrets that might be hidden behind my woman's unfathomable, tarnished silver orbs.

Elise is still the most beautiful woman in creation. She's on the porch swing with our four-year-old twins. I can just hear the confident pitch of her voice as she recites Sara and Sonja their favorite poem:

> Crosshatch draw the latch
> Sit by the fire and spin
> Take a cup and drink it up
> And call the neighbors in

*

Burl, by court decree, was a ward of the state; the bureaucracy was thus charged with both his care and the interment of his remains. They shoved him into a blast furnace and fired away until all that was left was a little pile of ashes.

How O'Riley, after being discharged for negligence (a slap on the wrist) had gotten ahold of those remains, or what kind of inch-worming sensation her conscience made creeping up her tight ass, for three years, I really don't care to know. She showed up here with Burl's ashes, one fall day, had them in a sealed canister.

O'Riley wasted little time with niceties. She spat up what brought her all the way to the Basin. She asked me about the tape

I'd erased. What Burl had said before I blotted out his confession and replayed the chaos of that day over his slow, arduous words.

I mulled it over Burl style for an eternity. In the end the whole thing had become surreal to me. I might never face up to the intolerable pain my brother had wrought on so many innocent strangers. Today was licking a sweet lollipop. Thinking back was finding a dill pickle in its center. I would have to spit it out someday, but not to Wretch. The guilt had become a cyst Elise and I would live with until our day of reckoning.

I made a few oyster-lodged-in-my-throat noises and watched Wretch squirm before I drew the latch and clasped it tight.

"Burl had geese and people all mixed up in his head. He didn't realize that geese are far nobler. Burl was *'loony tunes'* y'know."

***

Elise and I took the Burl of my childhood down by the goose blinds and turned him loose. When the late October sun first paints the cottontail marshes in flame, the geese come in whistling golden-winged droves. The monarchs of the sky sheer the wind to bank and veer over the blinds. No guns blaze to alter their course.

Their call is a wild, melancholy dirge. It is nature's wailing of the autumnal equinox. Fall is the time of dying. Their rhapsody is a composition of season's memorial to my brother, Burl.

******

TOY SOLDIER

The footbridge is 213 feet long. Its cable suspension catwalk spans the River Olo at an average height of 126 feet. The walkway is just wide enough to accommodate two adults crossing side-by-side. As the sightline visits the far end, optical misconception reduces the structure to the size of a rabbit's burrow.

Li scans the bridge with fretful doe eyes. The shortcut across the river chasm seems suspiciously fragile; as if a support cable might snap by the weight of a seagull, and the entire structure would plunge into the deep gorge. Her heart is lodged in her throat. Her breathing becomes erratic. Tingles, not unlike needle pricks, cause her armpits to itch.

Li is not going to impress Dun by being a lily-livered, quivering jellyfish. She edges behind him, a fist gripped firmly to his belt. He pauses and says "Makes ya feel a little tipsy, huh? It'd be rude and crude if I were to say, don't be afraid, Li, 'cause it's okay. I had the swingin' bridge phobia from the first time I encountered this diabolical contraption until I was eighteen. And then my blind tremors were replaced with a real, rational fear.

"I'm guessin' you couldn't spit if you had to. There's no need to reply. Just know that this is a sacred place — a sort of shrine — that no evil will befall you here as long as your motives are pure, babe.

"It's hard to interpret the music, but the bridge dances. When we step, the bridge dips and twists ever so slightly. A wave ripples from our feet. The ripple travels along the span until it reaches the anchor pins on the far side. Then the wave telegraphs back. Soon the waves are going and coming and the bridge is subtly doin' the twist. The cables stretch, retract, and twang. Mother Nature is strokin' her guitar. The gentlest breeze will make this rickety thingamajig sway your breath away. "Relax, and enjoy the rock 'n' roll. When your spirit lets go you'll be in step with the dance of the bridge."

Li doesn't feel the harmonics; just a deep dependency on Dun. And without warning, he's on his way. His stride lengthens. The bridge thrums, bounces and writhes beneath her feet. She stays in step silently mouthing; "*It's just a damn bridge, a damn bridge a damn bridge.*"

The bridge's tempo ebbs and flows through her being. Her feet tingle, even through the thick soles of her hiking boots. Her rocketing pulse backs down — a little. Finally she remembers to breathe. And then Dun stops at center span.

Li stares with him at the mist billowing from the boulder-strewn falls some one hundred feet below.

She witnesses the power and the fury transcend into beautiful rainbows. A spectacle so awesome, it's as magnificent as a panoramic mural in wild animation. Dun sees his past unfold before his eyes. Sensing this, Li stands transfixed, and finally diverts her eyes to focus on Dun's. He wraps his arm around her and the words roll off his tongue so softly, so gently, she wonders how she hears above the roar, wonders if it's really him speaking. But those words are too revealing to be imagined.

Li releases her death-grip on his belt and slides her arm around his waist. Perhaps she reads his lips…his thoughts? Dizzy broad.

*

"There once was a farm over there where that weed and briar patch has taken over: the Grebe place, Jon and his parents. His mom and dad were the god-damndest pair to draw to you'd ever deliberately do anything to avoid. Invertebrates, I believe. Jon's dad, I'm almost positive. The Mrs.? Well, I doubt if she had a spine, but whatever specie she was, she lacked human fiber, and that's presenting those two in the fondest light I can shine.

"But enough glorifying those two... I'm just gonna tell it the way I saw it. You probably ain't gonna believe it anyway...."

"I guess we shall see what we will see," Li replies in stilted anticipation of...?? ever reserved Dun has passed no clues as to what he referrers to — or where this is going. Why here? This frightening place is far from conducive to easy conversation....

*

"Fortunately for a boy like me (scared of his own pee stream) the Grebe adults were recluses. I only encountered the two weasel look-alikes once. That was the day I met Jon, the first day ever, of school, first grade, indoctrination day.

"School, to me, was being strip-searched, deloused and humiliated — like shovin' a wild animal in a cage. But I guess that's about my past and not particularly about Jon's story, even though his parents were. Those two left an impression of evil on my soul from the time I was six, until I was eighteen.

I don't know how I'm doin' this by the way; don't know how I can stand here with my arm around you and reveal to you what a wimpy little cowardly creep I was. But don't say anything. You didn't know me then. There is no way to compare me to the person I've become...because of Jon. So you're gonna want to hear this through to the end."

Ohmygod, Li is thinking, he wouldn't bare his soul to me unless he's forgiven me my trespasses. "Just one Question, Dun," Li says, holding dearly to eye contact. "Have you told this story to anyone else? I mean it sounds so private, so deeply personal."

"No. No one knows. No one will ever know unless you're not the girl I think you are; hope to Christ you are."

Li nods in a convincing manner. It's the moment of truth, and because he wishes it so, Dun's heart absorbs the love cast by her eyes. The words will come when it's time. For now, she silently vows she will never do him wrong again. "Go ahead. I'm all in."

Dun starts where he left off, his spirit renewed. To him it's as if an anaconda has released its suffocating grip. He can spew out a bit of the venom from his volatile past.

"I feared Jon's parents as much as I feared the bridge, but looking back, I guess all that scaredy-cat crap was intertwined. But swear to God, there was a forerunner of strange origins comin' at me. I felt it but could only worry it. Damned if I could get a handle on my own freaky id until Jon, *Soljir* Grebe's day.

"Other than facial features, Jon was not at all like his parents. His eyes were not cold and unholy. Not spiteful or shifty.

No, Jon's eyes were usually swollen and bloodshot, but even then, curious and mischievous. But there's no two ways about it, Jon was more of a misfit than I, even though I didn't know why.

"Where his folks were rails, Jon was fat. Among the usual taunts brayed by his classmates came the classic *Lard A' Mighty*. He was balding by the time he was eleven, a rotund freak in too small raggedy clothes — fodder for his peers, the meanies, the cruelest jackal pack of all. He dropped out after sixth grade. God only knows grubbin' for his folks on that piece of crap, hardscrabble farm was heaven compared to facin' those little heathen tormentors who could never put themselves in Jon's worn-out clodhoppers.

"Jon and I became something akin to friends. Don't ask me why. Maybe it was because our only neighbors were Jon and his folks: our one-way neighbor on the far side of a bridge I couldn't make myself cross. Jon, on the other hand, was not afraid of a damned thing, least of all a stupid bridge.

"Jon would come across near anytime he could escape the evil eye of his father. We always played war. Jon was obsessed with war. He was *Soljir*, named himself *Soljir*.

"War was the main obsession of a brain brim full of weird quirks. He had every bad habit imaginable. I doubt he ever bathed. He smacked and slobbered, belched and farted. He had a mining claim goin' in his nose, worked at his crotch incessantly, and dug at his butt as though his behavior was quite the fashion.

"Soljir was so damned wrought with superstition he was in constant turmoil — rats and bats and steppin on cracks were hexes absolutely imperative to deal with. We once skirted a field, backtracking and makin' a four-mile detour because a black cat ran across the trail ahead of us. He had two brothers he went on and on about. I thought they were imaginary. Soljir said they were twelve years older than us — that his two brothers had run away from home when Jon was four, maybe five. But Li, darlin', those boys were not imaginary — they just had better instincts than Soljir. They had the good sense never to come back — even after it was over, but it wasn't over yet, not for Soljir.

"Like I told ya, Soljir and I were something akin to friends. Akin, meanin' we played together but were never close enough to share anything even remotely personal. By the time we were thirteen, fourteen I was all warred out. Not Soljir. War was his reason to be alive, his fanatical obsession.

"My mother gave Soljir half a dozen volumes of *Histories of American Battles*. Those books were his bibles. He studied every battle that America ever fought. He was an authority on the geography and the noteworthy participants of all wars.

"Mom figured Soljir had a glandular disorder that caused his hormones to rage uncontrollably. And that's what made him so huge and so fat. I didn't give it much thought. I was into girls and cars by then. I neglected to even visit Soljir for a couple years. But I'd heard tales of his exploits. He made sneak attacks on neighboring chicken coops, and the chickens raised one hell of a ruckus.

"He was seen crawlin' along the dikes slingin' rock hand grenades that made huge splashes in front of steelhead fishermen along the big levee. He scared the bejesus outta those flatlanders, lettin' go high-pitched squeals. Soljir's notion of a rebel yell was blood curdling and effective as hell.

"Soljir grew and grew. By the time we were eighteen, he was six-six and maybe three sixty; a gentle giant but a nuisance in general. People talked about him from time-to-time, especially those riverbank steelhead and salmon fishermen. Some figured him for a dimwit. Said it was high-time to get one of those tranquilizer guns they use to down elephants, and juice up the dart with a double dose — attempt to subdue the efffin' freak.

"When I received my greeting and salutations from Uncle Sam, I was scared shitless. Mom, she was set on a college deferment, while I was thinkin' all kinds of crazy things, thinkin maybe it was time to grow up and step up to the plate, for chrissakes. I wanted to do what a man was supposed to do, y'see…but… There was always that *but*, that little scardey cat *but*.

"My thoughts eventually turned to Soljir. He was my age. As fate would have it, we were even born on the same day. If logic had anything to do with it, Jon Grebe had probably received his draft notice about the same time as I had.

"It was time for a parley with the Soljir. We could actually go off to war together for real. He was a giant. Nobody would mess with him. The Army would wash away the stink, and I could hide in his shadow. He could be my pile of sandbags when the shootin' started.

"I struck off for the Grebe spread determined to cross this very same freaky, swayin' bridge. I took the high trail that day, to avoid the cliffs you and I slithered up. We'll take the easy way back providing you can still stomach me…after the tellin'."

"Now listen Buster, you've got my heart-rate up," Li purses her perfect lips. "I'm stronger than the impression I left on the climb. I'm as mentally fit as the best of 'em, and I'm literally dying of curiosity. Besides, our eyes just made a pact my heart will never break. It will take something totally devastating to change my mind about you, Thomas Dunhill Hurdelman."

"Okay then," Dun sighs, "on with the strip mining of my soul.

*

"I'm headed out across the high trail sneakin' up on the bridge of my acrophobic and hydrophobic nightmares. I'm edging up, about a quarter mile off. And I hear the first shot.

"Hearin' gunshots around here ain't at all unusual; in fact it's the norm. I don't think anything of it. A second shot follows the first, and I think, good. Soljir is out practicing with his deer rifle. Got his draft papers. He's chafing at the bit, getting' his shit together to be a real soldier. The next shot is muffled and so is the next.

"The birds stop chirpin'. Even that's not unusual after a gun goes off, but there's a vacuum. The sky seems to change color. The air goes slack as the horizon slides into a dark void.

"I get this feelin', y'see. Gooseflesh crawls down my spine. I should turn back, but I'm caught in this unworldly place. My fear goes into hiding, I guess. It's unbelievable — as though a pile of chickenshit has evaporated from my shoulders — as if I'm levitated into some higher plane where only the brave dare to venture. It's a sixth sense — highly developed in 'Nam. The tunnel rats and ground pounders who survived it called it *bad juju*.

"The shooting has stopped. I haven't taken a hit but my gut doesn't believe me… Don't remember what pulls me onward… My mind says *NO*, but my feet say *proceed with caution*. The bridge that petrified me all my life is just a blur I hardly remember crossing. I'm on the other side, on the trail along the narrows, climbin' out of the gorge when I spot Soljir. He's comin down-trail towards me, holdin' back on a wheelbarrow to keep it from runnin' away.

"Soljir has a rifle slung across his back. The wheelbarrow is overloaded with what appears to be the carcass of a deer — until the gap between us closes. The carcass becomes the remains of two human beings; Soljir's mom and dad. Both are shot low in the vitals. They are as dead as the yellow, jaundiced sky.

"Blood trickles through rust holes in the bottom of the wheelbarrow leaving twin red lines behind his cargo. When Soljir stops to greet me, the blood splashes softly beneath the wheelbarrow to puddle a black stain on brown soil. The smell of offal is rank. If I hadn't been outside my body, I would've up-chucked my cookies.

Soljir sets the wheelbarrow down, snaps to attention, salutes and says, "I dint know the gun was loaded an' I'm so sorry my frien'."

"It's my cue to make like a shepherd and get the flock out of there. Soljir has surely gone completely batshit. But instead of hattin' up, I'm drawn to his eyes, and his eyes are as yours were at first light, Li. If anything, Soljir's a bit bemused, as if contemplating the enormity of his act and shrugging it off as a dirty chore he should have taken care of a long time ago, before it took on that ghastly odor.

"C'mon back down t' the bridge," Soljir says. "I gotta show you sumpin."

He squeezes by me somehow, wheelbarrow, cargo and all. Meekly, I follow, carefully avoiding the twin trails of blood stringing out behind the wheelbarrow — we both watch our step.

"Before long we're back to this spot, the center of the bridge. Changing grips on the wheelbarrow handles, Soljir dumps the contents easy as y' please. His parents flop out with a sound that lives with me today. The bridge tilts, pitches and yaws. Me, I seem to have developed sea legs. Soljir tosses the wheelbarrow over the main suspension cable as though the damned thing is a football. The toss easily clears ten feet. The splash is muted by the roar of the Olo's falls, and the wheelbarrow is a vanished prop in a horror flick.

"Did y' know," Soljir says, "that Olo is a Chinook word? Olo means hungry. Kinda funny, ain't it?"

"It's anything but funny," Dun informs Li. "And the river's name is no mystery. The local's call it the River Hungry. But I don't enlighten Soljir. My throat is constricted, my mouth too dry to speak.

"Soljir Jon offhandedly grabs his father by his collar and by the ass of his baggy bibs and pitches dear ol' Dad over the swaying cable. The gruesome carcass plunges ass over teakettle and is swallowed by the churning depths of the rapids far below.

His mother wears a raggedy, blood-soaked dress. He heaves her up by her arms and wallows her around until his huge hand is centered flat on her belly. Soljir shot-puts his mother up and over and into that liquid agitator as if her limber carcass is a bag of rotten spuds dumped in the mouth of a giant garbage disposal. A streamer above her gross carcass, her dress is a failed parachute. My eyes squinch — she's gone. I never knew her name — didn't care to.

"Soljir wipes his bloody hands on his pants and apologizes for the mess on the boardwalk. I stare spellbound after the carcasses. Nothing rises to the surface. The River Olo swiftly digests its meal. But I imagine I can see those bodies rocketing downstream until they're bashing into the cliffs on the north shore, the waves grinding them to tiny bits — crab meal.

"Soljir, in his high-pitched effeminate voice, stands alongside me. He too stares into the maelstrom. He finally says, *"Every word ever spoken floats endlessly through the air. This falls is the place where the sound waves of history bivouac and regroup. The voices, the battle cries, float on the wind through time's passages. The sound comes to the falls and the mist is a poultice drawing the words through history's archives.*

"The words come out in a whisper hard to pick out over the roar. Hear Nathan Hale? If you tune your ears, his words come together."

'I only regret that I have but one life to give to my country.'

"*Listen up. It's John Paul Jones. He shouts above the Bonhomme Richard's cannons:*

'Sir, I have not yet begun to fight.'

"Soljir is with Farragut damning the torpedoes and opening the throttles:

'Damn the torpedoes. Full speed ahead.

Soljir stands at attention alongside General Douglas MacArthur at the Philippines:

'I shall return.'

"He's with the US Marines on Iwo Jima, raising the flag on the summit of Mt. Suribachi — and he's off on a tangent that takes him through the halls of Montezuma to the shores of Tripoli — and everywhere in between.

"'Sighted sub. Sank same.'

'Take her down.'"

"Soljir pulls those voices out of the thunder of the falls and ends with Chief Joseph of the Nez Perce Nation:

"'*I am tired of fighting... From where the sun now stands, I will fight no more.*'

"Soljir Grebe seems to be home from his wars. He turns to me and says.

"I reckon you're here 'cause you got your draft papers."

"Yeah," I reply, wondering why my voice box works.

"Got mine too," he says. "Pa fetched them in the mail this mornin'. Ma and Pa read them papers first. Boy, did they ever dance a jig and have their last hee-haw over that letter."

*

Dun looks into the mist spiraling up from the gorge and says to Li, "My hair should be standing on end, but isn't. I feel no fear, just a bizarre numbness. I stare blankly into those easy blue eyes of his, my mind as stupefied as my stare."

Li has no words, but had she; she would not have the means to communicate them.

At any rate, Dun is as lost in his tell as Mt. St. Helens when she blew her peak. Beguiled, he continues. "Well, Soljir, still staring me in the eye, willing me to figure it out, says, "I can't go and take the physical, y' unnerstan'."

"I don't understand, but manage to step in shit by uttering some ill-conceived crap about a freakin' corpse bein' able to pass an Army physical. I keep my bead focused on his eyes, wishin' I could outrun a bullet. Unfortunately, I can't move my feet. Fortunately, Soljir ignores my blather, just goes on telling his story in mechanical, robotic fashion....

"Farm wasn't so bad when I was little. Looked up to and enjoyed my big brothers. I dunno if you recall, Dun, but they up and runned away when I was four or thereabouts.

"Ma and Pa called me out to the woodshed after m' brothers'd been gone a spell. The folks, they had it in their heads that my brothers, Elwin an' Clay, weren't a comin' home to help with the milkin' 'n' plowin,' 'n' such no more.

"Ma had a needle an' some catgut thread. She'd fetched a dishpan full' a scaldin' hot water an' a bar of lye soap.

"Pa, he had 'im a coil of rope, a big hook bladed knife and a bottle of 'shine. I tried to run, but Pa was too quick. He wrestled me down and tied me up so I could hardly wiggle. He stuffed a sock in my mouth so I couldn't scream no more.

"Pa jerked down my pants 'n' under drawers. He pulled the cork out'n the bottle with his teeth and poured ice cold whiskey on my sack. Ma helt my peter agin my belly whilst Pa set out to do what he did with that razor-sharp blade.

"I passed out then. When I come to, Ma had me scrubbed down with the lye soap. Pa's cut was sewed shut, the blood no longer spurtin', but I hurt so bad I puked for days, and couldn't walk for a time after.

"I was never gonna be a man, y' unnerstan. And there's my folks fightin' over the jug, cussin' over who deserved the dregs. Ma won. She said without her, there wouldn't be no boy to fix. They were drinkin' to the fact that I wouldn't be a runnin' away like Elwin and Clay done."

Li is hugging her stomach as if she's taken a rapier slash through her entrails. Her expression says what her mouth cannot.

Dun is beyond sensibilities. He continues, "Soljir up and shrugs his suspenders. The man-child unbuttons his pants. He drops his drawers to display his shriveled penis. There is no scrotum; no testicles nesting within — and his pants are up before I can form a mental image of a lifetime shamed.

Soljir hands me the rifle he'd propped against the rail and says, "You do what you gotta do, Dun. And I'll do what I gotta do. But when you get down there to Fort Ord, please tell them soldier boys I surely wanted to be a patriot."

"Before I can reply, Soljir is climbing the guardrail cables, wrestling his giant frame through the lattice work. He shinnies on up where the downrigger-strands are spliced into the suspension lines. With the agility the obese frequently possess, he vaults atop the suspension cables anchoring the bridge. He stands balanced to that high-wire, but sways precariously over the falls. When he gets completely balanced, he stands at attention, salutes, and performs a jackknife to rival the cliff divers of Acapulco.

"I can only stare in horrible fascination. His giant frame sails between those sheer outcroppings and strikes headfirst in the narrows with a sickening *SPLAT!*

His remains are swallowed in the hungry maw of the River Olo. I witness his spirit rise in a fine spray that becomes a fast dissipating rainbow. The whitewater pulses red with his blood, but is instantly purified — all in less time than it takes to say it to you. The River Olo swallows the filth, the abject shame Jon Grebe's forever young mind never could.

Dazed, I pick up his rifle and sling it into the rushing falls. Lighting splits jagged cracks in a bruised sky. Thunder rolls in belated warning. And here I stand, a lightnin' rod smack dab in the middle of a jim-dandy web of electrical conduits. The rains beat down like, well, *crazy*. I feel no fear, and think I know why. Soljir gifted me his courage.

The downpour flushes the blood from the catwalk. Soaked to the skin, I walk away as though I imagined it.

***

The inhumanity, the injustice is beyond the realm of anything Li has experienced…or so her silent prayers would have it. As tears run rampant, Li's hand reaches up under the back of her sweatshirt. She unhooks her bra. Her hands burrow up her shirtsleeves one-by-one. She slides the bra-straps down her arms. Out of a sleeve, she gently tugs her bra free.

Dunhill Thomas Hurdelman, ex Green Beret, and decorated veteran of three tours in Vietnam, snaps to in military correctness. He salutes as Li crosses her heart with her right hand. She releases the bra to the updrafts created by the majestic Olo Falls. With pink bra cups inflated, the undergarment dances beyond the falls as if a butterfly. The bra meets its waterloo in the rapids far downstream. As inadequate as it is, Li wishes her sacrifice were at least red, white and blue.

******

THE PINK ZEBRA

My brain is a swarm of mad hornets. Dark thoughts zing in all directions. And the humming. If only I could stop that unmerciful humming. I'm too terrified to pee, or even to scream! And I'm seeing things that no longer exist. I'm seeing Pam as though she's here, only she's gone, and has been, for six years. We were sisters. She was my everything. I'm not afraid of seeing her. I'm afraid of *me*.

The electric humming transfers to the mania within. I was twelve when my sister walked out the door, never to return. No calls, no letters. Not a hint of her scent. Pam and I were born on the same day, six years apart. Pam and Nan. Maybe we should have been born seven years apart. Rolling sevens might have changed our luck. Six has proven not to be my lucky number.

The hums reverberating from everywhere subtly transform into female voices. Their messages are anything but clear. Am I supposed to fill in the blanks? Finish their sentences? To top it off, the girl-voices are demanding, and antsy. I pull my shirt-front over my head and play ostrich. It's almost midnight. My heart pounds like crazy. There's no respite. In a few seconds it would've been Pam's 25th birthday — will be my 19th.

Mom is blotto on the sway-back divan, hip-huggers undone. She hasn't bothered with underwear. A heavy swatch of kinky hair seems intent on escaping an even darker abyss. She snorts. A crusty nostril inflates and pops a bubble. She'd chugged her beer to the dregs, lit a doobie and dropped it beside the long-necked dead soldier. The joint's remains are an imprint burnt halfway through the filthy carpet. The room stinks of cat shit, urine, and roach (which takes me to pack rats nesting). Tomorrow is probably moving day. We move so often our welfare checks are addressed with *Forward to* stamped on the envelopes. My once gorgeous mother surrendered all, the day Pam vaporized.

It's time to slip away, at least ala my father. He'd cut and run with a married woman six weeks after Pam's disappearance. Mom once referred to dad's new love as the local *sperm depository*. I suspected she wasn't paying compliments, but never knew exactly what she meant until recently.

TV sets raised me after Mom stopped living and Father fled. Cathode rays shot up my brain so that reality is just another illusion and Hollywood is truth. The voices have me now. The ragging is steadily leaching into my brain, eroding my willpower. I tearfully shut the door behind me. Why bother locking it? One whiff and bye, bye bad boys. "I love you Mom." I sob and then I'm gone.

By midmorning I'm driving my beater Falcon by rote. The voices are hard at it, wailing above the acid rock blaring on the radio. The ladies are getting down, egging me on. I have driven across Nevada. California is a blurry desert before me. Heat risers shimmer above what appears to be pools of water out where the road is no wider than a serpent of electrical tape narrowing to infinity.

If the voices keep me awake, I'll be there before midnight. If not, I'll pretend like tomorrow is today. Who's going to care? Me, or my submersible camera? The camera is the exact same model that the voices told me to lift. And I did — from a man-made beach in a town with a bridge that is no longer falling down: Lake Havasu. A snowbird magnet — an imported fairy-tale that connects a man-made island to a world gone mad. Jesus. And I'm crazy?

It's time to gas up again. I can only hope there are no creepoids hanging at the next mini-mart. Being 19, stacked, and good looking is a scourge. But I'm not to be deterred. Thanks to the tube, I'm a black belt in Karate, and an 'A' student in several forms of martial art ball kicking. Looks, at least in my case, are deceiving. Even my fawn brown eyes hide the meanness inside. I'm one cold-hearted piece of raven haired work — quick, silent, deadly, and as double-jointed as an Olympic gymnast. Just ask me.

Hours and hours of fighting sleep deprivation (and losing to weird hallucinations) and finally, the whiners insinuate that I've reached my destination, a turnout before a bridge on a country lane some five miles up from the mouth of the Little Monsoon River along the Central Oregon Coast. I don't know why I'm here, nor do I understand why I'm supposed to smear mud over my license plates. The voices don't answer questions; they just scream orders. But I'm one up on them. I remember living near here, in another life.

I mumble words in the Chinook language as I dismount. I remember to remove the disk in my appropriated camera and insert a new one before strapping the camera around my neck. What the hell for? I stop in mid-stride. Half breed that I am, I don't know from Katmandu about the Chinook lingo, but Pam studied the endangered language just before she disappeared.

Tremulous with grief and confusion I do the mud gig on my plates. No shortage of the sticky goo in Oregon.

A patsy on invisible strings, I head upstream. I wear the same cutoffs and yellow tank top I started out with. The tank top is one stiff coffee-with-sugar-and-cream stain. Feels like the cutoffs are about to disintegrate. I'll find a deep hole and scrub myself clean — clothes and all.

The sky is so bright it seems more white than blue. Is this a harbinger of my upcoming demise? What am I doing here? Where are those drama queens taking me? I hesitate, start to turn back....

Suddenly my sister, Pam's voice rises above the cacophony of crazed voices raising cane with my soul. "Find the rock, Sis, find the rock."

Pam. She was my sister, my surrogate mother. She was my mentor *my rock*. My everything. I am insane with grief. She taught me to laugh, to cry to count, taught me the alphabet, to tie my shoes, and dress myself. She helped me through the bloody anguish of my first period, and then she was gone.

I want to scream so loud the earth will shatter. Her voice soothes my freaking mind. "Go upstream. Find the rock and use it. You will find me. Peace will come with time. It will be over, but only because you are so amazingly strong, Little Sis. Do you not know that you are a direct descendant of *Wolf Weasel*, the slyest shaman ever to walk on two legs?

I've never heard of Wolf Weasel — can't say "Sounds like a plan" in *Chinook*. I resort to English. I repeat those words in my native tongue but they make no more sense than they would in *Chinook*. The Little Monsoon runs down a bed of river rock. There are trillions of stones. Which rock is *the* rock? What's this special rock for?

I wade on. The river splits around a tiny island; the roar of a waterfall beckons from the next bend. Suddenly I sense someone evil is watching me. Paranoia sounds its ungodly alarm. Shivers run through my spine. My bottom end clenches as the cowardly voices flee my soul, leaving me to…what? I bite my lower lip until it bleeds. As ordered, I keep moving.

Yeah, I know. I'm a walking mental case. There's no getting beyond it. I've been diagnosed by Mother as a bi-polar, paranoid schizophrenic. Mostly she calls me a manic depressive, but being paranoid doesn't mean some perv isn't *really* after me. Sure I'm moody, and outside my job flipping burgers, a social recluse. Doesn't everybody hear voices from time to time?

I splash upriver, fight the onrushing current and slimy boulders — search for my rock — try an indifferent gaze. Even though the serenade that ate at my conscience has stilled, I swear I hear the background music in a seat-squirming suspense thriller. Only I'm not thrilled.

Seems like Pam or one of those freaky bitches with her, would tell me what my rock is supposed to look like… The falls is suddenly before me. A putrid smell triggers my gag reflex. I stand in the shallows of some ill-defined eddy and try not to upchuck.

There, up ahead, is my rock. It's as round as a softball. It gleams turquoise in a riverbed of gray stones. I bend down and hungrily stretch for it. Something monstrous enters my periphery from the bushes above the bank. A huge man: stark naked and hairless as a pink, scalded zebra. *Zebra?*

He's coming Mack truck fast — screaming insanely. I cannot hear his curses above the roar of the falls or the blood pulsing through my veins. His crazed charge produces wild, splashing wakes; his eyes are maniacal. My fingers clutch my rock. He launches himself. I can't stop focusing on a face with no brows, no eyelashes. My arm comes out of the water; the beautiful rock is an outgrowth of my fist. In slow motion, I waltz a toreador sidestep. The mesmerizing stone swings a cleaved-rainbow arc — stops dead at the monster's hairless skull. I don't hear a *clunk*, but the impact sends sickening shock waves through my skeletal system.

The voices cheer more insanely than the madman's spasmodic twitches before me. Time begins again. My toes tightly grip the gray stones beneath my feet. My nerve endings twitch like a beached salmon approaching death. My hands shake; my knees quake. My lungs seem locked in paralysis. I can barely breathe. But I'm conscious enough to know the turquoise stone had done its job. The monster, after thrashing aimlessly, is face down in the deepening eddy, floating in gross, elongated circles towards the falls.

It occurs, as I vomit a chunky stream of junk food. The zebra stripes are bizarre tattoos, strange encryptions of numbers and letters in foreign font that entwine the thing's gross, pink skin. The monster is dead…his pink, hairless flesh subtly fades to bluish gray — and the ladies swiftly begin to harp.

I'm supposed to take *pictures* of the tats. All of them. It's imperative. It's about releasing the monster's victim's from purgatory or limbo or *something*. I balk.

My sister pleads. I have no choice. I dog paddle with the current whirl-pooling below the terrace-like falls. Near the falls, I slip beneath the surface. The *thing* is there, floating upright, or levitated by currents at cross-purposes. His arms and legs are spread wide. He pirouettes in slow-motion. I ease closer; give the camera time to auto-focus up close on perhaps hundreds of bizarre tattoos. And then the monster's face revolves to stare into my petrified soul. Washed of blood, the gash in his forehead looks all the more hideous. His features are bland: a round rubbery blob with cherub lips, flat nose with flared nostrils and pale blue, sightless eyes. Those opaque eyes are still grotesque, still portray ungodly evil. Click, click, click.

I shoot to the surface for air, but cannot swim away. The voices are at me as if I were running a gauntlet straight to hell. I refill my lungs and slip below the surface to continue my heinous task until I have close-ups of every single zebra stripe that encompasses his entire body.

The voices are sated. Exhausted, I swim to the bank and retrieve the precious stone I don't recall depositing there… My toes squishing with muck, I follow a fisherman's trail back to my home away from home. Now what?

*

On the run without a gun. Lamb it baa'ck to Arizona. Don't remember escaping the Little Monsoon River. How did my beater make the trip unassisted?

Time has eluded my senses. I possess a camera. The disks are proof. All it takes is a push of a button to remove them, one, by one, in reverse order of the way I don't recall loading them. Then a furtive interlude with a monitor I know nothing about. Yes, those horrid pictures await my disposition — rather the voices wishes. I'd sooner down a hemlock highball than confront the pink zebra again. It's time for a shower. Since arriving in Arizona,

I've been averaging six a day, and still feel like I've been rolled in grease and then soot and then covered with crawly/clammy vermin.

I read the paper every day. I peruse reports with dogmatic dedication. I watch the depressing news shows day after day. Nothing. Nothing about a missing hairless monster. Nothing about a floater washing up on the beaches near the mouth of the Little Monsoon River.

Finally in the lost and found section I read about a missing submersible camera possibly mislaid on the island beach at Lake Havasu. A substantial reward for its no questions asked return is offered.

Substantial? Oh my yes! A substantial stint in a Yuma prison cell until I'm extradited to Oregon to face a much greater charge. I can't dwell on it, but I hear the voices in the background. A hubbub. The mutterings of a lynch mob before the jury reads the verdict in an old war whoop flick. *Guilty as charged!* Or are my nemeses sniveling in Chinook?

Pam's voice rises above the mass mutterings. "Call the number. Arrange to meet the camera's owner. Do it Sis. Take the next step down the road seldom traveled."

I know I must do what Pam so passionately suggests. I sigh and enter the number poke the *Send* button and push *End* ten times. Maybe *eleven* is my lucky number. I didn't have my big girl panties snugged up on *seven*. I hear the *brrrt* five times. A sense of relief passes through me — but then someone says "Hey."

My metaphoric panties are up, but I'm caught tongue-tied and brain-dead. I try to fold the phone, but my hands don't work...I can make myself take pictures of a killing machine I slew with a beautiful stone, yet I can't face the music long distance? Maybe Mom has my number. Maybe I am loony toons. "I've got your camera," my interfering mouth blurts.

Ooh...kay," a masculine voice drawls. "Can we meet somewhere? Preferably on the island?"

I know what island he refers to. "Yes."

We skip the name game: instead, set a date: tomorrow afternoon. Three. I describe my wheels, fold the phone and try to conjure a picture of the man behind the voice. As I drive toward Lake Havasu, I keep coming up with a leather-faced, weather-cured cowboy driving a beat-up pickup truck... The Marlboro Man toting, instead of twin six guns, an expensive submersible camera?

*

I get to the rendezvous a half hour early. My paranoia is a day early. I need a shower in the worst way. I'm afraid I've forgotten how to talk. There are people all around happily going about their mock busy-ness. He comes at me from an oblique angle on foot. He's wearing Hawaiian shorts and a khaki vest. The vest is a curiosity in pockets with Velcro fasteners. The man is a hunk. He's about my age, probably a little older. He wears no hat. His hair is short, black and curly. In lieu of lace-ups he wears Jesus sandals — we have something in common — my complexion, his, deep tan. His eyes are gray, depthless and beautiful. There's nothing under the vest but constantly expanding and contracting muscles.

"Hey," he says. "You must be the girl who found my camera?"

I swallow. There is no spit, just a burning sensation in my throat. My tongue is stuck to the roof of my mouth. I manage to pry it loose and eke out a feeble "Yes."

"Ooh...kay," he says, 'where do we go from here?"

"I don't want the reward," I blurt. "I stole your camera. I, I needed it bad. Someone abducted my sister. That was six years ago. I've been, well, um, communicating with her, and a group of the perpetrator's victims ever since."

Suddenly the hunk's eyes are silver dollars. Was it something I said? "I was the bait and means to kill a serial killer. I did — with my turquoise stone. The perv, um pervert had strange letters and numbers tattooed all over his torso — cryptic. He was levitated in cross-currents made by a waterfall. The voices of his dead victims demanded I take pictures of *all* the tats. They seemed magnified by the crystal clear water, the tats, I mean. Where *do* we go from here?"

The hunk has a nervous tic. It makes his cheek twitch. It's with my unspoken permission that his mesmerizing gray orbs absorb my soul....

"Oh man," he finally says... "You're comin' at me with fastballs, curves, spitters and knuckle balls, all at once, girl. Tell ya what. Let's start over, okay? My name is Tom. Tom West. I do underwater photography. Mostly freelance. Sometimes I shoot for National Geographic, sometimes for scuba diving magazines. Currently I'm tracking hen bass nesting in man-made coops in this man-made lake. Bass fishing tournaments translate into big bucks. That's it for me. Your turn."

"I'm Nan, er, ah, Jones." On impulse, I stick my sweaty, sticky hand out the window. Tom takes it in his. His touch is firm and soft, and at the same time, electric. The current passes through my heart, and pulses down there. I turn crimson.

"Did you know your license plates have mud plastered all over 'em, Pam Er Ah Jones?"

Tom is flashing an odd look. Is this a test? "I was taking necessary precautions, um, according to the voices. I forgot to wash the mud off afterwards."

"Well," Tom strokes his invisible goatee, "If what you say is true, Nan, then I guess that would compute — somehow."

*

I pass through a period of time in a numb and mindless vacuum. I think Tom asked if I'd seen the pictures I'd taken with his camera. I think I said no. He said something about calling the FBI. I must've protested vigorously…the voices and I. Tom's easy allure compels me to follow his little delivery van to his motel room downtown.

*

I have converted into a brazen hussy while cast under Tom West's alluring spell. I step out of *his* shower wrapped in *his* Turkish towel. My hair hangs in ringlets plastered to my scalp.

I make my grand entrance as if I do this sort of thing every day. Tom has a laptop that is silently, ominously percolating. He has transferred my pictures on to a thumb drive thingamajig.

We sit tight together on a king-sized bed. I sense that the voices have somehow manipulated this scenario. It doesn't matter. It feels warm and natural; plus something I've never felt before. Could I be experiencing *sexual desire*?

The monitor on the nightstand lights up. I'm back on the Little Monsoon River. Suddenly, the pink zebra is levitated before us. His rancid stench once again pervades my senses. I want to vomit.

The monitor flicks through the awful gamut of evil I made possible. I'm shaking like a leaf in a blizzard. Tom loops his free hand over my shoulders. He says, "Oh Christ! It's what you said, Nan Er Ah Jones. It's unbelievable, but there it is, whatever it, is."

"The tats are a record. As suggested by my inner demons," I declare. I steady myself by placing my hand on his hot, muscular thigh. The heat engulfs erotic zones I was unaware existed. I shyly continue my theory, "Some sort of log book. It has to be. I think the voices are locked in limbo, or purgatory or something. *Something* about not being able to achieve reincarnation until they are freed."

The voices expect me to break the tat code and interpret the messages. Find their remains for their loved ones. It looks Greek, if all things I can't comprehend are Greek."

"Cyrillic, maybe," Tom whispers. "I don't think it's Chinese, or Japanese, any of those vertical alphabets. It's weird, but you did a great job shooting those pics, Nan.

"It was not me," I whisper back. I was someone else. I still am.

Tom places his hand on mine and gently massages. "Oh, it was you alright, Nan. You are an enigma wired fiddle-string tight. And you are a thousand times stronger than you let on. If you are not a marvel, then you are a hypnotist. You have cast me in a spell."

"I can't explain, but I am none of those things except for the, uh, wiring," I counter, instantly red again. "And if I hadn't connected with that first blow to Mr. Pink's head, I wouldn't be here puzzling over cryptic messages. I'd be tattooed — let's see — still plenty of room on his fat legs and calves. Looks like there's room for another string around his midriff."

"I don't know how familiar you are with the male anatomy," Tom squeamishly provides, "but that dude's penis would be categorized as a dinky dink, not to mention those hummingbird testicles."

I morph from red to scarlet, whisper, "Not what you'd call well endowed?"

"Huh?"

I'd seen porn on the web. I'd witnessed lewd shots of men whose private parts seemed impossibly huge. I lack experience, but the path we travel now, leads me to believe my virginity is about to go past tense. "Never mind. How are we going to translate the tats to English?"

"I don't know," Tom says. "I think we should sleep on it and hat up for Oregon and the Little Monsoon, first, well, second thing in the morning. Shake the local tattoo artists out of the tall timber. See who wants to claim bragging rights on the tats."

Tom looks at me as if I were a maple bar. He pulls me to him and plants a kiss on my lips. I'm overcome with lust…my tongue slides into his mouth… Yummy! I warned him. I am not me! Locked in embrace, we tip back on to the bed.

Such roving hands…my towel-dress surrenders without much of a struggle… Ohmygod!

Tom was taken with his umpteenth surprise a humid time later. And me? Well, I'm a virgin no longer. I'm sore, throbbing sore down there. My nipples are still *rock* hard. Now I know the meaning of *Hurts So Good*. Why had I been such a neurotic introvert since Pam was abducted?

I answer my own question and sigh heavenly again. I was waiting for Tom West to come into my life. I owe him. I made a down payment. I want to keep making payments forever. He seems willing. That, to me, is as befuddling as zebra tats.

*

We set out for Oregon in Tom's delivery van *third* thing in the morning. Morning lasted until checkout time at two. I'm pretty sure we slept some. I've never felt more alive.

We are eating up the miles and talking as though we've known each other since birth. I can't help wondering why. Why would such a handsome dude hook up with such a loser? Suddenly I'm aware of my neglected state. I need to purchase makeup. But what? And decent clothes. I must look like I just fell off a manure spreader. I need perfume and lipstick. Maybe eyeliner? And a hairbrush. I steal another glance at Tom. My mind returns to last night's sex marathon. I blush because I'm blushing.

Tom's hand slides from the wheel. It glides up and down, up and down my bare thigh. "We should find a room soon. Your vibes are lighting my fire."

His voice turns up the heat. We're a little shy of our goal of 800 miles today. About 500 miles. "Ooh-kaay."

At a motel room many miles from the Little Monsoon: our sense of urgency is distracted by our sense of urgency. I feel no guilt. Later, after the coed shower, I step out and wipe the steam from the mirror. Is the face reflected in the glass really mine? I am aglow. My obsidian eyes have a luster they've never displayed. I lean closer, look for flaws. My dark complexion holds tight to its secrets. Do I need teeth whitener? It dawns on me in a rush. Mirrors don't lie. *They turn things around...* "Tom?"

"Yeah"

"Bring me one of those tat printouts. I think I've figured out what the pink zebra was up to."

Tom steps into the bathroom beside me. He's as buck naked as I. We are not deterred — yet. I hold the tat printout Tom brought me to the mirror — it changes everything.

"Amazing," he practically shouts. "The pink zebra tattooed himself in mirrors!"

"I'm thinking he wanted to keep track of his precious souvenirs. He must've figured out a secret code. Thus, the creepoid psycho, serial murderer bastard had to become a do-it-yourselfer. The letters and numbers seem to mean something now, but it's only turned around Greek."

"Yup," Tom concurs. "We gotta un-reverse the process... Set the pictures up, all of them, so I can retake them through the mirror."

*

It takes all of the night and almost till checkout to finish most of the sequel. My hero had to adjust and re-adjust until he gets it by taping the pics to the back wall and clicking the mirror from the hall with a flash attachment with the lights out. To keep it unscrambled, he resorted to single tat focusing. I thought the night would never end, while hoping daylight would not come until the job was done.

Yeah, dawn sneaked in. We had to endure another night. But daylight was not entirely wasted. I attack Tom between short naps. It's only right. He owed me for the mirror trick.

*

When we head out the following night we are headed for Phoenix. Phoenix is apropos. The phoenix is a bird-symbol of tribal lore that lives a few centuries, sacrifices itself on a funeral pyre, then rises from the ashes to begin anew. We will find the answers in Phoenix. The pink zebra's victims, most importantly my sister, will be freed. All those spirits attached to caring families will rise from whatever holds them captive just as my spirit was set free by those said victims.

*

In the wee hours the highway is barren of night-birds flying on wheels. We are momentarily, virtually afloat.

Tom douses the lights. We fly alone under an umbrella of a kazzilion-million stars. It occurs to me that people are stars. That my sister has not yet been granted hers. And that the Gods that count the stars will decide when there is room for no more. That Mother Earth is the grandest phoenix of all. When the time is right, She will rise from the ashes of her upcoming pyre. I only hope the next species that inhabit her will be peaceful and… Oncoming headlights encroach from a few miles away. The spell goes south.

Tom reluctantly reignites the lights, and we are still here, on sick, sick earth…The words spew forth under their own volition. "I love you, Tom West."

Tom glances over. His reflection glows like Kryptonite radiating from the dash lights. He squeezes my thigh. "And I love you, Nan Er Ah Jones. I will forever."

We find the correct language and translate the symbols to English by goosing a super-computer at a university in Phoenix. Turns out the tats *are* Cyrillic. They all translate to surveyor's land descriptions. According to Tom, those states, counties, ranges, townships, chains, corners, quarter corners, and points and degrees on a compass, lead to burial sites.

Tom is knowledgeable enough to define the tats as legal descriptions. Unfortunately, legal descriptions are as foreign to him as Cyrillic before forcibly reflected through a mirror. And I wonder if one man could possibly accomplish all that measuring and calculating.

Tom says legal descriptions are readily available at county seats. The pink perp probably didn't survey one square inch. All the rapist/murderer was interested in was that last measurement from a known marker to point X. Pink animal had knowledge of plat maps. He simply copied the portion of the plat in question, and recopied its mirror image in private. He stood before a mirror and added those final, heinous measurements. It seems the pink zebra also knew enough about tattooing to do himself.

According to dates on the tats, we discover that my sister, Pam was the pink zebra's first victim. That other than sniffing out dates, states and counties, we are in over our heads.

We write a short explanation to go with the pictures. We make enough copies to go around. Through the US Mail, and by UPS and Federal Express, we anonymously send our evidence packets in clean manila envelopes to FBI agencies located near the gravesites.

We set out on a road trip trying to guess where the Feebees will initiate their investigations. The scope is broad, little chance of being near, but we will go crazy if we don't keep on *doing*.

Our nothing mission takes two weeks of meandering. And finally, results are leaked to the media.

Clothing and body parts are ID'd. DNA tests are fast-tracked. Dental records are checked. There are twelve victims in all — two for each year, starting with Pam. I was to be number thirteen. Flashbacks in pink, conjures elaborate visions, and I'm infected with a dose of heebee jeebees.

Pam's remains are identified as we are motoring down the Oregon Coast on highway 101. I hide in the blackened depths of my soul while a migraine stabs icepicks into my eyes. Tom guides me through the string of *whys* and *if onlys* auguring holes in my brain.

After jumping through the inanity of bureaucratic hoops, Tom and I bury my beloved sister in a cemetery on a small reservation where our family resided seven years back. When I return from Zombie-land, I recall that my first home was located near the river with the turquoise rock — or was my cherished stone a planted decoy?

I believe Pam was lured to that spot, and was slain beneath those very falls; taken by surprise, just as I might have been, had it not been for those supernatural forewarnings, and that beautiful turquoise weapon that Pam somehow provided. I kiss the stone for luck and burry my most precious possession alongside Pam.

I want to scream like a crazed warrior, but tears are flowing from Tom's eyes. He holds me very, very tight. Our tears intermingle and drop on the freshly-turned earth.

The news created by these horrible crimes is, of course, sensational. Bloodlust is a spectator sport in America — as long as the fans are not related to the victims — in the end, it hardly matters. The voices are free, as free as the phoenix.

Sensationalism never lingers. Someone more heinous will soon top the pink zebra's diabolical crimes. Pam is finally in a better place. I have Tom. His easy ways steel me from the darkness I embraced for oh, so long. The end of the trail is in sight. All that's left is to get Mom in rehab. This should be no harder than wrestling anacondas.

A couple years flit by — beautiful, multicolored butterfly style.

I'm an assistant camera person now. My job pays well, if sporadically. The fringe benefits outweigh flipping burgers a million-fold.

The FBI has not apprehended their serial killer. Tom and I know why. We are positive the pink zebra washed out to sea — that the bottom feeders feasted for quite a spell. I won't be eating dungeness crabs ever again.

My boss and I are on assignment in the Greek Isles, which are almost as beautiful as my life. Tom calls this gig a busman's holiday. Me? I can't believe any living soul could be happier, so absolutely positively free! Me, a married woman in a white one-piece, swimsuit/uniform, three months pregnant!

Oh yeah, least I forget, my last name is not Er Ah Jones. It *was* Sparrow Hawk. *Now* it's West.

*****

STOOD UP

They say it's never late till two and then it's too late. Two and too are on a collision course. It's time to come clean. I mean it's high time to tell my wife the truth, right? After four decades, and a few too many shots of liquid courage, I've worked up the intestinal fortitude to 'fess up. Meanwhile the storm outside rattles the shingles . . . Or is it the rat-a-tat-tat of distant small-arms fire? I've stepped in shit with this PTSD thing, and the house sways. Although flat on my back in bed, I feel as if I walk the power lines suspended along the highway out there in the black sizzle of wind. If I screw this up and fall, the juice will pop back on. I'll be electrocuted and cut in two. Cut straight through the depths of my soul before she knows what happened all those years ago…and I gotta go back a little further than Vietnam, for chrissakes. I feel like Elvis's; *It's Now or Never.* Tomorrow will damn sure be too late. I'll never get this close to the black torment in my head again.

*

It's been said that if you remember the '60s, you weren't there. Shame on me. I remember the damn sixties.' — the worst and best decade ever. Paula Wren was there with me. No, that's a lie. Paula was never with me except in dreamscape.

It's hard to believe, but Paula must've been born with those sensual, expressive, melancholy brown eyes. 'Course I never noticed her eyes or that perfect figure until I sensed she studied either me or my profile with an altogether different look in her eyes. She was built to perfection. Paula stood about five-eight, had long legs broad, muscular hips. A terrific athlete. An honor roll student, for chrissakes…one fine rack that put the completed package in perspective. Paula. Untouchable Paula Wren. She had an air about her though. She told all the lotharios that hit on 'er that she had a boyfriend from out of town and this stranger nobody ever saw was her one and only.

But after I caught her givin' me that come-hither stare, I was *gone* — y'know what I mean. I'd catch her unaware once in a while, and my heart would make like a pinball machine. We were seniors when I finally said do or die, and I asked her out — in my own chicken-shit way.

We had one class together — English Lit. I passed her a note. Asked if I could drive her home, maybe later check out a flick.

She passed one back. It said no. I have my own car. Meet me at the *Pit (local drive in hangout)* after school if you want.

I met her. She came out of nowhere, opened the passenger door and slid in beside me kinda furtive-like. And when she slid in, she slid right up tight to me.

Besides being dumb-struck, and tongue-tied, my heart was doing its thing again. She started talking right off. Said she might go out with me. It depended. Could I keep it a secret? Would I write a story about myself? And leave nothing out. Who was I really, y'know, like inside, where my spirit lived. Did I get along with my parents?

A freakin autobiography, but in brief; she would read it and score it. She would do likewise, she said. No putting our best feet forward. No lies, no exaggerations.

She said maybe after I read about her road to eighteen, I wouldn't want to go out with her, after all. She wouldn't tell me where she lived, wouldn't share her phone number. Crazy as it sounds, that's how it all started with Paula and me.

*

What I didn't share with my wife, and never will, was the kiss. Paula leaned in even closer. She palmed my face with her hot hand. Her lips brushed mine and then settled for just an instant. That kiss was wet and sultry. The tip of her tongue darted out and traced a swift oval around my lips. Then she was gone. I will feel the mystique of that fleeting kiss for the rest of my days.

*

I thought about her and writing about me until my underdeveloped brain seized. But I would suffer through. Paula meant too much to me not to give it a shot. I started out tryin' to be cute — but it wasn't long before my stubborn pen guided itself — that was forty-five years ago, give or take. If I would've known what was goin' down…I might not have ever… Jesus! I still don't know what I would have done.

Anyway, that intangible need pushed my pen, and it all rolled out of the catacombs in a conscience I thought was permanently sealed, y'know, forever. My autobiography begun something like I said — cutesy…..

*

I was born at an early age. Eventually I grew to such a height that my feet would touch the ground. Soon as they touched, I took off like a rocket, only horizontal. I had no memory of this, or anything else, for a year, maybe two. I have a flashback of the alien who claimed to be my father hosing me down with ice cold water from the garden hose because I filled my diaper. I must've been barely walking, maybe a year old.

Mom came outta nowhere. She caught Father in the act. By then I'd turned blue from the cold. I don't remember if I cried. Maybe. But I didn't like to give him any satisfaction. I remember that. Anyway Mom put the kibosh to Father's hydraulic pressure cleaning job.

I must have been six or so when I figured out father had the tomcat syndrome. As you know, tomcats will kill all the males in a litter of his own making, if he can find where the female cat hid her litter. Since killing me outright might tend to give him more grief than he could rightly handle, he decided on a course of random beatings and endless put-downs. Perhaps he thought I'd commit suicide and save him the effort of wearing me down. I wasn't inclined. But I often wondered why he hadn't up and named me Sue.

When Mom went off on him for the way he treated me, he called it "Constructive criticism."

I was thirteen when I got my fill of "constructive criticism." After recovering from a particularly ruthless beating and mind-strafing, I went out on the pathway to the barn. I dug a hole. It was six feet long and three feet wide and six feet deep, give or take. I wheelbarrowed the dirt out to the manure pile, dumped it and covered it with manure. I drove long nails through two-by-sixes. The nails stuck through those boards an inch or more. I placed those boards in my hole, pointy side up.

I covered the hole with slats and loose hay. It looked like I'd dropped a bail there. It'd broken open and I'd gathered up all that I could.

He fell in that night. Mom heard him hollering for help. When we arrived, he was pretty much stuck to the boards.

Mom and I, we got a rope around him and we pulled him out. We pried the boards off. I never saw anybody bleed so much. The ambulance showed up a little after we got him cleaned up. Mom told the EMTs that Father was working on a harrow he had jacked, and blocked up. The harrow fell off the poorly set blocks.

I went to check out my handy work at the hospital a couple days later. For a good-lookin' man, he looked like hell. He started to say something. I beat him to it.

"If you ever beat me again, you better kill me 'cause next time I won't fool around."

"Pretty chickenshit to lay a trap for your own father," he gurgled.

"Almost as cowardly as a two-hundred pound grown 'father' beating the shit out of his six-year-old boy," I said. "Think about that while you're healing up." It was the first time I swore in front of him.

He never ratted me out. He never touched me after that. The head trips tripped over his tongue. I caught him staring at me a few times. His eyes told me all I needed to know.

I was free then. Free to do what I wanted. I started going out for sports. I still milked the cows in the mornings and cleaned up after. Mom took the evening shift. Father cleaned up the barn when he got home from his job at the nerd factory. It was Mom's farm by inheritance. She filled out the papers to make it mine when she passed.

It slowly dawned on me. I'm smart enough to do anything I want to. I'm going to be an honor student, a four-year letterman in baseball, three in football and basketball.

Getting on the honor roll was a challenge, and I have a need for speed. I race outlaw cars on dirt tracks in the summertime — no wins so far, but Paula, what a rush.

I bought the outlaw race car and my Baja Bug with my share of the farm money. By Mom's order, the profits are now split three ways. In the fall we harvest the crops we plant in the spring or the previous fall. The milk is steady income year-around, but the crops — that's where the real money is.

Well, that's about it, Paula. I'll take on anybody I catch abusing a child. And as you know, I won't fight fair.

I hope I don't come across as a perv. I ain't. I pray I don't scare you away 'cause I gotta admit I have wet dreams starring you, and I never thought I could tell any... you just gotta know what it took to say that, huh, Paula? There. I fell on my sword for you, so cross my heart, hope to die! Swear to God, Paula.

*

I don't know how I worked up the balls, but I gave her my life story the next day. It didn't take her long to read it. During lunch break, she said she'd be happy to go out with me. But she hadn't done her autobiography yet. She still flirted outlandishly, but wouldn't give me her number and address. I melted a little of her ice, but it seemed like my defroster was still on probation.

*

We were to meet at the waterfalls on the Roaring River Scenic Highway the coming Saturday. She would present me with her story there. I was so twitched I felt like popcorn in a red-hot skillet, and Saturday was an eternity away.

So while I had her attention, I told her about my street-legal dune buggy, since we'd be riding in it. When I bragged it up I called it an *all-terrain vehicle*. She giggled and said the best all-terrain vehicle she ever heard tell of was a bear. A bear, she said, could swim. It could climb trees and outrun anyone it had a mind to. She couldn't see a dune buggy climbing a tree or swimming a river, and would look ridiculous climbing a tree.

I really dug Paula's sense of humor. I laughed my ass off trying to envision the two of us riding a big ol' black all-terrain bear. But who am I to clue' you? You had much more time to know her. I was still in the dream stage....

The meeting was set for 1:00 in the afternoon. I think I was up at 1:00 in the morning. I couldn't get her out of my mind. The wait was sheer agony.

The cows were a little surprised to see me before daylight. Carrying a flashlight I herded 'em into the barn anyway. Milk production was a little down that morning but maybe it would pick-up in the evening.

I washed and waxed the Bug that couldn't match a bear right after I finished milking. The low-slung dunes cruiser sat on tall wheels with paddle tires for sand traction in the rear, balloon tires on the front. She had roll bars; had bucket seats with seatbelts like those on Indy cars. Her hopped-up engine would goose her up to a hundred-plus in a flash.

I even had a spare racing helmet Paula could strap on. And then rain squalls hit. Wouldn't ya know it! Damn. I wished I had her number. I'd call her and tell her to bring raingear. Those April showers were blowing off the ocean in the middle of May....

I showered, shaved, brushed my teeth, splashed on the Old Spice, and blow-dried my Elvis do. Admiring myself in the mirror,

I decided to trade-out the paddle tires on the Bug for balloon tires fore and aft. The sand would be wet and packed, so plenty of traction, and the highway would be rough on those rear paddles. I wanted to strut my stuff, not jar Paula's teeth out.

I finished the job in a big-ass hurry — which made it go much slower — fumbling around, chasing elusive lug nuts, wasting motion.

Just before hopping in the shower the second time, I glanced at my watch…where had the last hour gone? I could still make it if I redlined the tach on every straight-stretch. Jesus. I had to square myself away.

*

I hit the Scenic Highway at a high rate of speed, hardly noticing the old beater sitting in the turnout at the Y.

As you are already aware the Scenic Highway is one crookedy, gnarly bitch. The curves are switchbacks, hairpins and horseshoes. The supers are either nonexistent or bassackwards. Even with the extra shocks on the Bug, I power-slid and used both lanes to negotiate the road. But time, tide and love wait for no teenage rock 'n' roller. I maxed out on the short straightaways, hoping to hell I was the only fool, or flatlander on the road — which was slick with rain. The sun popped out to reflect blindly off the sheen. In my rush I forgot my shades — and the helmet visors were clear plastic. With my eyes squinched, I could see the shoulder. I wheeled and spun-out a time or two. I fought the blind-spots like a madman. My eyeballs would have hangovers before I met Paula at the falls.

But one more curve with a reverse super and I was… The torrent shut off. The sun shot a million flashbulbs off the pavement and the heat created steam. I couldn't see squat diddly, but even that was more than I understood. I stiff-legged the brakes, still playing blind man's bluff. The tires broke traction. I slid a broady and fishtailed into the guardrail above the falls. The tall tires bounced the bug back into the right lane just as if I knew what made the world go 'round.

I glided into the parking area with seven minutes to spare and not so much as a dent in my rear fender. Paula wasn't there yet. So I'm elated, y'know…at first.

As you well know, Paula never showed. I couldn't bear to think she'd stood me up. I waited there a good four hours, the roar of the falls brought a black tumult of reruns. Funny, I never encountered a soul. I never felt alone in the universe. It was more like the world was watching me die a slow agony — tormenting a fool in love with a jezebel — and the falls became a roar of hollow laughter.

I finally boogied. She wasn't on her way — unless she was on a rickshaw out of Tokyo — I could've excused that, oh hell yes.

*

Pitch black and I glanced over towards my wife. She hadn't said a word. I knew she knew most of my story. After all it was nationwide news. But I knew she lie on her back as wide awake as I. I'd never shared my story with anyone, ever. Why now? I don't know. Other than my head is about to burst with secrets, secrets and, yeah, my great escape to those godamm 'Nam years.

Oh well, play possum if you want or need to, Baby. I couldn't stop now if stopping could save my mortal soul.

*

I patrolled the Scenic Highway from end to end, I dunno how many times. I wondered if Paula had encountered the suns glare on a blind curve, lost control and crashed over an embankment and into the river to be swept out to sea in a tin coffin… But I couldn't latch onto it. I couldn't find any evidence of such. Something beyond ESP was also rattling my cage, but I was wound way to tight to believe myself.

Suddenly it was two days later. The word was out. Paula was declared missing. I told the fuzz about our date — that Paula never showed. Without the slightest attempt, I became the number one suspect.

The cops went over my Bug with a fine-tooth comb because eyewitnesses saw me out there in it on the Scenic Highway. The car that I spotted at the junction of the main road and the Scenic shoo-fly was Paula's junker. It sat there until the cops impounded it several days later. I had never touched that car, but the cops did a million forensic tests on the damn thing and found nary a clue of my ever touching it. But did that get me off the hook? Oh, hell no. The sharks were part bulldogs. I was their bloody bone to gnaw into pieces and they did. Not because they ever found a shred of proof. But because they could; I was their best shot— a target. They fired away until Mom hired a lawyer. The rubber hoses in the form of all-night grilling's were begrudgingly, put to bed. God bless America.

Still, the word was out. The locals looked down their noses. Gossip was digested as fact. Nothing unusual there, I've learned the hard way. The temperature surrounding me was below zero. I was getting away with rape, murder, sodomy, and whatever else a bona fide serial killer does for recreation.

I found myself without a solitary friend other than Mom. I couldn't stomach the evil eyes boring into the back of my head. I joined the Army. Six months later…gone to Vietnam.

***

"I read every one of your letters, babe — some several times. I couldn't make myself answer them. I hoped you'd understand, but in your eyes my lack of response was probably a sign of guilt. I was so screwed up I re-upped. I did three tours in 'Nam. My MOS (military occupational status): leaping out of helicopters, wallowing through shitty smelling rice paddies and shooting at shadows that shot back. Slithering down tunnels behind dudes in black pajamas and coolie hats seemed easier than being tormented by sidelong stares back in the world.

"I finally cowboyed up. Vietnam was a sham designed to make Johnson and his cronies multi-kazillionaires — and to reduce a populace that might be inclined to vote Republican — just to see what change might do.

"Seeing you there at the airport when we disembarked... Wow! You were and still are the image of your beautiful sister, Paula. I thought the past had magically changed or I was living in a dream that turns out like the end of a flick."

"It was *my* movie too," Rachael murmurs. "I elbowed and squirmed my way to the ropes so I could see you in uniform. You were even more handsome than I remembered. And when Joe College spat in your face, my breath caught in my throat, but you were prepared I imagined for anything. The stone cold expression you wore never changed. You casually turned and spat in *his* face."

(That was uncool, as I recall). My name is Henry by the way. "I remember. Those kids were having the time of their lives. They had no notion of what hell could be. I was still fantasizing that you were Paula waiting there," I continued "What were you, an eighth grader when I hatted up?"

Rachael: "Let's not go there, Henry. The subject this horrid night is Paula. She was never heard from after that afternoon. There was not one sighting, even by the cruelest headline seekers, and that was about the only surprise for me."

"Yeah," I divulged. "She was with me over there though, through the worst the war had to throw at me. We shared in many a firefight, many a foxhole, no matter if it was crowded with scared shitless 'cruits, artillery barrages and night attacks. She kept me going. And Rachael, as much as I love you and always will, I see Paula's face as the lights go dim and the night creeps in. A symptom, I guess, of PTSD. A woman I loved but never knew."

Rachael said nothing

I'm one tactless remark over the line. I should quit while I'm behind but my case of hoof and mouth desease seems to accelerate. "Finally have a handle on it," I blurt. I studied it and studied it. I drove the Scenic Highway a thousand times a thousand, if only in my mind's eye.

"Paula was a runner. She left her car parked at the Y. She left plenty early enough to run to the falls and meet me there. I envision her carrying a battery powered transistor radio, the volume cracked wide open to the local rock station.

She knew the law. You run or walk on the left to meet vehicle traffic head-on. The cops found her dark glasses in her car. At times she was running as blind as I was driving.

"She nearly made it. When I slid out on that last corner, I felt the rear wheel bump something before I slammed into and bounced off the guardrail. My tall tire slid into her backside. She sailed over the guardrail and into the river. She was swept over the falls and out to sea. I never saw her, never knew it happened. I killed your sister. The truth blew in with tonight's storm."

*

The wind screamed in unholy terror. Visions of the Grim Reaper pulling back his scythe lit the night. The eaves rattled the shingles like cards being shuffled. Ever so subtly, the house swayed.

Rachael took a deep, shuddering breath. My wife said, "I found Paula's story. It was tucked inside her pillowslip. Her words were folded with yours. I don't know if she would have ever been ready for you to read it… Or maybe she wanted to enjoy a day of ultimate happiness with you beforehand. We'll never know.

"I ran away from home the day I found out about her awful shame." Rachael continues. "With Mom's consent, I lived with a friend. I was not going to be my sister's replacement. I never knew what went on under our roof. Nobody did. Hon, you would have been the first to know, had Rachael shared her story. If I would have only read your story, I would have known why Paula had the courage to finally put it on paper. Oh, God Henry! If only you would — we could have talked it out. But the war zipped you in a body bag with my sister!

"Our father began molesting — abusing my sister, Paula, the day she turned fourteen.

"I sent Paula's, um, autobiography to the police. I sent it anonymously. That was wrong. The police did nothing. I guess they discarded it as another fruitcake getting off by getting published, I don't know. I was just a scared kid. And Mom didn't — wouldn't get involved. I guess she couldn't overcome her shame, so nothing ever happened. Looking back, I suppose the law filed it away as another he said/she said.

"My freaky father must've followed Paula out to the Scenic Highway. I know, in my heart, that old bastard abducted and murdered and disposed of her remains… God. All she wanted was a normal relationship with someone she could love.

"And Henry, for Christ's sake Paula wasn't out for a run. She wasn't in tennis shoes, ragged blue jeans and a sweatshirt. She had on something nice for a nice guy she longed to impress. That story you just decided was real was a symptom of your traumatic experiences. Your brain is grasping at straws brought on by enough stress to put down an elephant. You did not hit her by accident. You did not kill my sister, Paula.

*

The storm swept through with dawn. Lights came on all over the house. As if a Vietnamese tunnel rat, I couldn't get beyond the darkness. I saw nothing but guilt smoldering in my conscience. I turned myself in the next day.

The DA was a hard-ass old grouch out of the old school. He kicked me out. I was a war hero, he said. My confession was pure speculation and wild conjecture. Negligent homicide would be impossible to prove, he said. He would not accept my written statement. I watched him tear it to shreds. He said I should learn to listen to my wife, said my self-imposed forty-five year sentence was totally unjustified. He knew who killed Paula. He read her life story forty-five years ago — reread it many times since. But no corpse meant no proof for a conviction.

I thought about it some more. Contrary to the DA's decree, forty-five years was not enough. But the rear tire on the Bug had to drop off the pavement and onto the shoulder before it hit the guardrail. *Maybe* that was the little bump I felt. I guess I'll never know, or ever let go....

**

After the DA, Rachael and I talked the night through. We decided whatever went down back then would not evaporate in booze. It was etched indelibly in our souls. The worst part of it was the fact that Rachael's father was still very much alive. I like to believe he was waiting for me.

My folk's had passed. Our kids were grown and gone. We still owned, and lived on the farm, Rachael and I. The next day I fired up the old backhoe. It seemed a long way to the backside of the old cow pasture. The price of diesel was outrageous, but I was old, and someone other than my father, had beat the shit out of me. Yep, I was too damn old to dig a 3'x6'x6' hole and cover it up again. But I damn sure wasn't just foolin' around this time.

******

GOING OUT WITH GRACE

Old saws cut true. The road to hell *is* paved with good intentions ...

Even though he'd arrived early, and set up as close as allowed, Trey Waukegan, at the ripe old age of thirty-two, doesn't hear the scuffling, is oblivious of pivoting bare feet squeaking in dry sand. He remains deaf to the grunts, moans, cheers and catcalls bantered through the net.

From behind Mirrored sunglasses Trey watches but doesn't watch the two-on-two ladies beach volleyball game. His head feels as though it's volleyed fourth and back between reality and the big what the *F? This-is-the-shit-that-always-happens-to-somebody-else.*

Trey consciously zeroes in when the ball is in the near court, however, and the slender, leggy wench with tied back shiny black hair leaps high and spikes the ball hard and where her opponents aren't.

The woman is tall, maybe five-nine or ten. She looks to be in her late twenties — too mature to be called a girl — a little coltish to be defined as refined. In a word, agile... No, awkward. Or both. Or maybe somewhere in between, right? Whatever. Doubtlessly she plays with real *zeal.* No, *wild abandon.*

The woman capable of breaking through Trey's self-absorption wears a Corvette yellow bikini over deeply tanned flesh. He admires protruding pelvic bones, thick and muscular gluteus maximus. Wide, perfect thighs, narrow shoulders, a brown belly with skin stretched over a washboard, mesmerize...

Those small breasts that Romanesque nose are the imperfections that to him, mark beauty. And her depthless brown eyes reveal glimpses of something mysterious he'd love to...perhaps, if things were different...pursue...

His thoughts wander to an old Gershwin tune popularized by Ella Fitzgerald. His mind plays back Linda Ronstadt's later version of *Someone to Watch Over me*…would yellow bikini be sympathetic if she could… Jesus Trey. You are such a lowlife candy-ass wimp! Get her out of your mind. Best you could do is hurt her. But if there is such a thing as kinetic energy, he'll pull for her — and she'll never know.

A puff of wind cast furrows across the bay as though wrinkles in a scowl. Trey shivers. A Cuisinart switches on somewhere in his skull. Deep in the labyrinths of his being, the present becomes a cannibal, eating itself alive. Were he a soldier, observers would call his disorder *the thousand yard stare*. Trey is not a soldier. Besides, his mirrored shades lock his glassy eyes in anonymity.

Trey swallows hard. His tri-year physical exam was completed a month back in a purple haze. He flashes back to the solemn-faced doctor's answer to his last question. It might as well have been a second ago.

"Mr. Waukegan, you have a year, more or less, before your motor skills begin to…fade. Your, ah, malady typically actuates in the bottoms of your feet. The illness advances rather rapidly, elevating up the legs and into the spine, paralyzing nerve and muscle cells as it grows."

"A sneak peak at the end of the line; a cyber-cookie you kill, yet it pops back up on you when you least expect it," Trey mumbles. "I don't need this now, not while watching a wild young thing perform sexy aero/acrobatics." He pushes his shades up his nose and wonders why he doesn't cry, and then his Red Solo cup of rum and Coke is down to the last trickle.

He waves (a futile gesture) to catch the eye of the overwhelmed waitress. Simultaneously, the volleyball is served by the opposing team. Launched to skim the net, but lofted by the stiffening breeze, the serve sails high. The yellow bikini should let the ball drift out of bounds. Instead she leaps high and tips it sideways. Its course deviated, the ball glides toward Trey. He stretches high in his lawn chair and without completely standing, catches the ball one-handed. Totally riveted, his periphery fails...The blurred yellow and tan image hurtles out of the back court. What happens next will ultimately alter what's left of Trey Waukegan's days on earth.

His head swivels in time to catch the surprise in her eyes. She tries to stop. Her feet dig into the sand, her forward momentum overpowers her will. She topples, arms splayed, lands on top of Trey in what would be later referred to as *serendipitous embrace*.

After the crash comes an interlude of silence. His chair is history; his crumpled shades are half buried in the sand: a monument to mark the scene of the crime. Somehow his hat, though askew, still sits on his head. A baseball cap — a caricature of a sports bra over a jockstrap — the caption beneath: *WE SUPPORT ATHLETES*. Unique, she thinks to herself. Witty.

She sits astraddle, gently brushes the sand from his face, then makes a fist, and lightly taps his forehead a couple times.

"knock, knock."

"Who's there?" His voice sounds a little strained.

"Diane," she replies. Her voice has a happy, mischievous lilt.

"Dianne who?" Trey obeys the long established straight man rule.

"Dyin to meet you." Her smile sets his heart to thumping so loud he's sure she hears it — feels it.

"I'm knock, knock, knock" he whispers.

"Who?" the knockout babe smiles and frowns at the same time.

Lord have mercy, does she ever smell, well, exotic. "Trey," Trey replies.

"Are you a trio, Trey? A multiple personality? A fugitive from the Cuckoo's Nest?"

"More like *Three-In-One Oil*. Mom's a hippy retread. She thought she had three choices as to who my sperm donor might have been the night of my conception."

Yellow Bikini's eyes say whoa! Too much information. But she's a quick-tongue artist painting her picture over his. "My name isn't Diane. It's Grace. You're a block or two off Broadway, but in a crowd I think I will trust your baby blues. Are you hurt? Other than that protrusion in your groin area?"

"Nope. Not hurt. Just abnormally normal. But yeah, that's gonna be embarrassing when you take your leave, Dianne. I mean Grace."

Normal? Grace slides what's left of the lawn chair from beneath Trey. "I'll like, pull it across your midsection as I stand. It's been, umm, real, I think."

Grace stands and pulls the wreckage across his midriff in one smooth action.

Trey. He doesn't realize he's talking. The words just spew out without forethought…"I love music," He stares unabashedly into her hypnotic, brown eyes. "Particularly big bands, blues and old time rock 'n' roll. Oh yeah, and Country."

An astonished, impassioned stare forges her features. "How 'bout Hank Williams? He wrote, *I'm So Lonesome I Could Cry*, all those years before we were born. His prophetic verses still pull me, y'know, there — and goose my goose bumps from hot to cold and back again."

"Pure poetic genius," Trey voices, surprised by his reply. "Willie Nelson wrote *Crazy*. That too is up there with Hoagie Carmichael's *Stardust*, in the musical genius department."

"Yeah. *Crazy*," Grace sighs. "That tender torch would have fizzled out if not for *Patsy Cline*…Are you aware that the word *Crazy*, in Willie's original version was *Stupid?*"

"Uh huh," Trey admits. "And Patsy Cline was Virginia Patterson Hensley. How Crazy is that?"

Crazy enough to do this all day, Grace says, "but you might've noticed they're taking down the net. Game's called. Crosswinds are just too persistent. Some of the spectators are still hanging around, like, waiting to see if we get a room I suppose. I gotta hit the showers, dude. Promise you won't go away. This is something special. We can't just, you know, let it blow by like those tiny grains of sand that are peppering my bod where my bikini ain't. We may never collide again."

Trey. A British expression enters his brain... *Gobsmacked*, he decides, I've been gobsmacked. "Later then," he studies her eyes, while wondering if she can read the guilt in his. "Today is the..." he doesn't finish his sentence. Whatever he was gonna say was, at best, insipid, and fortunately, Grace is already gracing her way across the sand.

Trey breathes in Grace's exotic contradictions of scents. He smiles despite himself, uses the remains of the lawn chair as a shield, casually stands — the envy of possibly every heterosexual male that witnessed the incident — how little *they* knew.

*

Grace exits the shower room dressed in white capris and a white top with spaghetti straps and an open midriff that displays a precious stone that winks in her bellybutton. She spots Trey by a dumpster. He has obviously straightened his dark glasses. He's dismantled his lawn chair and disposes of the flak as she arrives.

She wears shades. Her loopy earrings compliment matching silver bracelets. Her hair, still wet, is combed straight back Elvis style. As her do cascades down her shoulders, the dried ends curl in rebellion. Trey's heart skips a beat. "Great game; too bad about the wind."

"Thanks Trey," she responds guardedly, "I'm sorry. We're going to have to call this off. It's too chancy. I'm not saying you fit the bill, but there's a population of pervs, weirdos and, well, very strange normal acting creeps running loose, and... You know."

Oh, crap! Why did I go off on a Mom tangent with that stupid triple knock joke? Unfunny! Just creepy. Trey, the vile old letch with zero couths! He feels a hunk of dry ice do flips in his stomach. "Hey, I get your drift. No worries." He finger-nudges his crippled sunglasses, hoping at least they don't add to the serial rapist, or whatever, look. "I wouldn't take a chance on me either… About that silence of a shooting star lighting up a purple sky verse? Well, that line of Hank's was about your free spirit, Grace. I will never forget your face, your, um, ah… Listen, forgive my big mouth. I don't like me when I sound like a crybaby. That's just lame. Goodbye Grace. Have a good trip. That's an old fisherman's blessing. Have a good trip for the rest of your life and forever after."

Trey. He wears khaki cargo shorts, and other than his bent shades and amusing hat, nothing visible. He adjusts his Hollywoods once more. He refuses to let himself slump. Life doesn't matter, not for a walking death sentence anyway. He'll strut his stuff without a backward glance.

The sun casts his body hair into a fuzzy golden glow — as though his aura is *St. Elmo's fire* — repelling the hurt she never intended.

It takes Grace a minute to re-reconsider, and extend those long, graceful legs. By the time she slows to match his stride, he's out on North Shore Drive making tracks like, like Patsy Cline out walkin' after midnight searchin' for… "Jesus H. Trey. Slow down. Stop." She yanks on his arm. He stops.

"I left my purse back in my locker." She turns him around. He grins. Big oaf. "What do you do, Trey? What's your last name?"

"I'm Trey Waukegan. Same last name as Mom's maiden name. Do I get a new count? Is that strike one? I own the *F/V Blue Moon*. I live on board. She's moored up the river, yonder, at the Easy Slider Dock and Stowage. I fish some. I charter sightseeing expeditions, and crazy/wild adventures, some. I read as much as circumstances will allow, and I wander and wonder while I'm doin' most of what I do — except when I'm listening to music and or mechanicin' on the boat which is a hole in the water I regularly pour money in. And that's the skinny. If ya need a documentary, I have none such."

"I owe you a lawn chair, and obviously, a pair of what looks to be the remains of very expensive sunglasses."

"Can't accept either. It was the time of my life. Well worth a lawn chair and a pair of titanium Polaroid's. And I'm not talkin' *pervertese*, oh nay, not my gig. Well, maybe lightly of sex…in a loose definition of, of, God, I've got my tongue tied in knots again. And it's all because you are the best lookin', sexiest woman I have ever laid eyes on." Is that strike two? When will I ever get it? I wonder if I'll ever learn when to do what a clam does instinctively."

"What other things do you wonder about, Trey Waukegan?"

It takes Trey awhile — they stroll almost back to the club house before he replies, "Mostly the meaning of it all. And you know, did the guru of love really write the book of love? Or did a ghost writer do the job? Do the good really die young, or are the good secretly bad? When's the fish gonna bite? Where's the hotspot? What's your last name? Do I stand a ghost of a chance with you?"

He's taller than he looks. She stands on her tiptoes and kisses him. The kiss is sensual, meaningful, and wet. Before they break it off, their tongues are well acquainted, and Trey is once more in need of a collapsed lawn chair.

She bumps grinds and teases. You got that Hank Williams verse wrong." She nibbles his lower lip, nuzzles an earlobe. "It's falling star, not shooting star. I'm Grace Donisio. Maiden name also. Third generation American. My Pop's Carlos and my Mom's Angie. Pops is a good man. I think maybe you are too, Trey Waukegan."

Before he can reply, she breaks free to fetch her purse, which turns out to be, on life's finite scale, about the size of a VW Bug.

*

Back in the day, he'd worked the deck of the *Blue Moon* for the man who'd left him the boat, Trey explains to Grace. "The man who liked to believe he'd fathered me. I hope to God he had it right."

Blue Moon is sleek and beautiful — a stern picker — 130 feet of dignified agility.

During her guided tour, Grace is awestruck. She had no experience with fishing craft, but this is a *ship*, and it is really something. They walk the main deck; examine the removable fish-fighting chairs, the pop-up pole holders, the extra valves with quick-change couplers that accept automated line coilers and hydraulically operated bait choppers. Physically present is a hydraulic crab block that pulls the gear from the briny depths. "Modernized, customized mechanization," Trey explains. They stare at a praying mantis type gizmo, the *cherry picker* that stacks and unstacks the hundreds of huge king crab pots it takes to fish up North — in frenzied success — or not.

In passing Trey explains in brief, the hydraulics which operates the pumps that make everything come to life with — unimaginable power.

Grace of course, is lost from word one, but knows not to look it. And Trey shows off the retractable high-pressure hoses that *swab* her decks after every workday. He explains how excess water is washed out the *scuppers* to keep the deck semi-dry and *Blue Moon* from top heaviness and deep sixing in rough seas. Inside the main deck cabin are five plush staterooms that can sleep four each on long journeys. There's a compact galley; fully electric and equipped with myriads of modern conveniences. This gleaming place is a work inspired by the pursuit of saving time. The supplies in lockers, cold, frozen and dry, seem endless.

Trey guides Grace down the *ladder* (stairs) to the spotless engine room, to the musty fo'c's'le stowage, and machine shop. They climb back up the steep, narrow laddered (stairway) to the bridge, the highest enclosed point on board. The wheelhouse within; the vast array of computerized electronics, from radar to sonar, from visual readout depth and fish finders, to a GPS and an auto-pilot system a child could navigate to China and back, no sweat.

Grace is awestruck when the tour reaches the Captain's quarters behind the wheelhouse. Inside, there is no end to the stowage of books, maps, and charts. This is the home of the Sirius Radio System that's piped throughout the boat, to include her broad deck. "Sirius," Trey explains, "is serious satellite radio. You can listen to every type of music ever invented. You can hear worldwide news the second it's broadcast — all the news that is the news — and instantly."

The Captain's rack, to Graces estimation is of special interest. It's a double bed with sideboards, one she could admittedly bounce a dime off the spread...that, and that thing running down the middle... the bed seems huge compared to the narrow bunks stationed in the staterooms and, or crew's quarters.

The board that cuts Trey's bed in half lengthways befuddles her. Does she dare ask? Oh, yes. Curiosity often leads to trouble, but in Grace's case, well, she's gotta know.

"Okay. Everything is so, um, shipshape, and high-tech. The finished product is so opulent, literally mind-blowing," Grace continues. "I'm probably going to regret the answer to my millionth question, but why is that board cutting your bed in half?"

"Bin board. It keeps me in," Trey replies. "In a nasty sea *Blue Moon* flops from side-to-side, and head-to-toe. A person alone couldn't sleep if he could stay in the rack. Here in port, it remains partitioned because, well, I haven't had the occasion to widen my nest, not for a long time."

"Then why bother with a double bed at all... Oh! Forget I asked." Grace does an eye-roll and sucks on the earpiece of her shades. Her eyes draw Trey in, she pulls him to her. Her tongue slides around his lips. She whispers huskily, "I think the occasion is...um, take the board out, I mean...if you want."

"Yes ma'am!" Trey removes and stows the plank beneath the bed, He adjusts the radio to songs of love.

The tour ends with Grace disrobing Trey and then herself.... Trey swallows an overabundance of saliva as Grace shimmies out of her calypsos and sexily sheds her top. But for the twinkle of that navel jewel, she is all Grace.

*

The lust in those expressive chocolate eyes is spell-binding. The shower fails to douse the embers of a tryst neither of them care to let die.

"That was the best ever," she murmurs, "twenty-some hours of ecstasy, and I'm, like, wow, *still fluttering, um, strumming*, like, low-level *twanging*."

Trey nuzzles her exquisite neck. "But nothing is so good it can't be improved upon. We should practice, practice and practice much more."

"You are very dedicated," Grace murmurs. "I adore that in a man."

"In nature's plan," Trey replies while sponging her coppery back, "the good and the bad are in constant competition. It's bad's turn. Bad says that I've got a contract to fulfill. Some rich, overly pampered guys from the Midwest that call themselves, the *Extreme Adventurers* have chartered *me* and the *Blue Moon*. They want to play a highly modified, secretly domesticated...well, a micro-version of the TV series, the *Most Dangerous Catch*. It involves a cruise south to the Galapagos and then north, where we'll venture into the Bering Sea. The trip will take three months, more or less."

"So that's why all the stores," Grace concludes, turns and slides her greatest physical assets up and down his muscular physique. "Well, my blond and hairy boyfriend, you're gonna have a stowaway, a new deckhand or a pretty shoddy cook on board. I won't be used, abused and rejected like *Brandy,* the barmaid in a sailor's song. I go where you go. You're stuck with me for eternity because I'm stuck on you."

"If she was a bartender in 'seventy-two, Brandy must be in a nursing home by now. I wonder if she still pines for that dipshit sailor that loves the sea more than the perfect wench."

Trey has never felt happier or more gloomy and melancholy because of Grace's surprise fell-swoop. He recalls the things he'd alluded to about mortality versus morality. He should be confessing the godawful truth. He cannot. He'd chosen the low road when they first met. He'll stay the course, swallow his lies for now. Even a dying man should have a year with the woman he suddenly can't live without. And he damned straight loves Grace — would, for an eternity — defined as a year — more or less….

"Okay," Trey fakes a sigh, "deckhand then. OJT."

"What's OJT?"

"On-the-job-training. But be forewarned. The deck job is a tough, dirty, dangerous place. Salt water is brutal to the skin. Jellyfish will spray semi-liquid poison in your face. The slime will sling off running lines to leave welts wherever they smack you. No bikinis. Long johns, baggy clothes under baggier raingear with hood cinched tight. Boots and gloves gartered tight to sleeves — pant legs cinched tight to rubber boots."

"Maybe I should consider the Captain position instead," Grace teases.

Her eyes widen when Trey agrees. "Not a bad idea. The boat practically runs itself. The passengers are supposed to be deckies, ha-ha. Yeah, it'll be best if I stay close at hand. Besides, it'd save hiring an experienced man when we reach Kodiak, and load the gear… Are you sure you want to run away for what's gonna seem like a lifetime? No way to change your mind once we're out to sea. It's a mighty long swim between ports."

"I work for the City Parks and Recreation Department, for god's sake. Litter patrol, lover. I mostly dump garbage after I gather it up. I sweep sandy restrooms, an exercise in futility. I mop nasty floors, and I unplug and clean toilets not fit for service. I'm long overdue for a change of attitude and latitude as you ol' salts say. Besides like, dude, now that I've gotcha, well, you know the rest."

Grace is the first hire Trey has ever consummated with a kiss in a shower while standing at attention stone naked. He hopes to Christ it takes, because *HELL* is, he figures, his imminent destination — and he's sure he deserves worse. Lying by omission is a hideous crime — especially perpetrated on one so undeserving. There'll be a day of reckoning — self-serving bastard that I am, I can't stop myself. Grace. Damn me. Damn those innocent brown eyes of yours. I'm thinking with that ol' unconscionable appendage oft referred to as *Dick* and or *Johnson*. I'm the worst kind of sneak-thief there is. I'm stealing the very spirited life of the woman I'm pretty sure I fell in love with at first sight: selfish negligent homicide, by dereliction of morality!

Grace changes the subject as if to innocently eliminate Trey's wanton agonizing. "Can we take *Blue Moon* out somewhere, and seal our deal on her deck before your clientele mob us?"

"The best plan I ever heard. Can you untie the pier cleats by yourself, leap back aboard, and snug her down when we return? I know from certain experimentations that you are capable of some bizarre and interesting contortions."

She smiles sexily, and provides a hip bump as her reply. "Let me dress, then watch my smoke."

*

Sea sickness, on this her first sea venture, fortunately does not affect Grace, the athlete. The deck *do* is improvisational with an assist from the rough, ready, and misnomered Pacific, partnered by the *Blue Moon's* auto-pilot system.

Sleeping bags zipped together and spread on the deck provide shock absorbers. Bucking, yawing, rolling, and a cold, brine spray is furnished by a gathering westerly storm.

It's a shivering cold, passionately hot interlude taped by *Blue Moon's* video setup. Later, Grace and Trey watch the movie with critical eyes. Practice seems in order — if only time and tide would wait for one couple. It's not a miracle to be. And the triple X-rated tape is destroyed — consumed by fire — only the memory lives on.

*

The priority of taking care of business has put a damper on misbehavin'. There's much to be done, and the list of paper chores it seems, for a time, onus enough to unhinge a legal secretary. But eventually, the deadlines are met, licenses and permits are procured There's time enough for Trey to meet Grace's parents, Mom Angie, (*Just call me Mom*). And the hard sell; convince over-protective *Daddy Vincent that* what's going down is a done deal. The old school Italian has a hard time accepting what is out of his hands, but begrudgingly gains a would-be son-in-law in lieu of losing a daughter. And Trey is in over the top of his dying, lying conscience.

Grace meets, and adores Trey's mother Zoe, and his half-sister, Sunny, who, like three-choice Trey, was born under the wiles of free love's philosophy as explained in a song called *Love the one You're With* by *Stephen Sills*.

*

So, with Trey in a daze, the show's in motion. Grace has resigned her position with the city, granting the powers that be a half-hour notice. She and her dad, who's sure he's been smacked silly, and slyly conned into approving his daughter's death warrant, set her Chevy on blocks alongside his garage.

Surprisingly and assuredly because Grace is on board, Sunny, Trey's half-sister, signs on the *Blue Moon* as head cook. In so doing, Sunny and Grace are soon *BFF*.

The clientele of comparatively young, self-made millionaires are aboard and semi-squared away. They're good ol' boys (they claim). They all swear to have climbed the proverbial ladder the hard way, four rungs at a time, stepping on the fingers of the second-rate competition. But these guys are not to be stereotyped, and there, somewhere in those individual personalities, lies the chafe.

*

And now it's time once more to prove they've got what it takes. They're here to play a different and highly physical, version of the ol' danger game. And in their cocksure naivety, the rich have lost control. The mindless sea and its often deadly relentless whims, take precedence over mere mortals.

The clientele live in a world of smug superiority. Unfortunately for the hotshots, a ship is not a democracy or an aristocracy. The captain is the commander of those aboard. In a speech before all, Trey takes the time to convince those that balk, that aboard his ship, his rule is supreme. The *Extreme Adventurers* call Trey 'the push' and in his presence, "*Push*."

Its time, according to tide and schedule, to hit the bounding main. And as they pass the whistler buoy, the comparatively tiny hole in the brine is in the hands of Mother Nature, and the experience of owner/operator, Captain Waukegan: dependable/secretive liar-at-large. Meanwhile, Grace is practicing OJT. She learns to tie some basic knots, how to splice an eye, how to toss the grapple hook and line to catch a buoy. And she learns to run the hydraulic gear — to include the cherry picker — even if she just assimilates, she discovers she has a touch for operating hydraulics, and touchy controls quickly becomes an extension of her firm/light touch.

*

Trey sets course for the Sea of Cortez, for a billfish tournament warm-up. The Sea of Cortez is a paradise in a beautiful, translucent shade of blue. Though the sea invites, it is unsafe to swim in. The undercurrents are deathly strong. It's a jewel no man can dare possess. It's fun; and a mean temptation. The tournament meets winner-take-all expectations. The tide dictates the time to set course for Panama.

"It's so gorgeous," Grace sighs. "I could spend forever here, if only I could swim in that alluring water."

"Yeah," Trey mumbles. *If my woman only knew how short my lifetime is gonna be, I wonder where in paradise she would deep-six me....*

The *Blue Moon* is stair-step floated from lock to lock through the Panama Canal. She crosses the equator offshore of Brazil in the middle of the night. Trey has wheel watch. Everyone but he sleeps into yesterday. There is no ceremony, but Trey's imagination dreams up a dandy for the return crossing.

Cruising around Cape Horn proves to be an insane way to kill time. In contrast to the Sea of Cortez, Cape Horn is a nightmare. Due to rogue currents, hazardous waves, strong winds. And so near the South Pole, the constant threat of icebergs lurk just beyond the periphery. Cape Horn is known as the *Sailor's Graveyard.*

Mother Nature treats *Blue Moon* as though a verse from a song born of a movie. She's turned every which way but loose. Trey is self-obligated to stand a sixty-hour wheel watch. He's rummy for a couple days after, and hardly remembers Cape Horn

— only that he'll never repeat anything so inane ever again — on purpose.

If the pointy tip of South America becomes a collision of dreams and nightmares, the Galapagos Islands are an unbelievable befuddlement of hallucinations, truths and living fantasies.

Ask the *Extreme Adventurers* and the all-girl crew what cruising along the equator, visiting islands and seeing weird creatures, some six hundred miles from nowhere is like.

To Trey it's just carryover numbness — going through the motions — fuel, groceries, babysitting *Blue Moon* — loving Grace, performing maintenance, watching gauges reading charts, plotting courses, logging freehand what he could easily print and copy on a computer. Loving Grace…and still basically ignoring that little message lodged back there, out of touch with that common denominator called horse sense.

What Trey does remember is his love-struck dream while crossing the equator into yesterday, not so long ago — or was it hallucinations brought on by sleep deprivation? Either way, Trey should've known better.

In a bejeweled night off the Pacific Coast side of Ecuador, he makes his bid for Graces hand — well, not just her hand — her future pretty much in its entirety…and of course Grace, bearing no secrets, and being just as deeply in love, accepts….

There are no rings, therefore, no ring bearers. So Sister Sunny attends the bride and the wheel. The *Extreme Adventurer's Club* members bear witness, Captain Trey performs a ceremony that marries him to Grace. Meanwhile, *Blue Moon* is set on a zigzag course forth and back across the equator. The world wobbles on her axis. Neither Grace nor Trey knows precisely whether they are married today or yesterday. Only Neptune and his trident could say for sure, and he's a no-show.

On the way north, the paying guests are honored to take turns pulling four-hour wheel watches. Sister Sunny is unlicensed Skipper-in-charge while Trey and Grace enjoy a honeymoon between planned ports of call, keeping in mind that the captain is a closed door from the wheelhouse should a need for his abilities arise. And Trey, if not completely relieved of command, is in such a relieved state of mind, guilty thoughts of his upcoming departure from the living retreat for a sabbatical that is destined to end much too soon....

*

Even sailing uphill towards the top of the world, and into yesterday, the plot stays on track. Time, although it seems to stand still, moves on and so does that little hole in the ocean called *Blue Moon*. Before it registers with Grace and hubby, *Blue Moon* has power-floated her, and the rest of this unusual entourage to a waterway known as the *Inside Passage*. And for now, and at least for a ten-day cruise (including two planned stops) through the Passage, it's smooth sailing, north, for maybe a third of the way to their semi-final, and most foolhardy event.

*

The *Shelikof Straits* are the next nasty hint of what lies in wait. The seas are rough and *Blue Moon* runs in the trough, or *ditch*, as Trey calls running sideways through mountainous rollers.

Three days in Kodiak to recover while purchasing, fuel, bait, groceries and loading king crab gear and *Blue Moon* is heading to the *Aleutians* and the *Bering Sea* beyond.

No one aboard other than Trey knows when they travel beyond the North Pacific and enter the Bering Sea. The open ocean is just as hostile on the North Pacific side of an imaginary line. But welcome to the alleged *world's most dangerous fishery*. Smooth sailing on the *Blue Moon* is only a distant longing. Its late summer, but no one has informed Mother Nature. She makes her seasons at will, and remains basically enraged.

*

Two weeks of a crew of greenhorns assimilating crab fishermen and the next to last leg of the trip is in deep do-do — The Bering Sea apparently despises pampered rich men. Her winds scream. Her waters froth. *Blue Moon* bobs like a cork in a washing machine on the whup-ass cycle. Is this the kind of weather the Extreme Adventurers seek to conquer? Well…

The deck is as usual in organized mayhem. Trey, the only journeyman fisherman aboard, is more than thrilled that the end is in sight.

Grace has the wheel during this shift. She watches the deck as a crab pot comes to the surface just as rogue wave is about to break over the starboard gunnel. Over the loud-speakers, she shouts, "Look Out!"

Trey and three of the four *extreme* greenhorns working the deck crouch-down and hold tight. The last *Extreme Adventurer* standing is a superior being called *Mac*. (Possibly short for MacArthur). *Mac* might just be the victim of a personality disorder, and sees himself as the conquer of the Philippines. He stands amidships, arms folded and gawking. The rogue wave breaks high over *Blue Moon's* rail. How dare this belligerent comber sweep holier-than-thou *Mac* off his feet! But that's the way it goes in the Bearing Sea; first your attitude, then your dignity. *Mac* is rolled, as if drunkenly, across the deck. In less than a heartbeat the *Blue Moon* reverses her roll, as does a few tons of flooded deck. In disbelief, *Mac* regains his feet if not his equilibrium. Tilt. He fans the air, and runs backwards. He, trips over the pot launcher, and disappears in a reverse full-gainer, head-first over the starboard rail. And the Bering Sea readies her maw to swallow another overbearing fool into the *Deep Six*.

"*MAN OVERBOARD!*"

As stated in the regulations, *Mac*, now bobbing in the churn, wears a life preserver. With one extremely lucky toss, Trey cowboys a doughnut lifebuoy over the greenhorn's head. As the man overboard clings to the ring, Trey lashes the preserver's throw-line to the rail. Meanwhile, the crab pot swings with the wild whims of the sea. Single handedly, Trey manages to secure and clamp it fast to the pot launcher. The victim's *extremely* inept *deck-mates* stare in petrified fascination.

Motivated by Grace's shouts, Sunny takes the wheel. To prevent the victim from becoming chopped crab bait, she neutralizes *Blue Moon's* twin screws. Simultaneously Grace, forgoing the ladder (stairs) leaps some twelve feet to the working deck and immediately activates the cherry picker's control panel. She guides the machine's boom to hover near the spot of the accident.

The cherry picker is the pre-discussed steel/hydraulic praying mantis look-alike. It's weird head and a swiveling/extendable boom substitute for a body. Its beak is a hook attached to a cable. Above this beak resides a spare tire hat which is actually a shock absorber thingamajig having to do with the cherry picker's primary function of stacking king crab traps (pots) high above the deck.

Grace lowers the beak. Trey climbs onto the beast and locks his legs through the hole in the cherry picker's spare tire hat. Grace picks Trey off the deck. She maneuvers him and the cherry picker's boom over the side; near the spot where the man overboard (*Mac*) is being cold water-douched as though the victim of a Salem Witch's trial.

Meanwhile, neutered *Blue Moon* bucks, tips precariously, and rocks, and rolls rhythmlessy from port to starboard, from stem to stern and back again. Through her rigging, gale-force winds whistle a timely dirge.

Grace cannot see the drama enfold over the side. Sunny, leaning out *Blue Moon's* aft wheelhouse window, employs hand signals to guide the boom Grace gingerly operates. With eyes locked on Sunny, Grace maneuvers the cherry picker's beak, as close to the man overboard as the deck rail will allow. A wave surges. Life-vested Mac, bobs up. Trey hangs by his knees from the tire-hat, and upside down, swiftly attaches said hook to the lost crewmember's lifebuoy. The wave recedes but Mac does not. Skipper and *Extreme* Adventurer are locked in death's embrace as, cautiously, they are hauled back on board.

It goes down so fast it's as if it never occurred. *Mac*, in teeth chattering shock, is flopped on a warm bunk and covered in a pile of blankets to squelch the onset of hypothermia.

Perhaps a lesson is learned. *Mac* is still in shock, but gains a touch of pink to his translucent cheeks. Not ten minutes ago, he was a doughnut-hole escapee from the *Deep Six*. Tomorrow, he'll swagger and own bragging rights — just another day in paradise for a privileged elitist who once again believes his station in life exempts him from becoming crab bait.

Trey's female crew has proved their immeasurable worth. He is back at the helm, but his knees begin to knock, and, as that expression about the net worth of *tits on a boar* comes to mind, he knows he will never, if he were to live forever, charter a trip as foolhardy as this again.

From *Blue Moon's* position somewhere in the North Pacific, until she ventures to home port, wheel watches will be divided between Grace, Sunny and himself, Trey announces. And he will take the wheel watch on to Kodiak, "by god."

A following sea with humongous breakers cresting as far as the eye can see, wag the dog. Unable to unwind, Grace visits her husband at the wheel. When she talks of the averted disaster, he answers in grunts. When she questions him he answers in single syllables. Exasperated, she stands behind him and massages his shoulders. Eventually she feels the tension recede.

"I don't want to lose you," he mutters. "You are all I ever...."

"You couldn't run me off with double the *Extreme Adventurers*," Grace replies, leans in, plants a hungry kiss.

"That's not exactly what I meant," Trey, stares at the radar screen and sees nothing. He continues, "Sunny thinks you are the greatest woman…or man, since Lady Godiva. She told me about you jumping off the wheelhouse deck to the main. That ain't funny honey. That's a twelve foot drop onto a very hard pitching surface. You could've crippled yourself for, well, forever."

"There was a need for speed. Besides, I leaped when *Blue Moon* was rising on a comber," Grace replies. "It was like stepping off an escalator. She just rose up to catch me. Easy peasy."

Trey envisions it in his mind's eye. "Sunny is right. You are one of a kind; an amazing woman, more marvelous than any super hero." He pulls his woman onto his lap… Somehow, despite heavy clothing, arrangements and accommodations immerge. After a timeless passage, Sunny is called to the wheel. Grace and Trey retire to the Captain's quarters for a short interlude that will not bring sleep, but talk, and they rehash the madness that led to a man flopping overboard.

Funny thing: Trey was stacking gear when the incident occurred. Just three pots left to board, stack and tie down out of a scant twenty (which turned out to be a gross overestimate of what the Adventure Club members could handle in a day).

Grace and Trey finally drift off for what seems like moments. Sunny raps on the door. Trey humps into a shirt, slips on pants, arrows his feet into Romeo slippers. He's refreshed. With the aid of a gallon of coffee, he guides *Blue Moon* past Woman's Bay, through the channel and on to the transit dock.

Even though they have their memories locked in videos, the big money boys have lost all interest in king crab fishing in the Bering Sea or anywhere else, other than a cozy fish market

None too soon, the *Blue Moon* and entourage will be heading down the hill towards the finish line… to home port and Trey's last trip… ever…

The Extreme Adventurists sit in the galley, drink hot buttered rum and stare into the *fickle Fates*.

*

Moored at Kodiak, The would-be crab bait candidate and his closest associate pack their duffels and desert the *Blue Moon* to catch an airliner east. Sailing, *Sailing Over the Bounding Main,* and playing deck hands, has become a pain — and it's a long, long way from the last frontier to a decent bully pulpit.

Trey suffers mixed emotions he fails to analyze. Or perhaps a mutiny is a welcome diversion for an over-stressed mind. Two days — offload gear, boil crab legs, seal those appendages in vacuum bags, divvy among Extremists. Procure fuel and groceries — no bait required — mooring lines are cast. Endure sideways seas across *Shelikof Straits*, Southeast of Anchorage, enter *Inside Passage* — a couple overnight respites — one quite memorable — smooth sailing, followed by a trip down the Strait of Juan de Fuca, a couple more days of rock and roll in and out of the continuous troughs later, and Sunny, Grace, Trey and paying crew, are tethering *Blue Moon* to her stall at *Easy Rider Dock and Storage*...

A trip beyond the equator, back past the beginning to somewhere southwest of Dutch Harbor in the Bering Sea, and back to the point where *Blue Moon* originally ventured forth — no stowaways — only two ship-jumpers and it's a done deal — except for that voracious cannibal eating away at Trey's conscience.

*

Trey: The *Extreme Adventurers* were reduced to so much debris to recycle. Sunny too, had collected her pay, made like a baby and headed out. The trip had lasted close to four months. The sister's-in-law that never started out as such, endured, persevered. They'd also pocketed ninety-three grand apiece. It would go down in the log as a successful excursion — Trey imagined maybe that would make it all worthwhile — if anything other than the woman tethered to his conscience was worth a four-month ride on a merry-go-round.

Ah, Grace... She has the mettle, Trey reasons. She possesses the never-give-an-inch spirit. She is ambidextrous of mind and body. Her love for me, though instantaneous, as mine for her, is strong and true. Her adoration surely manifested during the trip. Inescapable togetherness on a moving microcosm that plays havoc with body and soul is capable of snuffing any romance and turning it into abject hatred. This happening is one personality flaw from an awful reality. But it never happened. And that too, is mostly on Grace. Damn, Trey contemplated, it would have been better if the tables had turned. Grace would have stomped up the ramp and left me with a black eye and a broken heart. "I Don't have a yellow backbone. I have no spine at all! I'm just a yellow bellied dirty bastard!"

*

Grace: She imagines she knows the man she loves — and she does. Except Trey...she shakes her head. Perhaps Mom Chloe is capable of clairvoyance — and named Trey, Trey because he has *three* personalities... One for me, because he is always here for me, and one for *Blue Moon*, the object he built for himself and treats with such profound respect...But... I can't make myself be jealous of an inanimate thing. Still, there is another id lurking in the shadows...or perchance this being hides beyond my periphery, yet no matter how I yearn to, I will never draw it out of hiding... Not without playing dirty. And if push comes to shove, I fucking will!

*

Whatever is out there in hiding seems to be manifesting at least in Grace's eyes. Without benefit of prior knowledge of the subject, she frets herself into, well — I Guess That's Why *Elton John* calls it the *Blues*....

But it's Trey, not Grace, who takes up the habit of goin' walkin' after midnight searchin' for…whatever resides in his conscience that steals his concentration and fixates those baby blues on something only he can see. Trey is a knock-knock joke no more. He doesn't see, he doesn't hear. He's become the man on the stair, the man who isn't there. She loves him. She knows he loves her. She would not let him destroy something that only comes once in a blue moon — and how ironic is that?

When she gets a chance, perhaps when he is chipping paint and repainting by rote, she will play him a song — the hopped-up version of *Blue Moon* — she'll play it over and over until he picks up on the beat — and the words mean reality. Or does reality apply anymore?

*

Trey does ten miles the next night. He can feel the first dreaded symptom of his deadly disease. His feet tingle. He goes over the things he's done in secret. He has signed his life away. Grace owns everything now.. She owns *Blue Moon,* and *Blue Moon* is free and clear. There's cash in the bank, gold in a safety deposit box — a double indemnity life insurance policy — *double, but only for accidental death.* Well, there are ways…if only time is not collapsing, folding like a *Dear John* letter. He has to stop seeing her in his mind's eye. But how's he gonna do that? It's a stone black moonless night, and she's as visible as a neon love sign in a yellow bikini. The images play in his soul as a love flick — one for the big screen — obviously not to be.

As daylight encroaches, Trey takes leave of the North Jetty. He walks up North Shore Drive to the Iron Bark Boat Builders. He knows a welder there. Gyp Brogan is an old high school nemesis. Brogan: the meanest sonofabitch that Trey has ever had the displeasure to meet in a back alley after school.

Gyp Brogan made the big leagues as a pistol totin' holdup man supporting a top-dollar drug addiction. And once that rat poison they call *meth* eats up your ha-ha pleasure sensors, there's no return to sender. Not even for Gyp, who served nine of fifteen hard, and then convinced the parole board, and the boat works owner he's rehabbed.

The tide is flooding, but it'll take a while to fill the bay — the smells do not desert Trey's senses. Salt born odors that used to be a whiff of magic elixir — as were the keening of the gulls. Gray fog billows in concert with Trey's equally soundless breath. He wonders of the relentlessness of his disease — of the morbid circle of life. Morbid and as randomly fucked up as though God chose who goes first by the eeny-meey-miny-mo, catch a fisherman by his toe system… which is the exact-same modus operandi employed by rotten little third-grade, self-centered bullies. And the gulls become flying children. They squawk and squeal, and wheel in disorganized circles. They'd peck and claw at an outcast because they are themselves, racists.

In an assault of ear-splitting metal-to-metal collisions, the sputtering and blinding flashes of arc welders, Gyp Brogan, in greasy, pinstripe coveralls, steps out of a mini-door built into those giant doors. The door slams behind him and the brutal invasion ceases in mid-clang. Brogan gimps along the twin railroad tracks that disappear inside the giant doors. But Gyp heads to the opposite end of the boat launch, where the tracks vanish into the bay alongside a huge dock, and the home of a rusty derrick with a tall gantry that delicately puts the finishing touches on next customer in line's floating dream.

Gyp is a crane of a monster himself. Brogan. He has a face that resembles welding slag, only grayer. His red-rimmed, squinty eyes are soulless, and could stare down a vulture. He's probably six-five, and weighs, spark burnt coveralls and high-top, steel-toed work boots laced up, maybe one-fifty.

Brogan would have been a major league tryout — if not for being his own worst enemy...

A stick match flares, highlighting a nose that resembles a pointy pus boil. The match is dropped to fizzle in the brine at the rising tideline. A cigarette glows red.

At first sight, Trey decides that Gyp will not be a welder much longer. He says, "How ya doin' Gyp'?

Brogan twitches inside his skin. He had no notion he has company until his beady eyes focus on Trey. "What the fuck you care," he snarls through what's left of his meth rotted teeth.

From a back pocket, Trey withdraws a square of folded bills. "Got a deal for ya. There's twenty large here." Trey smacks the bills into his own left palm. "Twenty-five more where these come from."

"So?"

Trey glances over at a pickup with a lift kit and tall tires. He knows the old do-over belongs to Brogan.

"So...ya still can swallow a longneck in one gulp, huh, Gyp?"

"I ain't that old. I still got what it takes. What the fuck you playin' at?"

"I hear tell you used to throw empty beer bottles clean through stop signs"

"Still can fuckface." Gyp scratches at a five-day growth of whiskers that might be inflicted with mange. "Just get my truck goin' a hunert 'n' let 'er loose. But you ain't talkin octagon. What, besides a stop sign you got in mind?"

"Well, that's all you gotta do. Pretend my head is a stop sign. And no need for the bottle. Use the truck. But you only get one shot, one pitch, one strike."

"So you want me to do you in? Ain't that a fuckin' whatchacallit? Enigma in a puzzle in a conundrum stuffed up a fair-haired dipshit's ass."

"Not for you to reason why," Trey responds. "There's a couple catches though. You gotta do it today. Within the next hour. Don't think twice. Two down, full count. Throw your money pitch."

You're on!" Brogan snatches the folded bills out of Trey's hand. "Gimme the other twenty-five, fuck head."

"It'll be waiting for ya. It's kinda like payday should be. I'll trust you for half a day, you trust me the other. But if it doesn't go down today, you're SOL for the other twenty-five." Trey whispers the details and slips away unseen by prying eyes.

A mile beyond the boat works North Shore Drive ends at a washout. There's no traffic beyond Iron Bark other than the occasional lost flatlander. Trey walks the left shoulder, which is the bay side of the road. The incoming tide slows the river's quest to be swallowed in the big pond.

*

The exhaust on a diesel engine resonates ominously. The image of Grace is a picture show in his mind's eye. The roar of the diesel engine cannot erase or even dilute Grace's image — yet Gyp's truck sends a message that sounds like a klaxon in Trey's brain and that electric impulse screams, *DANGER. MISTAKE!* Trey dives sideways as the truck's brush guard clips his shoulder....

*

Grace vomits in the Captain's toilet. This is the only time Trey has stayed out through the night. But worry is only a contributing factor as to why she land lubbers up last night's dinner.

The radio, tuned not to Sirius, but to Amy in the AM; local News and Rock-A-Billy, gets down in the nearest speaker in *Blue Moon's* state-of-the-art system — *Eleanor Rigby* — in bluegrass.

Right out of left field she hears a news *Flash-Bang*.... Grace wipes her face and listens intently. Her heart beats like a jackhammer with the hiccups. She's dumbstruck for an instant, but then a terrible truth socks her flush in the *epiphany* department of her unique brainpan. She knows who Trey's doctor is! It's the same SOB Amy in the AM is ratting out! She' knows she's gotta find Trey before it's too late! And the *Eleventh Hour* stalks hand in hand with the *Grim Reaper*...Grace throws on her dirty jeans and sweatshirt, leaps into her rubber boots and sprints out the door; finds herself on the pier wondering which way to go...her knees and feet hurt. *Blue Moon* did not rise up to absorb her leap this time. Hand wringing doesn't help. Epiphanies come once in a blue moon, and not a blood hound around. Had he walked out the jetty, or upriver?

The jetty seems more likely. She scratches her head. Not many places to go on foot upriver since the road on this side washed out in the floods last... An explosion rattles her even more. It seems to be a gunshot. The report echoes through the river gorge. She can't decide where the sound came...and BOOM! Another blast... Upriver! Grace leaps back aboard *Blue Moon*, runs back up to the wheelhouse deck, and retrieves Trey's truck keys. Meanwhile, she hears three more gunshots. "Fuck, fuck, fuck."

After that second leap she can hardly trot. But she gets to the truck. It starts. It's obviously an archaic rust bucket... A four on the floor. Why the hell hasn't she learned to drive a stick? It can't be that hard. Teenage boys delight in it. Go, Grace. Hammer down! Where's reverse?

*

Trey knows he's in very deep shit. Gyp should cut 'n' run. But not. He wants the rest of the dough— needs it — like any addict needs a fix. The first shot ricochets off a boulder a foot over his head. He's gonna have to belly-crawl to the bay and swim underwater like a porpoise with a purpose. His shoulder hurts like sin dipped in jalapeno poisoned arrows.

Trey gives it a sea lion go. His shoulder isn't cuttin it. Under stress, his arm flops like a dying eel — the socket grinds like a peppermill. He's gonna have to propel himself on his back, pushing with his feet. "Mutherfucker!" At least it's downhill — slightly.

Screaming demented obscenities, Gyp cuts loose another .45 round. The bullet splashes sand and pea gravel an inch from Trey's head.

"Fuckin' loser sumbich," Trey mutters. "Couldn't hit an elephant in the ass with his pistol at that distance…" Wasn't that some dude's famous last words? Something along those lines, Trey imagines, and Trey heel-pushes like there's no tomorrow. "Gotta make it…can't hurt Grace without an explanation, lame as it will be. Trey you're one unnecessary sorry fucking bastard!"

"BANG!" Another ricochet — too close. Depraved vulgarities fill the air, overpowering the squabbling gulls. Come to think of it, the gulls have vanished. "I hope that pistol's only a six-shooter…and Brogan has no more ammo. Maybe Gyp thinks I'm armed… Damn me, I'm not."

Trey feels the icy water numb his head. A couple more pushes and he's bound to either give birth or float.

*

Grace has Trey's rust bucket wheezing, muttering. She studies the shifting pattern diagrammed on the shift knob. "Okay. Push in clutch, follow directions to reverse… No sweat." She pops the clutch and buck-stalls the engine. "Ohmygod! You gotta do this Grace." And to herself: Don't lose your cool. Life or death, you brain dead guinea. Anybody over ten can drive a stick…"

*

Trey squirm-pivots crabwise until he's parallel with the bay. He rolls onto his side — and feels a sharp pain in his hind quarters. A bee sting? More like a Portuguese man-o-war jellyfish nailing his rump... A simultaneous loud bang..."Oh! I guess I was wrong about hitting an elephant in the ass at that dist... Well, at least I'm not dead — yet. You never hear the one that gets ya — *they* say."

Trey rolls into an ice-cold wet place. And the sting in his hip intensifies ten times over to become waves of agony. "Candy ass," He mutters, his teeth clenched.

*

After a few stalls and buck-jumps, Grace is out of the parking lot and headed for...Jesus! She wishes she knew what and where. But whatever is coming down, it's upriver. "How do I get oughta low?" She looks to the diagram, shifts, sort of, veering to the right and frittering a mailbox, *Splat.*

She makes North Shore Road without further damage — except for the engine that seems almost powerless. She's heard the expression, *lugging it.* She needs to downshift before she stalls. And her eyes shift from diagram to road and back again — a raised pickup roars straight at her. The driver of the beater is driving like an crop duster. And she fits the shifter into a gear, and overcompensates; drifts to her left oblique. She glances up in time to clip the oncoming speed demon's front fire.

The speeding truck swerves into the far ditch, bounces out, fishtails in the gravel and lurches back on the asphalt. Out his open window, the macabre-faced driver screams a diatribe of extremely vulgar language. He regains control, but doesn't stop. He speeds up.

Grace is beyond thinking about it, nor has she the time to memorize pizza face's unique verbiage. She should have brought one of Trey's pistols… Again, she fiddles with the stick, lets out the clutch. *Click*…She's momentarily thrilled that she's found what she thinks is third. It seems to be the perfect gear. She must be doing 70 when she goes airborne over the railroad tracks at *Iron Bark Boat Works.*

*

Trey tries to dog-paddle upside down. But with a bum hip and a crippled arm on opposite sides of his body, he doesn't leave much of a wake. He swims in elongated circles. Mostly he prays for God to watch over Grace. He has never felt so fucking cold. The only sound he hears is his teeth banging together like a drummer gettin' down on speed.

Trey is determined to live and wonders why. He imagines Gyp will eventually work up the gumption to walk up to the edge of the bay and perform the death knell. He keeps kicking with his good leg fanning water with his right arm, circling, circling Thank God the water is too cold for sharks. He seems to be leaving blackberry ripple trails behind….

*

Grace kills the engine by braking hard. She doesn't bother to switch off the ignition. In the middle of a road that goes nowhere, she leaps from the seat of Trey's pickup. What for? Women's intuition, for crying out loud? Her head swivels fro and to and back again. Finally, on the flaccid water, her eyes focus on what appears to be a seal. The seal flounders as if injured… "Oh God!"

Grace whips her cell from her back pocket. She shakily punches in *nine-one-one* as she runs for the tideline shouting "TREY! TREY!" a thousand times over. The gulls return to squawk their protests, "No trespassing, no trespassing, bitch, bitch, BITCH!"

"Hello. Please state your name and where you are calling from. What is your emergency?"

*

Trey hears shouting. He's warm, finally, and cozily approaches euphoria. He wishes those fucking *Extreme Adventurer* sonsabitches would let him get some sleep... Grace? Trey kicks and paddles a few pathetic strokes. He thinks he hears something splashing. Do sea lions eat people? "Grace?" His voice sounds as one with a very hoarse toad. Grace does not speak gibberish — as far as he knows — but there's a lot he doesn't know about his bride... Trey smiles; or is his a salty grin?

*

Grace shouts at the 911 operator, "North Shore Drive, as far east as it goes. My husband is drowning. He's hypothermic! Send Paramedics. Gotta get his temperature up! HURRY!"

"Please stay on the line. An ambulance is being dispatched. Don't go in after him. Placing yourself in danger would only —"

— Grace tosses the phone a little higher on the shore. The dispatcher is still yammering. Mrs. Waukegan pries off her kneeboots, squirm-wrestle-kicks free of her tight jeans. The sleeves inside out, she throws aside her sweatshirt — no bra to contend with — and splashes for the depths.

*

Trey lies on an air mattress. The mattress floats lazily in a South Pacific lagoon called *Waikiki Beach*. With only his face above water, he drifts in and out of consciousness, hearing but not hearing obnoxious sounds that pester the shit out of him. And then someone dares to scream his name.

Pesky gulls: Flying varmints. I'll be flying soon...and someone or some demandable thing has the audacity to grasp him beneath his chin and pull him out of his reverie... "Grace," he croaks.

"Oh, thank God! You're alive. Stay that way! Stay awake! I've got you. I'll have you on shore before you know it!"

But what if I'd rather stay here? He doesn't voice his argument. He wouldn't hurt Grace's feelings for anything. He's gonna try his best to endure whatever she thinks she's up to. And his ears pick up the faraway sound of howling vermin, a lot of them. Or not. A lifetime later the indignant noise closes. Trey decides the obnoxious caterwauling is what's called an *EMT vehicle* these days.

Shit. There's no going back. He might as well swim along with Grace and be done with it. Are her teeth chattering? Isn't that an oxymoron? Who can figure women?

***

Trey's eyes squint and blink. He stares into an extremely bright light. He tries to roll from his stomach to his side, but something impedes any hint of progress. He is hotter than the hubs of Hates. His throat is parched. But memories, not cool water, flood his conscience.

Someone shadows the light. He blinks rapidly, finally focuses. It's Grace. His wife, *Wonder Woman* incognito!

"Ohmygod, babe! You've come to! I'll get your nurse. I'm gonna be crying for a while now, so bear with me, please? She kisses him square on his cracked lips. He's ready for more — he thinks — but she's gone as if a dream. Her tears run off his face, blend with his, so he knows she's real... wishes the salty tears would trickle into his mouth....

The nurse rubs ice chips on his lips — allows him to chew and swallow a few pieces. Jesus. His chagrin has gotta be palpable. He ekes out, "Grace, I-l love you. I'm so sorry."

Grace bawls loudly in reply. Hers is typical stress release after the fact. She wishes she could hold him to her bosom and never let him…

"You've been through a harrowing experience," Nurse Talbot says. "Both of you. And Grace, I don't know how you knew to treat your husband so, um, professionally — to disrobe both of you and, well, meld together for warmth. Severe ventricle fibrillation is often deadly, even after a person is rescued from hypothermia. You were right to get him out of his wet clothes and cover him with, well, what was available — even if it had to be quite embarrassing for you. I must say I wonder if I would have been so cool under similar circumstances."

At least you have a respectable rack; Nurse Talbot, Grace thinks to herself, and sobs, "He's my husband."

And that explains that, even though Grace has never heard of *severe ventricle* whatever, besides, we're beyond that now.

Grace Waukegan envisions what a chore it was getting sopped clothes off an uncooperative lump, and then lying in embrace with Trey… Displaying it for all to see. Somewhere along the way her thong had disappeared…Yeah, the queen of the flashers… until a couple EMTs showed, thank God. The good guys wrapped both Trey and Grace in dry blankets. And a litter ride later, the rescuer and her saved hubby sped off to the emergency room.

Naked on the beach, Grace thinks to herself. Both of us? Yep, and little ol' me flashing all —matted, tangled hair — and nipples as hard as hot frozen chili peppers — I hope that damn journalist wimp who attempted to put words in my mouth missed the visual aid thing. The article is gonna be bad enough in the paper — even if there's no picture! Poor Daddy! He's probably dying of embarrassment!

*

Trey recovers in his cabin aboard *Blue Moon*. His recuperation is unbearably slow. The surgeon says it'll take more than a day to get over the extraction of a flattened .357 slug discovered lodged in his gluteus maximus. His shoulder ball is back in its socket and hurts like it should whenever he moves. Grace wanted to move him to one of the stateroom bunks downstairs. He politely refused. He crow-hops up and down the stairs as a form of self-punishment. His emotions are cast in triplicate: guilt, self-loathing, and leery respect of the woman he holds such profound love for. His mother should have named him Corrigan, *Wrong Way Corrigan*.

He stands braced on crutches and stares through the wheelhouse windows into an empty void. His savior returns from the post office with a bundle of papers Mrs. Grace Waukegan had to sign for. She locks herself in their private quarters, and speed reads through her unexpected mail. Her lips form a singular line. Her dark complexion seems cast in jaundiced yellow. She's on a mission — again.

Trey braces himself for incoming. He knows full-well what Grace deciphered from a batch of legalese. And Grace is on him like a hawk on the chicken he is.

"Whiskey Tango Foxtrot," (what the fuck) "Trey?" She's rolled the papers in a weaponized club she holds at the ready.

"Yeah," Trey says.

"Yeah?" Grace replies, "You sign all your physical assets over to me, including *Blue Moon*, and all you have to say is 'yeah?'"

He stares beseechingly, pleadingly, and above all, *sheepishly*, into her angry eyes. "I'm dying, Grace. It's a done deal, according to medical science and a series of tests that don't lie."

"Why do some clueless males of the specie think they have to sing a home version of a lonely lanky dipshit in a tune called "Along Came Jones?" Duh! "We shall now play a little game of name that really shitty tune." Grace turns on her smart phone, switches to a conference call and finger dials a recorded passage she's managed to dig out of a local radio station's archives. Grace Waukegan has been a busy, busy girl:

'Local Doctor, general practitioner, Dr. Clarence Baldenhiemer was arrested this morning, and charged with criminal misconduct and related charges. The prominent physician allegedly substituted deceased patients' charts for live, healthy patients records, X-rays, MRI readouts, etcetera. Baldenhiemer's motive? To claim those chosen healthy patients were dying of incurable diseases. The purported reason for the duplicity was to study how those perfectly healthy people would react to death sentences.

'Doctor Baldenhiemer, apparently the victim of a mental breakdown, diagnosed an unknown number of his patients with incurable, terminal illnesses because', and I quote, "I'm justified by my study in psychosomatic behavior. National Healthcare is a farce. Populations of decadent citizens are programmed to become hypochondriacs and sob sisters. The lies perpetrated by our government officials have leached into society and became, within itself, a deadly disease. I simply needed a cross-section of humanity to confirm my suspicions. And I have. The proof lies in those who have chosen a second opinion. Can't anyone take a (bleeping) joke anymore?'

'The doctor was forcibly restrained from further self-incrimination. He is now in custody awaiting a bail hearing.

'The preceding was a summation of events released by authorities. If anyone listening is or was a patient of Doctor Clarence Baldenhiemer, and diagnosed with a terminal illness, we at KRAK Radio urge you to visit a competent diagnostician forthwith. Reporting live from Port Halcyon, this is Gloria Finnstar reporting from KRAK Radio where the news is simply the news. And now, Johnny Cash serenades you from the austere walls of Folsom Prison.'

*

Trey seems incapable of processing the canned newscast. His face scrunches into a bizarre study of contradictions.

Grace is not playing patty-cake. She continues to fume: "Because of that BS about everything being fair in love and war, I'm not going to shame you by bringing up your original dump-on-Grace campaign. I guess I gotta chalk that one up to an incurable desease. Even worse it's contagious. I caught it the same day you did. Now wipe that *gee-is this-where-I came-in,?* befuddlement off your face, Trey Waukegan. There's no place to hide from God's truth…

"And if you're thinkin' about pleading amnesia," she continues, "I didn't just fall out of the skiff and miss the water, y'know. I took the liberty of having your blood drawn while you were under sedation. I had the plasma frozen and sent to a reputable lab back east. You are, my poleaxed darling, other than recovering from being shot in the ass and a torn rotator cusp, bruises and lacerations; in perfect health. Lucky you. And lucky you *did* claim memory loss when that local excuse for J Edgar Mueller questioned you. And since twenty-five grand is missing from *our* safe, I suspect you ordered your own assassination. Don't answer that. I wouldn't admit to whatever law that sorry act would defile.

"I strongly suggest we go on with our lives as if none of this occurred. I also suggest we prepare *Blue Moon* for a trip. Say to one of those lush tropical islands we bypassed coming up the coast of South America? Maybe a barrier island off Costa Rica, where we can enjoy a period of attitude adjustment. As you might realize from your fool hardiness, I own *Blue Moon*, so in fact, it's not a suggestion. It's an order."

That word, "Gobsmacked" has returned, Trey thinks to himself. At least I know I'm the luckiest shit-for-brains bastard between here and hell.

"Oh, and I'm yet to file my final indictment," Grace says. "Pay very close attention. Do you remember a starry night on our way back through the Inside Passage? We dropped the hook" (anchor) "in a mystical cove south of Petersburg. The night was so beautiful. The moon shone on the water, reflecting the image of the surrounding forest upside down. Maybe it was an optical illusion, but the water was blue.

"We lingered out on the bow until everyone on board was asleep. You went in and brought out our sleeping bags. There in the starry night surrounded by an upside down forest, we made love. It happened two months ago; that is according to my *OBGYN*. She's very competent and perfectly sane. I'm two months along. Was it truly a blue moon? Are we going to be okay?"

Yup. *Gobsmacked!*

*****

Well, you made it this far. Thanks for ridin' along. As most of my short stories are third cousins to fact, I hope you liked what you read, but have never experienced anything remotely similar.

Short stories are cool, and fun to write, but what an onus for a fumble-brained romanticist like me to weave into a book. Thanks go to my Mom, Mary Rose Herndon, for the imagination she passed on to me. Boy, could that independent, little Irish whiz, ever embellish a story! For me to carry forward her examples has gotta be genetic.

Other than noise, I doubt much comes from blowin' my own horn, but if you want to know more about me, I will publish more of my stories. I hope to get back to you real soon. Thanks again,

Steve

Special thanks to these very special people for sticking with me through thin, thinner and *OMG*: My Grand granddaughter Arwen Maule, for which these stories would never be published; Blaire Vohs: a brute for punishment for reading my deviated words without a whimper. Thanks Matt Vohs, Maggie Vohs, Annie Oakley, and my wife, Sally Sampson Herndon, for pushing my lazy ass along.

My deepest appreciation is reserved for every member of the "Pacific City Monday Writers Group!" Without you fine, generous, and extremely patient professional and amateur writers alike, I'd still be up that old proverbial creek bereft the standard means of locomotion.

Special kudos to:
Ginger Allen, Nancy Altman, George and Maria Cetinich, Lois Chandler, Brian Dowell, Julius Jortner, Virginia Prowell, _Diane Robinson_, William Reynolds, _Diana Sears;_ also, Jewell Miller, Bill Hart and Jim Kesey.

www.ingramcontent.com/pod-product-compliance
Lightning Source LLC
LaVergne TN
LVHW021809060526
838201LV00058B/3299